Murder at Northanger Abbey

Sequel to Jane Austen's
Spoof on the Gothic Novel

Shannon Winslow

Henry and Catherine were married,
the bells rang and every body smiled; and, as this took place
within a twelvemonth from the first day of their meeting, it will
not appear, after all the dreadful delays occasioned by the
General's cruelty, that they were essentially hurt by it.

To begin perfect happiness at the respective ages of twenty-six
and eighteen is to do pretty well; and professing myself moreover
convinced, that the General's unjust interference, so far from
being really injurious to their felicity, was perhaps rather
conducive to it, by improving their knowledge of each other, and
adding strength to their attachment, I leave it to be settled by
whomsoever it may concern, whether the tendency of this work
be altogether to recommend parental tyranny, or reward filial
disobedience.

– Jane Austen, Northanger Abbey –

AUTHOR'S FOREWORD

*O*f all Jane Austen's novels, *Northanger Abbey* traveled the most circuitous route to publication. Similarly, the title and heroine herself underwent identity changes before finishing as we know them today.

Jane Austen wrote *Northanger Abbey* primarily in her early twenties (in 1798 and 1799) as *Susan*, the name of the lead character. After some later revisions, Jane happily sold the novel in 1803 to Crosby & Co. of London for ten pounds, thinking she would soon realize her ambition to be a published author. Much to her consternation, however, Crosby & Co. never bothered to publish the book. Finally in 1816, Jane's brother Henry was able to buy the book back for his sister for the same price. Had the publisher realized that he possessed a manuscript by the anonymous author of the by-then-very-popular novels *Pride and Prejudice* and *Sense and Sensibility*, he surely would never have left it sitting on the shelf for years, much less parted with it again for such a paltry sum.

Jane subsequently changed both the heroine and the title to *Catherine*. But by this time, her health was unfortunately in decline. Through Henry Austen's efforts, the novel (now called

Northanger Abbey) was finally published together with *Persuasion* in a four-volume set after Jane's death in 1817. The set was prefaced with Henry's "Biographical Notice," at last identifying his sister as the author, not only of these two last-published works but of the other four novels that had preceded them.

Knowing this background helps us to appreciate *Northanger Abbey*'s unique place in the Austen canon and its teenaged, somewhat-naïve heroine. Austen conceived the story when she was quite young herself, before she had experienced much of the world or any success with her writing, and at a time when the novel was still not fully accepted as a legitimate literary form. Thus, it is brimming with youthful humor and fun, early examples of Austen's patented ironic wit, and even a protracted, unapologetic statement in defense of the novel itself (chapter 5 of *Northanger Abbey*).

This latter is probably the most overt example of where Austen occasionally comes out from behind the narrator's mask to address her readers directly – a technique not uncommon at the time, but now long out of fashion and termed "author intrusion." The final words of *Northanger Abbey* (quoted a page or two back) represent another excellent sample. Austen tells us that she personally doesn't think General Tilney's interference harmed so much as promoted Henry and Catherine's eventual happiness, and that we readers must decide for ourselves the lesson to be learned from *the tendency of this work*.

To my mind, catching these occasional glimpses of the author at work behind the scenes only adds to the period flavor and the rather tongue-in-cheek tone of *Northanger Abbey*. So it seemed to me that any true-to-form sequel should do the same! With this in mind, *dear reader*, I hope you will enjoy my occasional, intentional *intrusions* as well as the playfully mischievous flavor of this work.

PERFECT HAPPINESS

$\mathscr{N}$o one who had ever seen Catherine Morland in her infancy would have supposed her born to be an heroine. Her situation in life, the character of her father and mother, her own person and disposition, were all equally against her in the beginning. But when a young lady is to be an heroine, no perverseness of circumstances can prevent her. Something must and will happen to throw a hero in her way, and Catherine Morland's case was no exception.

Having thoroughly prepared herself for heroism in her adolescence by the industrious study of every novel – sentimental to thoroughly horrid – she could, by fair means (or even mildly foul) lay her hands upon, Catherine herself was hardly surprised when adventure and intrigue found her the moment she set foot outside her own sleepy community of Fullerton. It was inevitable that such a fate would overtake her, she believed, and oh, how she had longed for it! She had quite counted on it. Indeed, if nothing whatsoever had happened in Bath, if love and adventure had not been expectantly waiting for her there, she would have been exceedingly disappointed. She would have thought it unfair in the extreme.

The fates, rather than behaving in that fickle manner they have often been known to do, instead smiled on Miss Morland. Love and adventure *did* find her, as she had always foreseen that they would.

It was only now, many months later, that she had difficulty believing it. Parts of the story began to feel like an implausible dream: those early heady days exploring Bath with the inconstant Isabella Thorpe, being introduced to Henry at the assembly rooms completely by chance, her uneven acquaintance with the rest of his family, the surprising invitation to Northanger Abbey, and finally her violent expulsion from that place with Henry following, resolved on marrying her.

It must all be true, however, Catherine reasoned when she blinked awake this particular morning, experiencing the same feelings of dawning pleasure as many other mornings before and since. Sun flooded in at the windows, filtered through the sheer draperies hanging there, and giving her a clear view of her surroundings. This ceiling over her head was certainly not the water-stained ceiling of the crowded bedchamber she had shared with her sisters in Fullerton. This bed was more comfortable too, and the bedclothes finer and sweeter smelling than those merely serviceable examples which had enfolded her throughout child-hood (and which she had had the duty of laundering herself).

No, the dream was become reality, and this was Woodston parsonage! For the most conclusive evidence of that fact, she slowly turned her pretty face to the left, blushing becomingly in anticipation as she did so. Just as she had hoped and suspected, it was not any mere sister's visage that then greeted her eyes but a medium skinned, rather handsome, and decidedly masculine face instead.

"Good morning, Mrs. Tilney," he murmured low.

"Good morning, Mr. Tilney," Catherine returned, smiling as if she possessed a delicious secret too good to tell.

"I trust you slept well." The lift of his eyebrows as he said it and his slight smirk afterward hinted at his particular reason for thinking she had spent a pleasant night with him.

Taking his meaning and a moment to remember, even more rosy color flooded Catherine's cheeks. "Yes, I did, thank you," she said, and a girlish laugh escaped her lips in spite of herself.

It still seemed to her somewhat of a miracle that Henry Tilney was there in her bed, and that he was truly her husband – a miracle that needed constant confirmation. The sight of him, albeit exceedingly agreeable, was not enough. Hearing his familiar voice, still rough with the effects of sleep, was yet insufficient for her. She must consult her other senses as well.

Henry had quickly learnt this about his young bride – her need for continual reassurance – and he was always happy to oblige her with every positive proof of his presence and his love that she required. Toward that end, he now pulled her close and proceeded to bestow kisses here and there upon her person – affectionate to passionate according to what was wanted – and to furnish whatever other personal attentions seemed advisable.

Catherine, sighing contentedly and abandoning herself to his capable ministrations, wondered if there could possibly be any felicity in the world to equal it.

Mr. and Mrs. Tilney quit their bed sometime later – much later, in truth, for neither of them really had any pressing reason for rising promptly that day. Catherine did not even bother to summon the servant to help her dress, accepting her husband's offer of assistance instead. She knew from recent experience that it would take twice as long that way, probably even longer than if she had tried to manage the whole affair herself. Henry's large hands were not particularly adept at lacing stays and doing up tiny buttons. And then there were the predictable stoppages and digressions along the way...

Ah, well. None of that mattered when there was no hurry at all. Henry only had some minor parish business to attend to that day, and Catherine could continue her work in the drawing room at her own pace.

The drawing room had been an instant favorite with her from the occasion of her first setting eyes on it those months before. General Tilney himself had brought her to Woodston to see Henry's home, at the time making ill-disguised allusions that it might one day be *her* home as well.

"Oh, what a sweet room!" she had involuntarily exclaimed to Henry upon seeing it. "But why do not you fit it up, Mr. Tilney? What a pity not to have it fitted up for use! It is the prettiest room I ever saw! If this were my house, I am sure I should never sit anywhere else!"

Such were her irrepressible sensations at the time. She remembered that Henry's answering smile seemed to convey his amusement and pleasure at her unguarded effusions.

"I trust," the General had said with self-satisfaction, "that it will very speedily be furnished; it waits only for a lady's taste!"

She had blushed and blushed, not only at the thought of being Henry's wife one day, but at the obvious preference for her shown by a man of importance like General Tilney. The general, of course, had shortly thereafter changed his mind, withdrawing his good opinion of her when she turned out not to be the heiress he had supposed. But as for Catherine, she had never retracted her high opinion of the drawing room at Woodston parsonage; it was still her *favorite room in the world.*

It was so prettily shaped, and the large windows reaching all the way to the ground seemed such an extravagant feature, one more expected in a house of real consequence. Although she had yet to finish properly fitting it up – there would be new paper for the walls, of course, different curtains, and a stylish sofa had been ordered – she had temporarily installed a small table and two comfortable chairs directly facing those extravagant windows, where they could sit and enjoy the bucolic view in the meantime.

Before she could settle to her work, Catherine once again paused before those windows to consider the scene, as she had done an hundred times before. But this day, she flattered herself that she was seeing with a more educated eye, as she had been recently studying some extracts from a large volume on the subject of the picturesque. Consequently, it occurred to her for the first time that there was some small imperfection in the view before her. Although there were a succession of hills at the back to give depth, and a cheerful green meadow at the fore, both generously embellished with grazing sheep, hedgerows, and a scattering of apple trees, to Catherine's newly enlightened mind, there was still something wanting.

Although Catherine's knowledge of art was very thin even now, she had at least learnt enough to know that every landscape should contain a point of particular interest to draw one's eye. There was a charming cottage amongst the trees, it was true, but that could only properly be seen when the leaves had fallen. The sheep were always present, but they could not be depended on to always arrange themselves just so. And besides, sheep were far too commonplace to serve. No, it should be something else, something less ordinary but just as serene. Then an idea struck her, and she knew at once that her instincts had been correct. It only remained for Henry to be convinced as well.

Catherine lost no time. Finding Henry in his book room, she took him by the hand and propelled him to the drawing room without bothering to answer his questions as to the cause of her obvious excitement.

"There!" she said pointing through the windows to the precise place suggested by her imagination. Henry looked, but when he failed to respond with appropriate perception and enthusiasm, Catherine was forced to go on. "There must be a picnic to take place *exactly there*," she said. "Cannot you see how charming it would look, Henry? That is the very thing to complete the picture!"

Henry laughed. "My darling girl, is this what has you so agitated – the need for a picnic? Well it is a fine autumn day, and I have no dislike for eating out of doors. We may take a picnic wherever you say, but why amongst the sheep, darling? Surely under one of the trees to the side of our own lawn would do as well or better."

"No, Henry, you are missing the point. It must be exactly there for the sake of correct composition. A young couple, like us, sitting on a blanket, is needed to add the point of particular interest and complete the view. Look again, and I am sure you will see that I am right."

Henry obeyed but remained mystified. "I suppose you are correct in thinking it would make a charming picture, but not one that is within our power to contrive. We are not likely to convince any young couple to continually picnic there just so that we may always have the pleasure of looking at them."

"Of course not," Catherine said patiently. "We must do it ourselves."

"But... But I'm afraid I still do not understand, my darling," said he, his brow deeply furrowed. "One cannot be in two places at the same time – here to observe the pretty scene and there to be observed..." He trailed off.

Really, sometimes he surprised her with his lack of imagination. So she explained. "I know that much, Henry; I am no simpleton. But once we have picnicked on that spot, I will ever after be able to see it in my mind's eye when I look out of this window. Even many years from now, when we are quite old and gray, I will picture us *exactly there*. Wait!" Catherine ran to the cupboard in the next room, returning with a dark blue blanket, which she handed to her husband. "Now take this and go out into the meadow. I will direct you to the correct spot from here. Meanwhile, I will have Mrs. Peabody make up a basket with a few things – just bread, wine, cheese, and cake, perhaps. Then, when everything is ready, I will join you and we will have our picnic."

Henry, wisely, made no further protest. He took the blanket and set off out of the door, across the lawn, and down the lane to where there was a stile to give access to the meadow beyond. Every few minutes he looked back, waved, and waited to see Catherine's direction for where to proceed. Soon enough, she joined him and they ate their modest repast together there, talking and laughing, and then lying back on the blanket, holding hands and gazing deep into the clear blue sky for what seemed like hours.

Although Henry Tilney had gone along with the idea simply to indulge his wife, in the end he was forced to admit – to himself, at least – that her plan, unexpectedly, bordered on genius. Not only had he enjoyed himself immensely, which hardly surprised him. He was soon to discover how right Catherine had been as well, for never again would he look out of the drawing room windows without picturing their lovely picnic *exactly there*, just as she had said.

Mrs. Tilney currently had few demands on her time. Henry had kept the old housekeeper and her husband on, and although Mr. and Mrs. Peabody were getting along in years, Penny was now added, as a maid of all work, to assist them with whatever needed doing.

Catherine had at first insisted that she was perfectly capable of helping with chores, indoors or out. As the eldest daughter of a large family with limited means, she had been necessarily conscripted for more and various tasks as she grew. She was therefore not unfamiliar with the everyday employments required to maintain a household in good working order. But since she was the wife of a gentleman now, it was not thought fitting for her to be seen hanging out the wash or feeding the pigs any longer.

Catherine had accepted all this without question when Henry explained it to her untutored self. He was older and from a family of higher rank, and so he must know what was best and most seemly, she reasoned. In truth, it was no very severe sacrifice to relinquish these things to other hands, for Catherine had never really been fond of doing laundry... or of pigs, for that matter, at least not since she had been eleven or twelve.

New demands would surely fill her time as she became more acquainted with what specifically was expected of her as the rector's wife, although she already had a reasonably good idea of this from witnessing her mother's work in the Fullerton parish. And later there would probably be children too. Not that young Mrs. Tilney was in any rush! She had had quite enough experience of that sort of thing with her six younger brothers and sisters to desire beginning to care for her own brood of offspring just yet. For now, it was pleasure enough to dote on her handsome husband and hum her way through each day, making ambitious plans for improvements to the house and gardens without ever actually accomplishing very much at all.

Regardless, Henry would kiss her, tell her what a clever wife she was, and say something to make her laugh every single day. When she thought or spoke about it, which she did quite frequently, Catherine declared herself to be "perfectly happy." What would come tomorrow or the next day did not overly concern her.

What came, in fact, was a very unexpected invitation.

- 2 -

AN INVITATION

"*W*hat do you make of it, Henry?" Catherine asked. They were standing in the hall, both staring in wonder at the invitation Henry held in his hand, as if it might have come from another planet, when in fact it had originated less than twenty miles away.

"It is about the last thing I expected," said he. "I am amazed enough that my father should contemplate such a thing at all – giving a fancy-dress ball on All Hallows Eve – let alone that *we* should be invited to it."

"Perhaps this time he has decided to really forgive us for marrying," Catherine said brightly. "Perhaps the invitation is his way of showing we are now truly welcome to Northanger Abbey again."

"I suppose it is possible," Henry said, sounding dubious. "It would be more like him than a straightforward apology or an admission that he had been wrong in any way, which I should never expect from him in an hundred years. Still, I cannot be quite easy about it either. I wonder…"

"Do you think Eleanor will be there?" cried Catherine of a sudden, interrupting her husband. "Although I know I should call

11

her Lady Astley, now that she is married and a viscountess. Oh, how I should love to see her again!"

Henry laughed. "Your mind leaps ahead so rapidly, my darling, that I cannot keep up. While I am still considering if we should accept this invitation, no doubt you have already decided what costume you shall wear to the event and what feats you shall perform to amaze the crowd."

"I have done no such thing, Henry! It is only that I so long to see your sister, as I daresay you do just as strongly, if only you would admit to it. We owe so much of our happiness to her, and we never had the chance to thank her properly!"

"My dear Catherine, although I agree that my sister is everything that is virtuous and kind, you should not imagine she married a man of title and fortune just to throw my father into a more charitable humor for *our* sakes. You know yourself that she had long been partial to Jonathan."

"Yes, but that is even more to the point, Henry. Cannot you see that? For Eleanor to remember us at such a time of long-awaited personal jubilation, to think of speaking to your father on our behalf when her head could have easily been too full of her own concerns and happiness for anything else... That shows how truly amiable she is."

"Is that what it shows? How stupid of me not to have seen it. You must forgive my thick-headedness, my love. Men are so dense when it comes to social niceties. These things are far beyond me. Once again I say what I told you long ago in Bath, that no one can think more highly of women's superior understanding than I do. As you will recall, it was (and still is) my opinion that nature has given women so much understanding, in fact, that they never find it necessary to use more than half of what they possess."

Catherine crossed her arms and gave her husband a stern look. "I remember it very well. But you said it only because you liked to tease me."

He leant closer so their faces were just inches apart. "That is another thing that has not changed, my dear. Whatever makes you blush must prove irresistible to me, for you are irresistible to me when you blush." He soundly kissed her to confirm his point. Afterward, Catherine paused a moment to catch her breath and clear her head. "Very prettily said, sir. But now we are married, you have other more pleasant ways of making me blush."

"I know!" Henry said with a lift of his brows and a significant gleam in his dark eye.

"So you may safely leave off teasing me so often as you were used to doing."

"Hmm. There is some merit in what you say, I suppose. But now, as for this invitation," he said, tossing the card carelessly onto the hall table, "I am inclined to ignore it. I do not trust my father, and my instincts tell me he has something more in mind than generous hospitality and restoring family harmony."

Seeing the instant disappointment in his wife's countenance, he gathered her into an embrace and continued. "There, there, Catherine. You did not marry me for my distinguished family connections; I am quite convinced of that. We have no need of the grandeur of Northanger Abbey. We are very free and very happy here on our own at Woodston, are we not? That is more important than all the fancy-dress parties in the world. To preserve our peace and independence, I should be quite content to never set eyes on the abbey or my father again. Think no more about that vile man. He does not deserve another moment of your consideration."

A person unfamiliar with the regrettable family history might well be shocked by this apparent display of filial disrespect. Be assured, however, that Henry Tilney had more than adequate justification for his disregard, primarily for his father's offenses against members of the weaker sex under his control – Henry's mother, his sister, and his darling Catherine – not those against himself. Although General Tilney, thrown into a temporary fit of good-humour by his daughter's brilliant marriage, had briefly softened toward his younger son and his choice of bride, giving Henry permission "to be a fool if he liked it," it was an incomplete forgiveness. The general had never favored the young couple with as much as one word of civil acknowledgement since.

So when Henry Tilney denounced his father with these spirited words, he meant every one of them most sincerely. And yet his resolve against accepting his father's invitation would ultimately prove no match for the forces at work to overturn it.

First and foremost, there was Henry's exceptional affability, which very naturally called him to be on good terms with everything and everybody within his circle of acquaintance. Then there was his genuine curiosity to see his brother and sister again, and to discover what his father was up to with this proposed ball. There was his tender affection for his new wife that urged him to indulge her wish to attend. And finally, he could not help being drawn back to the source, back to the place of his birth, the only place he could still clearly picture his beloved mother and remember their time together. Despite what Henry had said, in a very real way Northanger was still home to him and always would be.

Moreover, even had none of these influences continued to work on Henry's mind over the next few days, even had every single circumstance been strongly against his accepting his father's invitation, something must and would have happened to overrule them. Something must and would have occurred to assure Mr. and Mrs. Tilney's attendance at the ball that All Hallows Eve. It had been ordained. Events that absolutely required their presence were soon to unfold at Northanger; that was the material point. Catherine and Henry's days of heroism were not over and done with yet.

As the reader has probably foreseen, Henry Tilney soon

relented. He judged that, if the invitation came as a genuine olive branch extended to him, it would be wrong to spurn it, putting to an early death that budding opportunity. Who knew but what it could be the last chance to make peace with his father? Better to risk erring on the side of forbearance, Henry decided. He could be generous. He could even forgive. If his father meant to turn over a new page and begin behaving with more kindness and respect, Henry felt it was his clear duty – as a son and as a member of the clergy – to encourage him in such reforms, regardless of what had gone before.

Carried along by this whisper of fresh optimism, his mind soon began suggesting pictures of a new family harmony, off in the not too distant future. He saw all his nearest relations charmingly gathered for Christmas at Northanger: his sister happy as never before, his brother settled by marriage to some sensible woman, children playing at their feet, perhaps one of them even being dandled on his father's knee. It was possible. And such images were irresistible to Henry's noble heart. If there were even one chance in a thousand of such a thing coming to pass, he would not be the one to spoil it.

When Henry announced that they would be attending the ball at Northanger after all, his grateful wife rewarded him with praise for his generosity and with extra affection enough to thoroughly convince him he had made the correct decision... and also to be on the watch henceforth for other ways to similarly please her.

Catherine was eager to begin making plans at once, and yet she was wise enough to temper her enthusiasm out of respect for her husband's ambivalent feelings. Although the invitation had specified *fancy dress*, Henry's lingering reluctance held so far as to refuse to take any extra trouble or expense on his father's account. There would be no money or time spent on elaborate costuming, he declared; they would get by with ordinary evening attire supplemented with masks alone.

Catherine, who was satisfied just to be going to the ball, did not much mind the diminution of the intricate plans that had already been forming in her imagination. Those excellent schemes could be reserved for another day, for she dared to hope there would be other balls in her future.

"I will make the masks myself," she told Henry. "It will be no trouble; I am handy about such things. I can use bits and scraps I have tucked away in my sewing box for the most part, so it will cost next to nothing. And I will enjoy the challenge."

"Clever girl!" Henry said, smiling at her and giving her cheek a gentle pat. "But I have something already – a plain black mask I have worn before. That will serve very well for me. Do whatever you like for yourself, though, and by all means make an entertainment out of the job if you can. Should things turn out badly at the ball, that may be the only pleasure derived from the occasion."

Henry said this last part more or less in jest, but in the weeks and months to come, he would often look back on the statement as being all too prophetic.

3

APPROACHING A BALL

*C*atherine had genuinely intended that her preparations
for the ball should cost her husband "next to nothing."
But as she proceeded, she found that she really owned no gown
that was entirely appropriate, at least not without significant
alterations. And as for her mask, sadly, her store of ribbons,
feathers, and silk flowers turned out to be likewise deficient for
the purpose. Therefore, *some* expenditure could not be avoided,
she informed Henry. After all, "one cannot be expected to make
bricks without straw!" Shops must be visited. Purchases must be
made. She promised to compensate for it, however, by doing all
the assembly herself, thereby saving the cost of hiring a dress-
maker or milliner for the fancy work.

"It was worth every farthing," Henry declared when he at last
beheld his young wife coiffed and attired for the ball.

"Do you mean what you say?" Catherine asked, once more
finding she required his reassurance. Do I really look...
acceptable?"

"Acceptable? What an idea. My dear Catherine, you look
positively divine! But that is only my immediate, first impres-

sion. If you insist, I will examine you more circumspectly and give you my honest opinion."

"Oh, yes, you must do that!"

"Very well, then." Henry took a deep breath and steadied himself for the important task at hand. When he was sufficiently prepared, he told her, "Step back, my dear, and turn round once or twice... slowly, so that I can obtain a comprehensive view... That's it... Once more... Now, let me look at you."

Facing him again, Catherine nervously awaited his assessment.

Henry started at her feet, where the toes of her white dancing slippers could just be seen peeking out from under her lace-trimmed hem. The gown itself was a pale pink muslin – her best, he knew, and one he had seen before. But nobody else would recognize it with the way the sleeves had been cleverly remade and with the new gauzy overlay she had added to the skirt.

His perusing eyes moving upward, they stopped and held at Catherine's exquisite décolletage. He watched, for a moment spellbound by the quickened, rhythmic rise and fall of the rounded fullness there as she breathed in and out.

"Henry, is there something amiss?" Catherine inquired, her hand moving self-consciously up her gown and coming to rest in a protective way over the area that had apparently caught his attention.

"Hmm. You have made a change here, I think," he said, stepping close enough to run an inquiring fingertip along the inside rim of the low neckline.

"Yes..." she said uncertainly. "Yes, I... I removed the lace that used to be tucked in behind. You see, I thought... But maybe it was a mistake. Maybe it is too much. Oh, dear! Do you think I had better put it back? It can be done in the work of only fifteen minutes if you advise it."

Rousing himself, Henry shook his head. "No, not at all." Speaking as much of her modest endowment as of the cut of her neckline, he added, "In my opinion, it is neither too little nor too much. It is exactly right, that is unless you mind people looking. Because men will surely look, my darling, and I daresay they will all envy me as well."

"I'm sure they will do no such thing," said Catherine, extremely pleased nonetheless.

"I tease you not, my dear." Moving close and beginning to nuzzle her neck, he continued absently. "But *must* we go to this ball? I should much rather keep you all to myself."

"Stop that, Henry," said Catherine with a half-hearted attempt at sternness. "We have sent our acceptance to the invitation, and we must certainly go to the ball. Now, let me see what can be done about you." She pushed him off a little and busied her hands with straightening Henry's cravat while continuing to enjoy his undivided attention.

Despite her firm words about going, there was real temptation in the idea of remaining at home alone together instead. And she knew that if she were to look too long into the depths of Henry's eyes or let her imagination drift... But no; not tonight. Catherine called herself back to the business at hand. After all, they had so much time ahead for that sort of thing. They were still in the early days of their marriage – their honeymoon period, in truth – and there would be years and years of connubial life to come, years and years to discover the meaning of two becoming one.

Stealing a glance at Henry's face, Catherine wondered what he would look like when he was forty, fifty, or even sixty years of age, in his prime and beyond. He did not take after his father as to looks – or temperament either, thankfully – so no clue could be found there. She would just have to wait and see as the months and years revealed themselves. Not that such a trifle as looks really signified. Henry could grow wrinkled and lose all his hair, and she would love him just the same; she was sure of it. All she cared for was that they should be together forever.

"Now, my dear Catherine," Henry said, interrupting her private reverie. "Since you insist we *are* going to this ball, I suggest we depart without further delay, that is if you are finished fussing over my appearance and yours."

One more tug at her husband's cravat and she was satisfied.

And so, off they went, Mr. and Mrs. Tilney in their modest closed carriage with old Mr. Peabody driving them. Mr. Tilney would undoubtedly have preferred the gig and to drive himself, since the weather appeared favorable at the time of their departure. Yet he could hardly have expected his wife to endure the chill and inconvenience of the October night air over so long a distance, or the risk that it might rain. Besides, one must arrive to such an event in some kind of style.

In addition to the clothing they wore, they brought extra with them as a sensible precaution against any unforeseen events. This had been Catherine's idea. The moon would be nearly full and light their way, should they desire to return home to Woodston that same evening. However, she hoped all would go so well that they would be invited to stay the night, as surely Eleanor and her husband the viscount would be planning to do, since they came even farther.

This was all speculation, of course, because they in fact had no information whatsoever about who would be present or how long anybody would remain at Northanger. They knew not General Tilney's true intentions in giving this ball or how events would transpire. In many respects, they were walking blind. Initially, that seemed part of the adventure – the thrill of the unknown – and for the first half of the journey, Catherine felt quite as happy as a young lady on the way to a ball can be supposed to feel.

However, doubts and forebodings began building inside her breast as they approached the place of her prior mortification. Northanger, she cruelly reminded herself, was where she had been embarrassed by Henry's discovering her foolish imaginings

– about his mother's death and so much more – not to mention his father's unceremoniously ordering her from the house. Dreadful!

Henry had well and truly forgiven her; of this she was confident. But she could not entirely forgive herself and would not enjoy being reminded of these things again at every turn. *Down this dim passageway, I imagined a ghostly presence. In this room, my foolish fancy made secret manuscripts out of ordinary laundry bills. Up those stairs I crept without permission, thinking I should discover some mystery of Mrs. Tilney's demise.*

Catherine shook her head resolutely. She must not allow her mind to stray down those dark corridors again. She silently but earnestly vowed that this time she would keep a firm grip on reality, not imagining ghosts and murder plots round every corner. She would not tremble with equal parts excitement and alarm at every unexplained sight or sound, as she had done before.

She further pledged that she would remember only the good from her previous visit to Northanger. There *were* many good things to remember, after all, most particularly that it was at Northanger where the first attraction between Henry and herself had ripened into love. That single fact overpowered all the others. She would look forward to what could be built on that foundation, not backward to her childish mistakes.

Henry, who sat close beside her, holding her hand, gave her a quizzical look. "You are oddly quiet, my dear Catherine," he said. "Where is your enthusiasm for this ball that you have been overflowing with these many days? Have you exhausted your supply just before we have need of it? We will be at Northanger in only a few more minutes, you know."

"Yes, I know," Catherine said, trying to sound more calm and confident than really was the case. "I recognize the landmarks along the way. It is nothing more than a small attack of nerves, I assure you." Then all her pretenses failed and she turned pleading eyes on her husband. "Oh, Henry, suppose your father still hates me. I do not think I could bear it. Or suppose I do something unforgivably stupid again. I suddenly have the most fearful presentiment of catastrophe."

Henry laughed and pulled his wife closer. "What could possibly happen tonight that would justify all this anxiety? It is a ball, after all, which is hardly a matter of life and death. The worst that can happen at a ball is somebody forgets the steps to the *Allemande*, breaks a plate at the supper, or discovers her gown has a tear."

"I suppose you are right." But a moment later, she continued just the same. "Perhaps we should have made more of an effort with our attire. We may be the only people there in ordinary eveningwear. A mask alone does not quite constitute 'fancy dress,' and the invitation *did* specify…"

"Catherine, Catherine, be easy," said Henry, not waiting for her to finish her long list of misgivings or to build her mountain of worries any higher. "I care not what the invitation says. I can promise you that you and your gown are quite perfect. And as for your mask, it is a work of art! I daresay no one will believe you created such a masterpiece yourself from only a few scraps and feathers."

"It was nothing," Catherine disclaimed.

"You are too modest, my dear. And as for this ball… Well, I know I had my reservations before, but I begin to believe it will be well worth the time and trouble, just for the pleasure of dancing with you and to see you properly admired. You are destined to be heralded as an angel the moment you enter the room, and confirmed as one by your behavior before the night is out. Everybody will adore you, without exception."

"Even your father, do you mean?"

"Even my father. He will have no choice." The carriage rolled to a halt. "Now, here we are. Enter the house with your head held high, Catherine, and have no fear. Tonight will be a great triumph."

While waiting for Mr. Peabody to open the carriage door and put down the step, Henry considered that perhaps he had laid his praise on a *little* thick. But Catherine looked much relieved, and that was the important thing. Besides, *he* thought Catherine as lovely as any angel. If others could not see it, that was their loss.

Henry handed his smiling wife from the carriage, both of them feeling ready to take on the world. At that very same moment, the first sound of thunder pealed in the distance.

4

MEETINGS AND GREETINGS

"*H*enry!" cried Lady Astley, the former Eleanor Tilney, rushing forward when Mr. and Mrs. Tilney were barely in through the door. "Catherine! Oh, I am *so* pleased you have come! And here is Jonathan," Eleanor added, drawing her husband, the viscount, into the merry group. The reunion was everything for which they could have hoped after months of separation. Affectionate words and embraces passed from one to the other and back again.

With Eleanor, of course, there was no reserve, despite her new title. But Catherine did not know the viscount well. Still, he was very pleasant and attentive, and it seemed to her that he had grown an inch or two in stature since the occasion of her last seeing him. Yet surely he was beyond the age when that could be. Perhaps it was only that he had come into his own, she considered, his bearing and manner expanding to fill his new role amongst the ranks of the nobility. Or perhaps it was more the confidence engendered by having a worthy wife he loved at his side. And no one could be more worthy and more deserving of her good fortune than Eleanor.

Just for a fleeting moment, Catherine imagined what it would be like to be married to a titled man instead of a parson, to be called 'Lady' something or other instead of a mere 'Mrs.' But no, it was the grand surroundings; they had put silly ideas in her head, for unless the nobleman were Henry – an impossibility – she would never trade her place for the highest in the land.

While the two young men, who were old friends, talked amongst themselves, the newly minted viscountess turned her more particular notice to Catherine. "How well you look, my dear. That gown is most becoming. Now, may I see you in your mask? It looks very cleverly done."

"Oh, yes! I quite forgot," said Catherine, hurriedly slipping her plumage, which had been perched precariously atop her head, into its proper place.

"That is the perfect touch – not the least bit overdone, which is a novelty tonight, I must say." Lady Astley herself wore a gold-colored gown evoking the idea of an Egyptian queen without being unnecessarily ostentatious.

Catherine could contain her effusions of excitement no longer. They would overflow without further delay.

"Dear, dear, Eleanor. Oh, pardon me! I should have said Lady Astley. But how I have missed you! I hope we shall have much time to talk tonight... or even tomorrow. Your brother and I are prepared to stay if we are invited. And I supposed you and the viscount would be as well, since you have come so far. How is your father? I am not afraid to admit to you that I have been nervous about seeing him again. I cannot tell you how much I appreciate all you did for us in that regard, but I still am not satisfied that he has entirely forgiven us for marrying. Do you think he has?"

"Gracious!" Exclaimed her companion. "I cannot answer as to all that. I can only tell you I should be very pleased if you would call me Eleanor, same as before, and also that my father seems in excellent spirits tonight, perhaps helped along by wine. So I think you may approach him without much trepidation. He is just over there," she said, nodding across the hall to a rotund, bearded man in a royal robe, velvet doublet, garters, jewels, and a hat with an ostrich plume sprouting from it at a rakish angle. He stood with feet apart and fists on hips, staring in their direction as if impatiently waiting.

Catherine's mouth dropped open in amazement. "That is General Tilney? How is it possible? He was not nearly so large a man whenever I knew him before!"

"Oh, Catherine! You do make me smile," said Eleanor with amused affection. "It is a padded suit he wears, and he has grown the beard especially for this occasion. He is dressed as King Henry the Eighth. Do you see?"

"Oh, yes. How silly of me."

"Not at all. He would be very pleased to know how well his costume succeeded in disguising his true identity." Eleanor then addressed her brother. "Henry, you and Catherine really must greet your host without further delay. We will talk more later."

"Of course." Slipping his mask into place, Mr. Tilney tucked his wife's arm into his. "Courage, my dear," he whispered into her ear. "Courage and confidence." Then together they made their way over to pay their respects to the king.

"Good evening, sir," said Henry with a bow. "Thank you for the invitation. Catherine and I look forward to an excellent evening."

General Tilney gave a nod in return. "I am pleased you both have come. I have spared no expense, and I think I can promise you that the evening's entertainments will be something no one here will soon forget."

"How do you mean, sir?"

"You must wait and see, Henry. These things have more impact when they come by surprise."

Just then, a very pretty young woman approached and stood beside General Tilney. Was she dressed as the also-royal Anne Boleyn?

"Ah, there you are. Kindly do not stray off again," the general told her reproachfully. "I would like to introduce to you my younger son. This is Mr. Henry Tilney. You will remember me speaking of him. Henry, this is my very particular friend, Lady Charlotte Penninger. You may have met her some once or twice in years past. She is the daughter of my old friend, the Marquis of Longtown."

"Of course. How nice to see you again, Lady Charlotte." Henry bowed and then introduced Catherine.

They all proclaimed themselves extremely pleased to know one another. But as Mr. and Mrs. Tilney moved away, proceeding on a few feet in the direction of the ballroom, Catherine dropped a private word to her husband. "His 'very particular friend'? Do you suppose Lady Charlotte is meant to be the part of the evening we will not soon forget – the surprise your father has planned? Perhaps your father means to marry her."

"Surely not!" said Henry. "She is *very* young – young enough to be his daughter, as she *is* the daughter of his friend and contemporary. Quite pretty, though," he said, looking back, "and with that classic aristocratic air about her now that she is grown. My father is no doubt intending to show his guests that he is a man of consequence who can still attract the eye of a beautiful young woman. In that respect, he is no different from my brother. Look there."

Catherine directed her gaze toward the grand staircase ahead. There at the top, conspicuous in his uniform, was Captain Tilney, and beside him, just as Henry had implied, was an equally young and equally beautiful lady, although not dressed nearly as fine as Lady Charlotte Penninger. "Do you know who she is?"

"I do. Her name is Miss Virginia Holt. She and her family belong to this parish, so Frederick has known her all his life. I wonder what he means by bringing her here tonight, though. She is entirely unsuitable."

Catherine remembered what Henry and Eleanor had told her

on the subject from when it had seemed as if Captain Tilney might be courting her friend Isabella Thorpe, how the captain would be expected to marry some young woman of wealth and consequence. "Has Miss Holt no fortune, then?"

"No fortune and no name of importance. She is only the innkeeper's daughter. I like her well enough myself, but she will not satisfy my father's vanity as a daughter-in-law and future mistress of this estate. And I should be surprised if she genuinely suits Frederick's own ideas either. Perhaps he has brought her here on purpose to annoy my father."

"Or perhaps this time your brother is truly in love and does not care about the rest."

Catherine was thinking of herself and Henry's similar situation. She could not help but consider her own humble origins as being nearly as annoying to the general as Miss Holt's would be. Although the daughter of a clergyman must always be considered above the daughter of any sort of tradesman, the two of them were probably fairly equal when it came to the smallness of their respective fortunes. So would Captain Tilney's setting his affection on Miss Holt really be a much greater offence than Henry's setting his on Catherine? The only way Catherine could be easy was to remind herself that more was always expected of the eldest son and heir. Perhaps Henry, as only a second son, could be forgiven for marrying beneath himself whereas Captain Tilney could not. Her father-in-law had greeted them civilly enough only moments before, so that must be the case... at least she hoped so.

"In any event," continued Henry, "I shall not be the one to make her feel unwelcome. Come, Catherine, let us go up and greet my brother and his friend."

Before they could do so, however, they heard someone beckoning from the wings. "Mrs. Brooks!" cried Henry, immediately going to and embracing her like a long lost friend.

Catherine recognized the middle-aged woman from her first

visit. Mrs. Brooks was the housekeeper at Northanger, but Henry had explained that she had worked her way up to her current position from her earliest beginnings in the nursery, where she and little Henry initially formed their mutual attachment.

After briefly greeting Catherine too, Mrs. Brooks turned all her effusive attention back to Henry, saying, "Take that mask off for a minute, my boy, and let me get a proper look at you! Bless my soul! You look very well indeed. And you are happy, too; I can tell. I thank the good Lord I have lived to see this day – my young Master Henry all grown up and married."

Henry laughed. "I have been grown for quite some time, Mrs. Brooks, as you know very well. If, however, I look better than when you last saw me a few months ago, give the credit to Mrs. Tilney's influence, by all means."

"That must be so, for a man is never content without a wife. Well now, this is nearly like old times, is it not? With you, Master Frederick, and Miss Eleanor here together again, and the great house all lit up and filled with company." She sighed deeply. "If only your dear mama could be present among us like she used to be…"

"Yes, Mrs. Brooks," said Henry. "That is what everybody would wish above all things. Nevertheless, we mean to enjoy ourselves tonight, just the same."

Mrs. Brooks glanced about before continuing. "I only hope the master will do nothing to spoil it. Oh, but never mind me; it is my job to fret about such things. Now go on with you both. I could not resist saying 'how d'ye do' as you passed by, but I'll not keep you from the pleasures of the evening any longer. I had best be getting back to my work, in any case. It is a busy night for me, and there is no mistaking it, what with extra rooms to prepare and all the food and drink to oversee. It has been a long time since we had this house full, and the less experienced servants hardly know where to begin. The respon-sibility all falls to me. But we shall do very well in the end. We will not see the master or this house disgraced, not while I can help it."

Henry squeezed her hand. "You are a treasure, Mrs. Brooks," he said, "and I know we can completely rely on you. Furthermore, I hope tonight is the beginning of my being on better terms at Northanger again, so that it will not be so long between our visits here in the future."

"From your mouth to God's ear, Master Henry. Let it be so. I have always ventured to put in a good word with your father for you and your missus wherever I could. But he pays my opinions no mind, and I can ill afford to make him angry by persisting."

"Mrs. Brooks!" It was the cross and commanding voice of General Tilney, who had come up behind them unnoticed. "What do you do here? I am surprised at you; you forget yourself. It is not your place to annoy the guests."

"Father," objected Henry, "I am hardly an ordinary guest, and Mrs. Brooks and I are old friends."

"You are nothing of the kind. My sons do not consort with servants. Back to your work this instant, Mrs. Brooks, or I will find something more for you to do."

"Beggin' your pardon, sir," said the housekeeper, hurriedly withdrawing.

Henry opened his mouth to protest, but General Tilney had already turned away. Instead, Henry said to his wife, "He has no business to treat her in that cruel fashion, especially after nearly thirty years of loyal service."

As they moved off together, Catherine fished for a way to restore her husband's mood. "It seems Mrs. Brooks is a great favorite of yours," she said teasingly. "I noticed you were very quick to come to her defense. Should I be jealous?"

Henry smiled then. "Pray, do not trouble yourself, I beg you, my dear Catherine," he said in affected earnestness. "Still, your suspicions are not wholly unjustified. Mrs. Brooks *was* there before you. In fact, she is the first woman I fell madly in love with, there in the nursery these many years ago. And I daresay I never fully recovered from it. Although the age difference ultimately proved insurmountable for all practical purposes, I am still quite devoted to the lady in my heart. I would move heaven and earth to please her, I swear. That is the truth of the matter; now despise me if you wish!"

"Indeed, I do not despise you, sir," Catherine said, copying her husband's playful tone. "I find I must honor your constancy, and I believe I can reconcile myself to sharing your affection with Mrs. Brooks if I must. I only hope in time to inspire the same heroic sort of devotion myself." She then waited in the sanguine expectation of her husband's assurances that she had done so already. Instead, she heard something very different.

"This is a worthy ambition, madam," said Henry, "however unlikely it is to be realized. Although the goal currently seems impossible for you to reach, there is nobleness in continuing to strive against the odds. One must never lose hope entirely."

So little did this answer suit young Mrs. Tilney that she was compelled to give some clear remonstration. Mr. Tilney soon felt the point of her elbow in his ribs, as convincing as if it had been the point of a sword.

"You know I only jest, my love," he said in his own defense, laughing to add weight to his words.

Catherine smiling sweetly up at him, "As do I, my dear, each of us in our own way."

5

BROTHERLY AFFECTION

*T*hese thoughts were soon erased from Catherine's mind in her eager anticipation of the moment when they would at last enter the ballroom, which she had never seen before. It was one of the many rooms at Northanger whose doors had remained closed to her on her former visit. When General Tilney himself had conducted her tour, he had, for reasons known only to himself, deemed this and other sights unfit for her eyes – or her eyes unworthy of beholding them. Consequently, the ballroom had been a subject of desperate curiosity to her in recent days – a curiosity which her husband's perfunctory descriptions had failed to satisfy, though she had repeatedly queried him.

"Is it very grand?" she had asked him.

"Tolerably so, I suppose. I have never given the matter any thought."

"Well, how large a room is it, then? That, you must surely be able to tell me."

"Large enough for a rousing game of battledore of a rainy day, I remember." He laughed.

"Do be serious, Henry!" she chastised him.

"I am perfectly serious. As children, the ballroom was the scene of much fine sport. We would carry on until either we were caught at it or all the shuttlecocks became lodged in the chandeliers and out of reach. Frederick considered it a particular triumph if he could accomplish the latter before the former took place."

Henry smiled at the thought. A look at his silent and unsmiling wife, however, was enough to inform him that his answer was still unacceptable. "I beg your pardon, my sweet," he continued, "but what can I tell you? The ballroom is larger than the ballrooms in most houses, I daresay, but I cannot judge as to exact measurements. It never occurred to me I should be expected to know such a thing, since I am not in the habit of boasting about a ballroom or comparing the size of one to another. A ballroom is a ballroom. If it is large enough to accommodate a goodly number of enthusiastic dancers without danger of them repeatedly crashing into one another or tumbling over the onlookers, surely that is all that matters. In any case, you will see it for yourself soon enough."

Catherine had had no choice but to be satisfied with that... temporarily. But now the moment was nearly at hand when she would indeed judge for herself. She and Henry surmounted the final steps of the grand staircase, only to discover that Captain Tilney and Miss Holt had apparently moved on. Then turning to the right, at last the ballroom lay before them, this time with doors wide open.

Upon passing through that portal, which was magnificent in itself, Catherine's attention flew at once to the high ceiling with its two enormous, glittering chandeliers and then everywhere else, noticing not so much the people milling about but the room itself. She was all admiration.

It was grand and precisely to her taste – certainly not so large as the rooms where she had danced in Bath, but with a more distinctive atmosphere. For just as with so many other parts of

Northanger, one could never entirely forget that this was an ancient and somewhat crumbling edifice. All the fine furnishings in the world could not obscure that fact completely, nor would Catherine have desired them to do so. To her mind, the state of elegant decay, bleeding through here and there despite all efforts to the contrary, only heightened the appeal, testifying to romantic origins and a colorful past.

Briefly, she wondered what alternative purpose this space had served in Northanger Abbey's first incarnation as a religious sanctuary, if indeed the room had existed at the time and not been a more recent addition. Surely the monks or nuns who had originally occupied the building had no need of a ballroom. But it was only a passing question, and Catherine allowed it to do just that – to pass as her mind moved on to other satisfying observations.

In the gently decomposing expanse of plasterwork crowning the walls, she saw the remnant visages of angels and gargoyles peering down at her from above. In the persistent damp, which would never allow the up-to-date papers to adhere properly at the edges, she envisaged the tears shed by generations of former residents through whatever sufferings had pursued them in life and finally hounded them to their deaths. Light from the scores of candles deployed was yet insufficient to penetrate the corners of the cavernous room and chase away whatever shadowy secrets they concealed. In short, it was everything Catherine's imagination could have wished for.

"Well, what do you think of the place, now you see it?" her husband asked.

At this interruption of her pleasant musings, Catherine was reminded of her vow to put her wild flights of fancy behind her. So she simply said, "'Tis a very elegant room," with no mention of unearthly beings or generations of tears. And in truth, when she looked again, this time with greater detachment, she could not be sure that there really was anything so distinctive about the place after all. Perhaps it was just her mind playing tricks on her again, as seemed to always happen at Northanger.

"Very well then, let us get on with the necessary civilities and greet my brother, who is over there." A very few steps and they were in front of Captain Tilney. "Good evening, Frederick," said Henry. "You will remember Catherine."

"Yes, of course. Charmed to see you again, Mrs. Tilney," he said, taking and kissing her hand perfunctorily. "Allow me to introduce Miss Virginia Holt."

When the standard pleasantries had been exchanged, Eleanor came up to join them. "Miss Holt, if you and my sister-in-law would allow me to steal you away for a few minutes, there are some people I should like you to meet." Both of the young ladies eagerly went along, leaving the two brothers side-by-side, watching as they walked away.

Finally, Henry spoke. "I see you have taken even less trouble with your dress than I have, Frederick – a captain wearing a captain's uniform and no mask at all. Is that the best you could do?"

"Yes, well," Frederick began languidly, his hands clasped behind himself and slowly rocking from heels to toes and back again. "As you say, I aimed at taking as little trouble as possible. I did think of at least improving my rank for the evening to something surpassing my father's, but then nobody outranks a king, do they?"

"No one except God," Henry suggested.

"True; that would have been just the thing. But an accurate costume is so difficult to come by," the captain added with a smirk. "Besides, God is more in your line than mine." A short pause stretched into a long one, both men taking time to observe the scene in silence before Captain Tilney continued. "The old pater has really outdone himself tonight, concocting this scheme out of the blue. Makes me wonder what he's up to."

Henry smiled wryly. "You too, eh? I probably should not

admit it, but that was my first thought as well. In fact, I very nearly stayed away altogether."

"Lucky man to have a choice. That was never an option for me, unfortunately. Do you know, Henry, sometimes I almost envy you."

Henry glanced at his brother sideways, saying, "Envy *me*? What can you mean, sir? You would not have me believe you would really exchange your dashing uniform and your status as heir to Northanger for the chance at a religious life, would you?"

Captain Tilney laughed sardonically. "I, a country parson? We both know that would never do. No, I only meant your comparative independence. That is what I envy, not your vocation. You have your comfortable little world, such as it is, already established. You have a living secured that will meet all your present and future needs; you have laid claim to a respectable home of your own; and you have your pretty little wife all to yourself, with no one to disturb you. All this at a safe distance from Northanger. Even Eleanor has lately come up smelling like a rose – a viscountess, no less. And yet here am I, the eldest, still dangling on my father's string, forced to dance to his tune and do his bidding as long as he lives. I am a commander of men! Bowing and scraping goes sharply against the grain."

"So you are finally prepared to admit that Catherine is pretty, are you? The word does not do her justice, of course. I would say beautiful, but from you, who seldom gives a compliment, I will accept 'pretty' on her behalf."

Captain Tilney turned to his brother, hands on hips. "Good god, Henry! I nearly laid my soul bare to you just then. Out of all I said, is that the only thing you heard – that I think your common little wife is not ill looking?"

"That seemed to me the most important bit," Henry said, undaunted. "Anything in Catherine's praise will always engage my attention."

Both men, who had been almost unconsciously following the

progress round the room of the three women who most concerned themselves, now looked more deliberately at Catherine.

"Yes, she is pretty, I admit," said Frederick, "at least pretty enough that I shouldn't have minded giving her a tumble back in Bath, along with her friend. Although I would hardly have gone so far as to *marry* her as you did."

"Mind your tongue, sir!" Henry demanded sharply. "That is my wife you speak of so cavalierly. I warn you, I am prepared to defend her honor if you should make that necessary."

"Easy on, Henry. Easy on. Climb down from your high horse. I am sure I meant no insult to the fair and virtuous Mrs. Tilney. Attractive as she is, she and her reputation are safe from me. I am not completely devoid of principles, you know. Here I will cite you a Biblical reference and say that I am not as bad as King David with Bathsheba. When I can have my pick of all the rest in the world, why would I covet the only lamb of a poor man, and my brother's 'lamb' at that?"

Henry relaxed his guard. "I am impressed with your use of a Biblical illustration, Frederick, for I did not think you had been paying much attention in church. Still, I cannot say it sets my mind completely at ease."

"You should know my style of humor by now, Brother, and that I mean no harm. The thing is, I never could pass by an opening to get a rise out of you. Is it not the elder brother's duty to torture the younger? Nowadays, though, I am more likely to direct such devious ambitions my father's way instead. It is my only recourse, my only chance to rebel a little, to exert a false sort of independence while I wait to inherit. I will not be kept waiting forever; that is my other comfort."

"At that pretty speech, Frederick, I should rise up again and censure you for disrespecting my father in such a manner, as if wishing to hasten his death. But I refuse to give you the satisfaction."

"Very disobliging of you, I'm sure. But you would not be such a hypocrite as to pretend the old man has always been your friend either, not after the trouble he gave our mother and then his insult to the former Miss Morland. With that in mind, you could not have failed to appreciate the sight had you witnessed our dear pater's face tonight when I marched Miss Holt through the front door. With his friends and neighbors looking on, I daresay he will try to behave civilly to me, but it will be a severe exertion for him. For every two glasses of wine he consumes in excess, I and Miss Holt may take credit for at least one."

"Does Miss Holt know she is here only to aggravate your father? She is a sweet girl, from what I know, and I would hate for you to toy with her affections."

"Is it Sunday? For a minute there, I thought you were going to preach me another sermon. For your information, Henry, Miss Holt is here because I enjoy her company. And difficult as you may find this to believe – I know *I* do – she seems to enjoy my company as well. Neither of us has illusions for anything more, however. I must marry a lady of wealth and consequence; everybody knows that, including Miss Holt."

As pleased as Catherine had been to be taken under the patronage of Lady Astley, she was just as eager to return to her husband when the signal was given for the ball to commence. "How lovely," she told him as they joined the forming set, "that since we are now married, we shall not be limited as to the number of dances we share together."

"True enough," Henry cheerfully agreed. "No one will fault you for dancing with your own husband more than once." Then he gave her an arch look. "But perhaps you will very much want to take this singular opportunity of dancing with other men. I am sure you will find it tedious to remain with me all the evening long, when there are so many more intriguing partners available."

"Not at all!" Catherine objected, not perceiving that her husband was once again teasing her. "That is to say, I am sure I should not object to standing up with anybody who asks me. There may be some very pleasant gentlemen on hand, and since they are friends to your father, I would not wish to slight them. But I should ten times prefer to be with you, Henry."

"Dear Catherine, I knew if I went fishing for a compliment, you would not disappoint me. Now, as we dance, tell me to whom my sister has introduced you and what you think of them."

When the music began, Catherine fitted her communication in as best she could around the movements of the dance, being careful no one else could hear those things that were meant for Henry's ears alone. She told Henry of meeting Mr. Oberton, a neighbor and the owner of Compton Court, an estate adjoining Northanger. "From what he said and how he said it, Mr. Oberton does not seem to have entirely cordial feelings towards your father," she finished circumspectly.

"Ah, yes," Henry returned. "They behave civilly to one another in public – hence his presence here tonight – but there has been somewhat of a personal feud between them for years. Allegations of unlawful water diversions and accusations of poaching are regularly thrown back and forth across the disputed property lines. My father has had the surveyor out more than once, and hostilities lie very close to the surface, I am afraid."

"That would explain his inability to conceal his negative sentiments, I suppose. I was surprised he was not more discreet. And do please keep your voice down, dearest. It would not be advisable to be overheard."

"No need to whisper, I assure you, just as there was no need for Mr. Oberton to be discreet. His feud with my father is common knowledge. I daresay everybody here – everybody but you, my dear – already knew of it."

"Really? That seems very odd." Here, the movements of the dance kept the pair fully occupied for a time as they crossed in and out, to and fro, and passed down the set. At the next opportunity, Catherine resumed her account as if there had been no interruption. "And Eleanor introduced us to Lady Charlotte's father."

"The Marquis of Longtown."

"Yes, and General Courteney."

"No feuds there. I believe my father considers those two gentlemen his oldest friends. The story is that General Courtney introduced my mother, who was a very great friend of his, to my father these many years ago. And the Marquis... Well, one always feels more important if one can claim nobility amongst one's friends. Although I do not know either well myself, you should definitely dance with each of them if they ask you. Did you like them?"

"Dear me, I hardly know! They both behaved very handsomely, but I am so unaccustomed to coming face to face with men of such distinction that I could barely speak a word myself. They will have nothing flattering to say of me!"

"Never fear, my love. Gentlemen of distinction are not blind to the obvious appeal of a young lady such as yourself. Did you see anybody else worth mentioning?"

"Oh, yes! The most delightful creature: Lady Melanie Rice. There she is," said Catherine, nodding and smiling at an elegant lady of a certain age who passed by in the adjoining set. "Do you know her, Henry?"

Henry looked and nodded as well. "A little," he said. "Very well connected, as I recall. Friends in high places, especially in Derbyshire, I believe. Yes, she is well worth knowing. You found her charming?"

"Ever so charming! But now it is your turn, Henry. You must tell me all about your conversation with your brother while we were apart. Was it everything you could have hoped?"

After a pause to accomplish a particularly demanding figure

of the dance, Henry answered, "Perhaps not. Everything I could have expected, more like: bravado, sarcasm, irreverence, innuendo. You have experienced a large enough sample of Frederick's actions and speech to predict the rest. I take nothing above half of what he says to heart myself. The strange thing is, though, that I have the idea he might actually care for Miss Holt after all, as you suggested."

"How interesting!" Catherine exclaimed, her eyes wide. "Did he say so plainly?"

"No, not in so many words. It was more in how his gaze seemed to follow her as she moved about the room with you and Eleanor, and what he said about envying me my relative independence to act. I could be wrong, though. I do not pretend to understand what goes on in my brother's head. We are two very different sorts of men. He takes after my father, and I like to think I favor my mother."

"That is all the more reason I wish I had known her. If she was anything like you, I am sure we would have been great friends."

"I believe so, Catherine. I do believe so."

6

A CHANGE IN ATMOSPHERE

*H*ad it not been for the ferocious storm brewing outside in the darkness, the notice of which occasionally intruded itself upon the merrymakers inside, nothing about the Northanger ball could have been judged less than entirely agreeable. The costumes, for the most part, were creative and colorful. The orchestra, brought from London especially for the occasion, was definitely first rate. Those dancing carried on quite energetically. And even the lookers-on were doing their part to add spirit to the evening by heartily talking, laughing, and especially drinking.

General Tilney set the chief example in this last category himself. But as to the dancing, although he encouraged his 'particular friend,' Lady Charlotte Penninger, to dance as much as she liked, he preferred to preside and observe, periodically lifting his glass (which the servants were careful to keep filled) to his lips again. He was also nearly the only one who did not seem to find the blinding flash at the windows and the deafening clap of thunder that presently exploded straight overhead the least bit daunting. While others, including the musicians, ceased their movements to look fretfully up at the ceiling, half expecting it to fall in upon them, their host applauded and cheered as if the noisy interruption had been the highest form of entertainment.

"I do believe my father intends to take full credit for arranging this storm," Henry told Catherine, with whom he happened to be dancing again at the time. "Far less expensive than a display of fireworks and yet just as impressive."

Catherine turned and looked. "He does appear to be enjoying it tremendously. I do not mind a storm either. It is only unfortunate that the dancing should be interrupted." In truth, Catherine could not help thinking nature's cacophony fittingly enhanced the Gothic feel already established by the setting and date on the calendar.

When both the echo of the thunder clap and the resulting shock to the company had somewhat died away, the music and the dancing resumed, tentatively at first but soon returning to something approaching their previous level of enthusiasm. Mr. and Mrs. Tilney did likewise.

Catherine was thoroughly enjoying herself. She had danced with her husband twice, both her brothers-in-law once apiece, Mr. Oberton, General Courteney, and one other gentleman whose name she could not recall, never standing idle. Two dances after the supper break were already reserved with her as well, she was pleased to remember. Her husband's prediction had come true. Catherine knew she had been looked at, admired, and sought out as a dance partner. It was a triumph and all that she could wish for at that moment in the way of perfect felicity.

A few minutes later, however, the festive atmosphere was disrupted once more. The sky rumbled and flashed as dramatically as before, but to this, something still more distressing was added. An icy current of air cut through the ballroom, rattling windows, jangling nerves, and brutally assaulting chandeliers, putting out nearly all of their candles.

As darkness swallowed the crowd, several ladies shrieked and at least one collapsed senseless to the floor. To her credit, Mrs. Tilney did no such thing. She merely drew closer to her husband, thankful it was his and not some stranger's arms that were available to fold securely about her at that moment. "What is it, Henry?" she asked. "What has happened?"

"Do not be alarmed, my dear. No doubt somebody has carelessly left a couple of doors or windows open for fresh air. That has given the storm winds easy purchase. The situation will soon be rectified."

A commanding voice rose above the whimpering and nervous murmurs circulating throughout the ballroom. Although the speaker himself was cloaked in the same darkness as everybody else, it was undoubtedly their host, General Tilney himself, who spoke. "Ladies and Gentlemen," he bellowed, "please calm yourselves and listen to me. Although I myself consider this storm a bonus, as it adds to the mood more than I could have hoped to provide for you myself, I am sorry for any distress it may have caused. While the servants address the problem of the draft and relight the candles, I suggest we adjourn for the supper break a few minutes early. All has been made ready, and I am assured that the room is warm and well lit. Kindly make your way in an orderly fashion through the open doors."

A cheerful glow appeared to one side, and everybody immediately gravitated toward it. Catherine and Henry held back, however, allowing others to go ahead of them.

Close together in the darkness, Henry asked his wife, "You are not afraid, are you?"

"Afraid? Not with you beside me. In fact, I am inclined to agree with your father that the storm only adds something to the mood. It is All Hallows Eve, after all. I am only sorry to miss the rest of our dance together, but I suppose it cannot be helped."

"Perhaps you would be so good as to allow me another later in exchange," said Henry, beginning to nuzzle her neck, "that is if you still have any dances free. Your company is much sought after tonight, my love, just as I had foreseen."

Distracted but determined not to give in, at least not just yet, Catherine replied, "Well, the first after the break is reserved for the marquis, and the second for Sir Arthur Canbury, who is only a baronet. But I can put you down for the third, if you like."

"That is exceedingly generous of you, my dear, to grant such a kindness to a lowly clergyman with no title at all. Allow me to demonstrate my gratitude."

He did so with a passionate embrace and a kiss that made Catherine's susceptible little heart race. There was something thrilling in knowing they were surrounded by people and yet perfectly concealed.

"I would not do it for just any clergyman, you understand," Catherine said breathlessly when the kiss at last gave way. "If you were not so very handsome, you would stand no chance with me at all, I assure you."

They shared a low, conspiratorial laugh and then another long kiss. And if Henry's hands strayed a little further than they should have in public, and if Catherine responded with more fervor than what would be considered seemly, who was to know?

The average observer to events at the ball would have logically assumed that the most sensational aspects of the evening had passed by the time the company adjourned prematurely for the supper break. After all, the noisy tempest had already begun receding into the distance, and it was unlikely to return. General Tilney had entertainment of his own still held in reserve, however, to which nature's theatricals had been only an unexpected opening act. And yet even the general did not suspect to where it would all lead.

The supper was very fine. As he had boasted to Henry, the

general had spared no expense, offering his guests every delicacy one might imagine: negus, white soup, cold meats thinly sliced, along with pineapples and other hothouse fruits. It was as if with the extravagance of that one night's hospitality he intended to make up to his neighbors for his long years of inattention.

The general may have been the one who opened the purse strings for the occasion, but Henry knew Mrs. Brooks deserved the lion's share of the credit for carrying it off. Glancing over his shoulder, he observed her at the back of the room, hovering unobtrusively and yet near enough to be sure all was well. Catching her eye, he raised his glass to her in a private salute, acknowledging her achievement when probably no one else would, least of all his father.

The general sat at the head table with Lady Charlotte Penninger again beside him, and no one partook of the feast – especially the wine – with more enthusiasm than he did himself. In hindsight, many wondered how much of the shocking business that followed had been intended by him and how much the general overshot his original mark, urged on by the fortification of excessive drink. His speech was not much slurred, people later recalled, but there was a slight yet distinct swaying back and forth as he addressed them.

In any case, when most of the company had eaten their fill and before anybody could escape back to the ballroom, General Tilney demanded their attention by standing and repeatedly ringing his knife against the crystal goblet before him. This having the desired effect, conversations ceased, one by one, and all eyes soon turned to their host.

The general's discourse began mildly enough.

"I hope you are enjoying yourselves," he said. He then waited for some response from his eager audience.

Their manners did not fail. There was a rapid swell of applause and various cheers. "Hear, hear!" "A fine ball, General." "Well done!"

When he was satisfied, the general went on. "Excellent. It was my first purpose to show you all a good time. But there was something more. I thought this sort of gathering the perfect venue for making announcements as well. Say it once when everybody is present and be done. That was my idea, for important changes have occurred in my family, and there are more to come."

General Tilney paused for effect, taking the opportunity to imbibe a little more wine as well. His listeners, for the most part, sat in rapt attention, silently speculating as to what these announcements might entail. Henry, however, feeling instantly on his guard, slipped his hand under the table to find and hold fast to Catherine's.

"As you may know," the general continued, "two of my children are lately married. First, I will speak of my daughter Eleanor, who has done me proud by her marriage. I do not even mind that she now outranks me." He laughed at his joke and was joined by others. "On the contrary; it is exactly what I would have wished for." Directing his gaze to where Eleanor and her husband were sitting, the general raised his glass. "Please join me in drinking the health of the Viscount and Viscountess Astley."

The toast was well received, all answering with the expected shout of "To the Viscount and Viscounte" Soon enough, though, their attention turned back to the general, who was obviously only getting started.

"My younger son Henry might have done as well for himself and for the family if only he had listened to me!"

At this, the mood of the company immediately shifted. Smiles prematurely died, and uneasy glances began flitting in the direction of Mr. and Mrs. Tilney, who were naturally the most discomfited of all. There was nothing to be done about it, however. They were a captive audience and must listen to whatever followed or risk creating a worse scene. Although what came next was bad enough.

"Henry," said the general, now addressing his son directly across the short intervening distance, "you will soon feel the full weight of my displeasure. Since you have chosen to go your own way – following your own foolish inclinations and marrying beneath yourself instead of doing as your father wished – you will now reap your just deserts. The independence you claim cuts both ways, sir. Since you no longer recognize my authority over you, I am sure you are also much too proud to want my help any longer. So I hereby serve notice that I am withdrawing the Wood-ston living from you and will give it to another."

At this, a sharp, universal intake of breath could be heard throughout the room. The sharpest – fully a gasp – came from Mrs. Tilney herself. Turning to her husband, she whispered in his ear. "Can he do that, Henry? I thought the appointment was meant to be for life."

"It was," Henry answered levelly, returning his father's glare across the room without blinking.

"Ah, I see I have your full attention now," continued General Tilney. "It will not be easy, but my attorney assures me it can be done. He will be here tomorrow to begin the necessary legal proceedings. Let that be a warning to you as well, Frederick." His eyes scanned the crowd until they located his other son. "There you are," he continued with a sneer, "alongside the charming *innkeeper's daughter*, I see. You will marry to please me, sir, or your inheritance will slip away from you just as surely as your brother's. I still have it in my power to raise up another, more worthy heir if it becomes necessary."

By now, the violent murmurings of the assembly had nearly erupted out of control.

"One more thing before you go back to your dancing!" the general loudly declared. He was a man who knew how to give orders and have them obeyed. With his grip on the company now restored, he smiled arrogantly and turned to Lady Charlotte, holding his hand out for hers, which she reluctantly gave him. "I have saved the best news for last. I am pleased to announce that this lovely young lady has lately agreed to become my wife. Therefore, I invite you to raise your glasses once more, this time to the Lady Charlotte Penninger: the next mistress of Northanger Abbey."

7

HIDE AND SEEK

*N*o one is shocked when a rich man in his middle years takes a bride half his age. Such things are far too commonplace to raise alarm. So the company's hesitation to celebrate the general's final announcement had little to do with that and much more to do with what had gone before. Their host's unfortunate conduct had entirely spoilt the festive mood of the evening and thrown the whole party into confusion. The guests did not rightly know how to behave in such circumstances, at least not until General Tilney told them a second time, more forcefully.

"I said, raise your glasses to the Lady Charlotte Penninger!" They automatically if unenthusiastically obeyed, drinking the health of the prospective bride. "Now back to your dancing… I insist!" the general added when no one moved.

A hurried exodus then began. Lady Charlotte was first to flee the room, visibly shaken and crying. To his credit, General Tilney followed after her, presumably to offer her comfort.

Some of the guests, who had seen and heard and eaten quite enough by then, called for their carriages. But most returned to the ballroom instead. It had been restored to order by this time, with the musicians in place ready to play for anybody still prepared to dance, of which there were a surprising number. Fashionable private balls were few and far between in that part of Gloucestershire, and so this opportunity could hardly be squandered, despite the recent unpleasantness.

Henry and Catherine, however, each gripping the other's hand as if it were the last lifeline available, remained where they were, too stricken to move or even to speak at first.

"Oh, Henry!" cried Eleanor, rushing up to his table with her husband following, once the crowd had cleared away a little. "I am more sorry than I can tell you that my father should have behaved so badly! He cannot possibly mean what he says, though. That would be too cruel."

Sauntering up, Captain Tilney remarked dryly, "That was quite a performance. Do not you all think so? The old pater certainly knows how to create an unholy uproar."

Emerging from her stunned silence, Catherine blinked, looked about, and then asked the captain, "Where is Miss Holt?"

"Oh, she needed a few minutes alone to recover. It seems the old man's words have cut her deeply." The captain's eyes hardened. "Someone really ought to teach him that a gentleman cannot treat people in such a barbaric fashion without consequences. Abusing and humiliating people before a large company of their friends and neighbors? I would not have thought even *he* was capable of that."

"It may be only the wine talking," said Eleanor. "Let us hope he will remember none of it tomorrow, least of all what he said about withdrawing your living, Henry."

All eyes turned to Henry, who still had not spoken a word. Taking a deep breath to fortify himself first, he said, "I wish that might be so, Eleanor, but I dare not depend on it. He was not so impaired as to be unaware of what he was doing. In fact, he may have been planning this for some time – to punish me in the most public and painful way possible. You simply received the overflow of his contempt for me, Frederick, which you might have been spared altogether had you not provoked him tonight by bringing Miss Holt."

"Still, the general cannot be beyond the reach of reason," said the viscount, helpfully. "Surely he will repent of this evil plan in the clear light of day. He has had his revenge tonight and can now want nothing more."

Henry laughed sardonically. "What do you think, Eleanor? Did you find the man calm and reasonable when you wanted to marry Jonathan before, before he was made acceptable to your father by becoming a viscount?"

"Not at all," she said gravely. "He was harsh and entirely unyielding."

"And so I expect to find him now. Still," Henry said wearily as he pushed himself up to stand, "one must make the attempt. There is nothing else to be done. Perhaps if I grovel a bit and say my *mea culpa* convincingly enough, he will be satisfied."

"You mean to speak to him tonight?" asked Catherine, jumping to her feet in some alarm.

"Of course. Tomorrow may be too late, with his attorney coming and all."

"No, Henry, you mustn't!" cried Catherine, clutching at the lapels of his coat. "I fear some worse result. Let us leave this place at once, I beg you."

"And go where, my dear?" he asked, patiently but firmly peeling away each of her fingers in turn. "Your father-in-law has just promised to make us homeless. Besides, how could the situation be made any worse by my speaking to the man? It seems to me the worst has already occurred. Now calm yourself and stay here with Eleanor and Jonathan until I return."

Placing a reassuring arm about Catherine's shoulders, Eleanor said, "Henry will be prudent, and who knows? Something useful may come of it. As he says, he must at least try."

"Good luck, Henry," said Captain Tilney, shaking his head.

"You will need it, if by talk alone you intend to make a lasting impression upon the old man's hard head." He then made a fist with which he struck the palm of his other hand. "Personally, I would recommend something more persuasive be brought to bear. But that's hardly your style, is it? Well, I had best see what has become of Miss Holt. After all, I am the one who brought her into this madness."

The two brothers walked off in the same general direction to seek their different quarries. Catherine, watching them go, could not be easy. The evening, which had begun so well, had taken such a strange and ominous turn. Who could say what would happen next?

By this time, the supper room had emptied of other guests, leaving only the three family members along with a host of servants, who were clearing away the leavings.

"Now, my dear Catherine, let us sit down and wait quietly," suggested Eleanor. "I am sure none of us is in any humor to return to the noise of the ballroom."

Catherine acquiesced so far as sitting was concerned, but to wait quietly was entirely beyond her power. Her agitation would not be soothed away so easily. "It is my fault," she cried. "Poor Henry! None of this would have befallen him had I never come along. He might have married somebody else – somebody more acceptable – and never been in trouble with his father."

"Nonsense," said Eleanor calmly, with her arm still about Catherine's shoulders. "You did nothing at all. My father himself invited you to know his son, and if he is not satisfied with what resulted, he has no one to blame but himself. Although he will never admit it."

"But what shall we do? If the general carries through on his threat, where shall Henry and I go? We have little money to speak of and no other prospects. We cannot possibly go to my father. He already has too many under his roof, too many mouths to feed."

"Have no fear, my dearest," soothed Eleanor. "First of all, I am by no means certain that my father has it in his power to revoke Henry's living, even with an attorney's help. But if he does, Henry, with his excellent reputation, is sure to be offered another parish in due course. Until then, you shall not be homeless; you must stay with us. We have plenty of room, and we would be very pleased to have you. Would we not, Jonathan?" she said, turning to her husband, who stood a few feet off.

"I can think of nothing I would like better," replied the viscount graciously. "In fact, I will not hear of your going elsewhere, Mrs. Tilney."

"There, now," said Eleanor firmly. "Do you see? Even if the worst should happen, you have nothing whatsoever to dread."

Catherine did quiet her fears a little at this, sincerely comforted by the warm assurances of her friends. Although it would grieve her tremendously to leave her home at Woodston, she felt that acquiring Eleanor's company in exchange would go far indeed towards compensating her for that loss. And as long as she and Henry could be together… and not entirely destitute… little else really mattered.

The three of them waited in silence several minutes, as yet without any sign of Henry's, the captain's, or the general's return. Although Catherine was outwardly calmer, she knew she would not be completely comfortable again until her husband rejoined them. Regardless of the news he brought, she believed she could now bear to accept it. In the meantime, she could hear the music of the ball carrying on at a distance, reminding her that little more than an hour before, she had been dancing herself, without a care in the world. It seemed a lifetime ago for how much had changed since.

An odd sound startled Catherine from her contemplations "What was that noise?" she cried, eyes suddenly wide.

"What?" asked Eleanor.

"Did not you hear it? It was neither a moan nor a creak but

something in between, like the groan of carriage timbers while running over rough ground."

Then it came a second time and louder, followed by a thud and a rumble as if something ponderously heavy had been toppled and then dragged against its will.

"Now *that*, I heard." said Eleanor. "What do you make of it, Jonathan?"

"I hardly know," said the viscount, with a look of concern. "It certainly is odd, though."

A similar noise sounded once more, this time with the addition of a crash and a clatter.

"It seems to be coming from somewhere above," continued the viscount. "Absent the other men of the family, I feel obliged to investigate. You two will be safe enough here with the servants standing by." Then before his wife or sister-in-law could object, he dashed away.

After he had gone, Catherine looked about herself. There were indeed many servants still going about their business, although more fretfully now. They had apparently heard the noises too, whereas those in the ballroom had not, judging from the incongruently cheerful music that continued uninterrupted.

"It seems all our men have deserted us," said Catherine, getting to her feet. "Walk with me, Eleanor. Just a turn or two about the room. I cannot possibly sit still another moment, not with so many unanswered questions spinning about in my head."

Eleanor took her sister's proffered hand and threaded it through her own arm as they moved off along the outer perimeter, skirting the tables, chairs, and servants at their work. Their walk was not the aimless stroll of the carefree in a garden of a summer afternoon. This was more the silent march of dread a soldier might make on his way to war, feelings of dark foreboding for what awaits him there nipping at his heels.

Halfway through their second turn, Mr. Oberton from the adjoining estate, who looked quite disheveled with his cravat coming undone and his hair half drenched in sweat, nearly collided with the ladies when he abruptly emerged through the side door.

"Oh!" exclaimed Eleanor, starting back a little in surprise. "Mr. Oberton, I almost did not see you in time."

"Forgive me ladies," he replied with a hasty bow, "and please excuse my appearance. But I am glad to have found you nonetheless. I need to take my leave without delay, and yet I could not immediately locate the general. I will of course send a card of thanks, but in the meantime would you be so good as to convey my compliments to him at your earliest convenience? Please say that I enjoyed the dancing immensely."

Eleanor smiled warmly. "Certainly, Mr. Oberton. I would be happy to."

"Thank you, Lady Astley. I am much obliged. Good night, Mrs. Tilney." He bowed again and departed.

Watching him go, Catherine said, "Judging from his appearance and his words, he must have been carrying on very spiritedly in the ballroom."

"Yes. Well at least somebody was able to find pleasure in these events." Eleanor pulled out and consulted her watch. "Midnight," she said. "I wonder where my father has got to. Perhaps he and Henry are still in conversation. Let us hope this long absence augurs for a beneficial outcome."

Just then Henry appeared and strode towards them, looking nearly as disheveled as Mr. Oberton had been a minute before, and twice as agitated.

"Here is Henry!" Catherine exclaimed.

"Have you seen my father?" Henry asked of his wife and sister as soon as he had nearly reached them. "I have been all over this house, some of it more than once, without any success. No one seems to know where he has got to."

"No, he has not been here." said Eleanor, her brow furrowed.

"And now what has become Jonathan?" Henry continued in exasperation, looking right and left.

"We heard the strangest noises," answered Catherine, "and he went off to investigate."

"Good lord, what a night!" said Henry. "Everybody seems to have gone missing, including Mrs. Brooks. When I had no luck locating my father, I hoped she might direct me. But no, she was nowhere to be found either. Well, I suppose we shall have to send out a search party after our lost friends if they do not turn up soon. That is the trouble with this enormous, old abbey: too many places to lose oneself. Although it made for hours of sport when we were children, it has been a great inconvenience to me tonight, foiling me at every turn." Looking down at his wife and taking her hands, he sighed and smiled ruefully. "I have failed you, my darling. Shall you mind very much leaving Woodston, should it come to that?"

Gazing up into his face – the face of the man she loved almost more than life itself – Catherine thought she should never mind anything much at all, so long as Henry was by her side. "Of course I shall miss Woodston," she told him truthfully. "But a house is only a house. Another place will do as well if you are there with me."

Henry bent to kiss her. Before he could finish the job to his satisfaction, however, the night air was split in two by a heart-stopping, female scream – followed by another and another – coming from the vicinity of the front hall. Henry, Catherine, and Eleanor hastened in that direction to find one of the younger maids there, sobbing inconsolably. Since not one of the many who had arrived on the spot before them seemed to have been able to discover what her trouble was, Henry took charge of the situation. Going to the maid, he grasped her shoulders and shook them. "Look at me," he said with authority. She obeyed. "Now, tell me what the matter is. What has happened?"

Trembling all over, the girl thrust an unsteady finger towards the partially open front door. "It's... it's the master, sir," she cried out in anguish. "I think he is dead!"

Everybody gasped in unison. White faced, Henry flew out of the door while Catherine and Eleanor clasped hands together for mutual support.

The music had ceased, and the growing crowd – spilling down the staircase and collecting in the great hall – remained hushed in suspense. Other than a few whispers, communicating the little that was known so far to the newcomers, only the subsiding sobs of the unfortunate maid broke the silence. She was now comforted by Mrs. Brooks, who had turned up, no doubt drawn like everybody else by the girl's bone-chilling screams.

When young Mr. Tilney presently returned, no words were necessary to give confirmation to the girl's dreadful report. The truth was announced clearly enough by the heaviness of his step and his devastated expression. His woeful eyes first met his wife's and then his sister's, holding a moment with each before surveying the crowd of faces for the one other that he sought.

Finding it, Henry said gravely, "Frederick, would you please go for the magistrate. Everybody else must stay at least until he arrives. It appears that tonight there has been a murder at Northanger Abbey."

8

NECESSARY MEASURES

*A*ll the earlier noise and confusion was as nothing compared to the chaos that now descended upon the house. There was an immediate uproar, some turning this way and others that. People did not know what to say or how to behave, most having never before found themselves at the scene of a serious crime... nor had they ever hoped to.

Captain Tilney did not lose his head, however, and neither did his brother. They – two of those who had the most reason to be alarmed by the distressing event – were the ones to comfort the others by their surprisingly calm demeanors and business-like efficiency.

After briefly viewing the body for himself, Captain Tilney spoke to the assembly, raising his voice to be heard over the troubled murmurings encircling him. "It is unfortunately true; your friend and my father, General Tilney, is dead. It is too soon to call it murder, however. It may well have been an accident instead. In any case, my brother is correct. The magistrate must be informed at once, and no one can be allowed to leave before he arrives. Please try to make yourself comfortable until then."

At the same time, Henry sought out his friend, the house-keeper, saying in a low voice, "Mrs. Brooks, a blanket or table-cloth, if you please. Something to… to cover your master." Nodding and crying profusely, Mrs. Brooks scurried away. Then Henry turned to the butler. "Hastings, I want you to take two footmen and stand guard over the body. I hate to send you out in this wretched weather, but it cannot be helped. The corpse must not be tampered with or moved until the magistrate and his men have seen it."

Showing no outward emotion, the butler simply bowed and said, "Very good, sir."

Once these necessary measures were taken, Henry's mask of careful control began to slip. The whole evening had been a strain out of all proportion, which had gone from bad to worse – worse than he or anybody else could possibly have imagined. It was a nightmare, in fact, one from which Henry would have been extremely glad to awaken.

Instead, he looked to his wife.

Catherine was all wide eyed with shock and wonder. "Oh, Henry!" she said in alarm when he came to her. "What can this mean?"

"I hardly know," he said, taking both her hands with the restraint the situation required. "I cannot accept what I have seen with my own eyes, nor can I image to where it will lead. Rather than my father being dead, I should more readily believe he had been playing another one of his vulgar tricks on us. The odd humor he was in tonight, I would scarcely have put it past him."

"I understand what you are saying, Henry, but you know that cannot be so."

"Yes, I know. It is just that, as bad as it would be, I would prefer it to the truth."

The viscount had by his time returned, and Eleanor was weeping quietly against his shoulder.

"What a touching scene," said Captain Tilney sarcastically, joining them. "Husbands and wives comforting each other in their time of great loss. One unfamiliar with the facts might actually be convinced you cared for the dead man."

"Frederick!" cried Eleanor. "Your father has just died. Show some respect."

"Do not be alarmed, sister. I will do all that is right and proper on the occasion. But I will not play the hypocrite, feigning filial devotion that I did not feel. The general did nothing in this life to earn my affection, and I refuse to pretend otherwise. It is all nonsense that just because a man has died people feel the need to make him out some sort of saint. He was a nasty piece of work from first to last, and I, for one, am not sorry he is gone."

This time it was Henry's turn to object. "Frederick, do hold your tongue!"

"Are you so quick to give orders?" Frederick demanded. "Even to me? Has it not occurred to you, little brother, that this is *my* house now? I am the master here, and I am the one to tell the housekeeper and butler what to do, not you." His words had the desired effect. "Ah, I see from your confusion that you had not yet thought of that, had you?" Henry made no reply. "Nevertheless, I would rather ride out into the night air to get the magistrate than stay here to be looked at by our sad-eyed neighbors. You may do the hand holding, Henry. As a parson, that should be right in your line." The captain paused to look about himself, saying in a softened tone, "I do not see Miss Holt. Eleanor, do look out for her. Tell her what has happened and where I have gone."

To everybody's relief, Captain Tilney then departed.

"Who is the magistrate?" Catherine asked her husband, still clinging to his hands for security.

"My father was one, and I suppose Frederick will succeed

him there too. Funny. As he said, it had not yet dawned on me that Frederick was now master of Northanger. And it still seems impossible. It is one shock after another tonight." He gave a shuddering sigh. "In any case, my brother could not have presided as magistrate in the death of his own father. So the next nearest man is Sir Melvin Whitmore, some six or seven miles off."

"Is he a good man?"

"I do not know him well, but I believe him to be fair and sensible. I trust we are in good hands and that he will soon get to the bottom of this."

"And do you really believe it was murder, Henry? Mightn't it have been an accident, as your brother suggested?"

Henry frowned. "Frederick only said that to calm the crowd. He knows as well as I do that this was no accident – not with the position of the body. It looked every bit to me as if somebody had pushed him from the roof, pushed him hard considering where and how he came to rest."

Catherine gasped. "How horrible!" she exclaimed. "Perhaps, though, one way to die is much like another? It was over quickly at least, I suppose, and hopefully he did not suffer much."

As Catherine shed a few tears for her departed father-in-law and for his grisly end, Henry placed a comforting arm about her shoulders. "Yes, let us hold on to that thought. Whatever he suffered in this life – as well as his power to inflict suffering on others – it is finished now. Although, who knows how far reaching the ramifications of the manner of his death may be?"

Catherine sniffled and asked, "How do you mean, Henry? What far-reaching ramifications are there to be expected?"

"There will be an investigation, presumably followed by a coroner's inquest and a trial, if a suspect is identified. We will not soon see the end of it."

Catherine pulled away enough to look Henry in the face.

"But if it really was murder, who do you suppose could have done it?"

"I cannot say, my love, for in truth, I have no idea. In his life-time, my father made his share of enemies of one degree or another, some of whom were in this very house tonight. I have heard that when there is a murder, it is most often committed by someone close to the victim."

Henry said no more, but only gave his wife a significant look, holding her gaze for a long moment. Though Mrs. Tilney's understanding was not of a particularly brilliant order, still the implications soon became clear to her. And of course Henry must be right, for he always was. There were no strangers in the house that night, only servants and supposed friends. So if the general had indeed been murdered, it had to have been by somebody relatively close to him. But how close? That was the question.

They were both silent for a few minutes, and then Henry shook his head. "How ironic," he said.

"What is?" asked Catherine.

"I was just remembering how I once berated you for imag-ining there could ever have been a murder in this house – that in England, with our laws and with our religion, such a thing was highly improbable, even inconceivable. I believe I spouted some pompous nonsense about no one being foolish enough to attempt such a thing in an open society where everything is subject to the scrutiny of his neighbors and even the press. Yet now a murder has indeed taken place in this house this very night, and right under our noses too, under the noses of a host of neighbors and servants. And so far it appears no one saw a thing. Catherine, I owe you an apology."

Catherine took no joy in this supposed victory or in Henry's disillusionment either. She would much rather have lived in a world where he had been right, where law and social order kept such things as murder far away or confined to the pages of books. Whereas books one could close, set aside, and forget about, this was all too real for common comfort.

The family remained huddled together while the crowd began to disperse to various parts of the house. Some returned to the ballroom, where the musicians, whose services had been engaged and paid for until two o'clock in the morning, were now softly playing tunes more suited to mourning than dance. Some went in search of comfortable furniture on which to recline while they waited. The lucky ones were the few who had been intending to stay the night. They had assigned chambers to retreat to. Still, no doubt even they would have preferred the hospitality of their own beds at such a time.

No one was ill-mannered enough to complain aloud about their discomfort. A man had just died by violent means, after all. Their own inconvenience was surely nothing to *his*.

Instead, there was much whispering and mental strain engaged over the questions of who was to blame and how long their wait would be. Some said the magistrate would surely come within the hour, and then they would soon be on their way. Others said that could not be the case. Captain Tilney might cover the original distance in good time, but then the magistrate would likely need to be rousted from his bed. He would in turn send for the constables, the mortuary wagon, and probably a doctor. The entire procession could not possibly be assembled and transported to Northanger in less than three hours. Unfortunately, the proponents of this second theory would prove the most accurate. And each person present marked the slow passage of time in his or her own way.

Miss Holt turned up shortly after Captain Tilney had gone. Eleanor, tolerably calm herself by this time, took the girl under her wing, explaining the situation and giving what comfort she could. Miss Holt stayed with the small family party – Henry, Catherine, Jonathan, and Eleanor – as they waited out the hours sequestered in a small parlor away from all the others. There was not much conversation since too little was yet known to allow any useful speculation. As it was by this time advancing into the wee hours of the night – the morning, in actuality – eyelids became heavy and fitful sleep claimed nearly all of them at some point.

One person who did *not* join the Tilney family's vigil was Lady Charlotte Penninger, who was to have been their unlikely stepmother, had not events taken this ugly turn. Catherine had caught a glimpse of the lady following the announcement of the general's demise, and she thought that Lady Charlotte did not look so much as if her best chance for happiness had just expired. In fact, she looked more like one who has had the weight of the world suddenly lifted from her shoulders. Perhaps she had not wanted to marry General Tilney at all, Catherine reasoned. Even if she had before, the general had so badly embarrassed her tonight that she might have repented ever agreeing to the match. Either way, she had now been given a most unexpected reprieve.

Catherine secretly cherished similar feelings, for, once the initial shock was over, she could not help wondering if her father-in-law's timely death might have rescued herself and her husband from a disagreeable fate as well. Now, with no one to take it from him, would Henry be allowed to retain the Woodston living and the parsonage house that went with it? Out of the ashes, a flicker of hope kindled within Catherine's tender heart. The decision would probably fall to Captain Tilney now, she reasoned. And despite her low opinion of him, Catherine could not quite imagine him taking the trouble of turning his brother out only to cause himself the additional inconvenience of finding a replacement. No, perhaps the general's death would be their salvation.

Captain Tilney returned to the house first and was shown by Mrs. Brooks to the parlor where the rest of his family awaited.

"Sir Melvin and the others follow directly," he told them. "They will want to examine the body first. Henry, you had better come along. And Jonathan, I suppose you may as well. We will need several men to hold torches. Mrs. Brooks, could you summon the maid whose screams so effectively alerted us to the problem? Sir Melvin will want to speak to her, since she discovered the body. What is the girl's name?"

"Her name is Annie, sir," Mrs. Brooks informed him, blotting both eyes. "But could it not wait until morning? She was in such a terrible state after her ordeal that I sent her to her bed."

"Well, now you will just have to order her back out of it and downstairs," the captain said impatiently. "None of us should expect to sleep tonight."

"Yes, sir." With an obedient nod of her downcast countenance, Mrs. Brooks left them.

Jonathan and Henry rose to go with the captain.

"Shall I come as well, Henry?" asked Catherine, getting to her feet. "I am capable of holding a torch."

With a grim sort of laugh, Henry replied, "No, my love; you will not be needed. I know General Courteney and the Marquis will want to help. And there are Hastings and the footmen already standing by. Besides, what kind of a man would I be if I allowed my wife to be exposed to such a gruesome scene unnecessarily? This is not like one of the horrid stories you read. It is quite a different thing when it is real."

"I know that, Henry!" Catherine exclaimed, affronted. "That is not what I was thinking at all! I simply did not wish to be parted from you again so soon."

He smiled sadly at her then and briefly laid his hand to the side of her face. "It cannot be helped. Sit here and wait quietly. I will return as soon as I have any news."

When the men had gone, Catherine did not sit. She paced restlessly, grumbling to Eleanor and Miss Holt. "Sit and wait. Sit and wait. That is always the woman's unhappy lot, to sit and wait for news, to sit and wait for men to do what needs to be done, to play no part and have no say."

"Dearest, Catherine," Eleanor said patiently, "I daresay the men will find their lot in this regrettable business no less disagreeable."

"Oh, please forgive me, Eleanor! I do not mean to complain at such a time. It is just that I would so much prefer to be doing something – anything! – to this perpetual inactivity." Nevertheless, taking a deep breath to calm herself, Catherine reluctantly resumed her seat, clasping her hands together to keep them from fidgeting.

Catherine had been truthful when she told her husband she had not been hoping for a view of the grim scene of death. But once he was gone and she had nothing else to do, her mind involuntarily set to work creating detailed images for her of what must be transpiring outside.

She could almost feel the thick, damp darkness all about; see the leaping flames of the torches encircling the crumpled, motionless corpse; the garish color of the blood – surely there would be blood – particularly out of place in the gloom; the sober-faced men encircling the body, some looking profoundly absurd for their fancy dress costumes, now soaked and dripping with the rain. They would keep their voices respectfully low, she supposed, as they tried to puzzle out exactly what had happened. No doubt the dead man would be examined from all angles, perhaps poked and prodded, and finally rolled over so the other side could be observed. No one had yet said whether the general had been found face up or face down, she realized. What if the real horror was still waiting to be revealed and would take them all by surprise at that moment?

"Catherine?" said Eleanor, eliciting a small cry of alarm from her sister-in-law.

"Oh, excuse me, Eleanor," she said when recovered. "You startled me. I was lost in my thoughts."

"So it would seem. You looked as if you were miles away."

"I wish it could be so. Oh, how I wish we had never come here tonight!"

9

THE MAGISTRATE

*W*hen the viscount, Captain Tilney, and Henry returned to the ladies an hour later, General Courteney and the Marquis of Longtown were with them. Though they had shed their great coats before entering the parlor, the condition of the five men clearly showed that the rain brought by the earlier thunder storm had continued unabated. Their clothing looked quite drenched, and their hair – those who had any appreciable amount – hung down in sodden locks.

"Sir Melvin has finished examining the body and the scene," explained Henry, going to stand near his wife. "He has gone up to inspect the roof now – the point where it appears as if... Well, we are to wait here for the magistrate's preliminary findings."

"Do sit down, Henry," encouraged Catherine, patting the place beside her.

"No, standing will do for now. I have no wish to leave a water mark on the furniture." The other men copied his example.

The magistrate entered ten minutes later. Sir Melvin was a gray-bearded, bespectacled man of about sixty, proudly displaying in his stout proportions the unmistakable signs of a life-long devotion to rich food and drink, as well as the ability to afford them. He wore his wig (although slightly askew, Catherine noticed) to signify that he was there as an official of the courts. Not that anybody was likely to forget that fact.

"Now," said the magistrate decisively after being introduced to those few in the room he did not already know. "Is there anybody else who should be here – anybody else that was particularly close to the general – before I explain the facts as we understand them so far?"

The Marquis of Longtown, a dark-haired man of obvious style and breeding, opened his mouth. "My daughter, Lady Charlotte Penninger, was engaged to marry General Tilney. In fact, it had just been announced tonight. But I will keep her apprised of what she needs to know. I see no reason for her to be troubled with details that must upset her even more. This dreadful business has already proved a severe trial to her nerves, as you might well imagine."

"As you like, Lord Longtown," agreed Sir Melvin. "What about the other ladies?" he said, turning to the three of them. "Would you rather be excused as well? Some of what I have to say may indeed be too upsetting for the delicate of mind or feeble of constitution. I can always put my questions to you later if need be."

"He was my father; I will stay," said Eleanor resolutely.

"As will I," said Catherine.

Captain Tilney, who was standing beside Miss Holt, bent to speak to her quietly, taking her hand in his. "Virginia, spare yourself my family's drama. I am sorry to have dragged you into this affair, but there is no need for you to suffer more than you already have on my account. Go now. Wait in the other room, and I will come to you when I can."

"If you wish it, Frederick" she said, giving him a long parting look before leaving.

Observing this exchange, Catherine was so struck by the captain's altered tone and demeanor that she could not help thinking there might be something to Henry's opinion from earlier that night. Perhaps Captain Tilney did truly care for Miss Holt after all.

"Well, if that is settled," said Sir Melvin when the door was shut again, "I will get on with it. Doctor Shepherd will be doing a more comprehensive examination of the body at his offices, but there seems little doubt about how the general died. He succumbed to severe injuries inflicted upon his person by a fall from the roof. Not to put too fine a point on it, the specific cause of death will have been a broken neck."

This news elicited a few muffled exclamations.

"Be consoled that the end came swiftly," continued Sir Melvin. "He will not have suffered. Furthermore, the doctor agrees with me that it was likely more than just a simple fall. The man would have had to leap or have been soundly pushed to come to earth where he did – considerably away from the wall instead of near to it. We are speaking of a deliberate act, there-fore, and not an accident. Presumably there was no reason for General Tilney, newly engaged, you tell me, to have committed suicide tonight. So that leaves only one conclusion. Ladies and gentlemen, this was murder," he said with a climactic crescendo, "and going forward with the investigation, we shall treat it as such. Is that clear?"

With a subtle gleam in his eye, Sir Melvin looked round at the close circle of grim faces, every one of them respectfully nodding in silent acknowledgment of his official pronouncement. There were no further gasps or wails. It was what they had all expected him to say, no matter how much they would have preferred it were otherwise.

Sir Melvin seemed almost to be enjoying his role in the proceedings, Catherine suddenly realized. He liked the way all heads turned to him. He liked the attention and control, having command of an audience as he revealed his grisly facts one by one. He was playing up the drama where no additional suspense was really required, simply for effect. She could not like him for that.

A year ago, it would not have occurred to Catherine to suspect a man like Sir Melvin of such motives. As Henry had early on correctly diagnosed, she had formerly expected everybody she met with to behave pretty much as she herself would do. But Henry had undeceived her. People were more complex than that, and one must not be surprised when they did not all think and act alike.

Apparently satisfied that the weight of his words had been fully felt, Sir Melvin went on. "Very well. I have had a look at the roof and have established a theory as to how the crime occurred. Since there was a quantity of some unfamiliar type of fireworks distributed along the roofline, it seems likely that the general went up for some related reason and was taken unawares by his attacker there. We discovered definite signs of a struggle on the spot where the gentleman must have gone over – another confirmation of foul play. The parapet is quite low in that area, so it would not have taken a great deal of force to send a person over the edge, even a man of General Tilney's size. A well-timed push to upset the balance and over he went. In other words, we are not necessarily looking for an assailant of great physical strength to have done it. I daresay from that perspective, anybody in this room could have accomplished the deed… perhaps even one of the ladies."

This revelation served as an overpowering invitation for each person present to look about the room and picture the others, one by one, pushing the general from the roof, and asking, *Could he have done it? Could she?* Catherine, having a particularly fertile imagination, answered *yes* in nearly every case. Only to her beloved Henry did she grant a verdict of absolute innocence. And to Eleanor, of course. For Eleanor's sake, she would wish to extend the same freedom from suspicion to her husband the viscount, but she did not know him well enough to be certain.

Before Catherine could carry her imaginings any further, the magistrate was speaking again.

"One helpful detail is that we have a very clear idea of the time of death, since General Tilney was present at the supper, left the party at approximately eleven o'clock according to many witnesses, and then was discovered dead shortly after midnight. Is that correct?"

Eleanor spoke up. "Yes, Sir Melvin. I remember checking the time more than once during that period."

Others murmured their agreement.

"You see, I was waiting for my husband…" Eleanor stopped short, as if suddenly realizing that she had already said too much. "That is… we were all… Well, it is of no account. Do continue, Sir Melvin."

"Thank you. So this is how we will proceed. With Mrs. Brooks' help, the servants, including the extra people hired only for tonight, have been assembled in the dining hall. Meanwhile, Hastings has done the same with the guests, who are now gathered in the ballroom. The constables have begun taking down names, noting the whereabouts of each person during the hour in question, and anything they may have seen or heard that could have a bearing on the case. Afterward, most if not all of the guests will be sent on their way. Same with the servants; the temporary help can be released unless there is reason to suppose we shall have further need of them, and the permanent staff sent to their beds for some sleep, those that can be spared. They will be a busy lot in the days to come, no doubt.

"However, I am sorry to say that sleep is not in the near view for *this* group." He nodded to indicate the parlor's present occupants. "Or for myself either, for that matter, for I am nowhere near finished with this investigation. Thus far, I have only heard bits and pieces of what transpired here tonight. You must excuse me for a little while now. But after I check on the progress of the constables, I will want to hear a more comprehensive account of events leading up to the murder, while these things are still fresh in your minds. I must know your whereabouts and activities, and determine if any of you had a reason to want General Tilney dead. Or perhaps there is someone else you know of who did. Motive and opportunity. Motive and opportunity! That is the key to solving the mystery. That is what will lead me to the guilty party."

Again, Catherine felt a wave of distaste sweep over her at the magistrate's behavior, especially his air of superiority. He was very business-like and organized, very logical and systematic in his efforts. But to her way of thinking, he was treating the occasion as a game for his own amusement – a jolly riddle to answer, an exciting puzzle to solve – and he intended to win the prize, evidently by employing a tone of intimidation as one of his tools for success. *I must determine which one of you is the murderer. Motive and opportunity… That will lead me to the guilty party!* As if he were the only one with a vested interest in discovering the truth.

But this was no game. There could be nothing more serious, in fact. One man was dead, and the lives of the others might never be the same again.

Consulting his watch, Sir Melvin said, "We will reconvene here in this room in one hour. See that none of you fails to return. Until you are cleared of suspicion, you are all required to remain on the premises and at my disposal. Gentlemen, you might take this opportunity to change into dry clothing, if you have any. And you will all wish to see to your personal needs and take some refreshment. It is going to be a long night."

So saying, Sir Melvin bowed out of the room, leaving the small enclave to eye one another with varying degrees of discomfort and suspicion. Most, however, were little inclined to worry about the next man at that moment, but rather to consider the strength of his own position. The interviews would commence shortly. Information would be taken down as evidence. Explanations and alibis would be required. Bad luck for anybody without them.

Captain Tilney finally broke the tense silence. "Sir Melvin may just as well ask who did *not* have a motive for wanting the man dead. It would be a shorter list."

There was undoubtedly a certain macabre humor in the remark, and yet no one seemed inclined to laugh.

Catherine knew she was safe from suspicion, since she had never been out of the sight of numerous witnesses, but she gasped when it struck her that the same could not be said for her husband.

10

A SHORT REPRIEVE

With only an hour of freedom before their presence would again be required, everybody was suddenly in motion, the parlor emptying out as quickly as the narrow doorway would allow.

"Oh, how glad I am to escape those close quarters, at least for an hour," exclaimed Catherine to her husband as they exited along with the rest. "I thought I should have fainted for lack of air to breathe."

"Perhaps a larger room might have been chosen if we had realized how many people would ultimately need to be accommodated in it."

"I think the size of the room suits the magistrate's needs very well. I am sure he will prefer to have us feeling the walls closing in on us as he asks his impertinent questions."

Mr. Tilney paused in place, a hand on his wife's arm to stay her forward progress as well. "You do not care for the man, do you?"

Catherine sighed. "Perhaps he is a fair and sensible magistrate, as you say, Henry. I do hope so. But it seems to me he is enjoying his role – his position of power – a little too much.

When he looks at one, one feels the prick of accusation in his eye."

"He must be strict to get the job done, I suppose. We should not judge him too severely, at least not until we see what results he achieves. In any case, I am grateful to Sir Melvin for the opportunity to change out of these wet things. Come along, my darling," Henry said, taking Catherine's arm and proceeding slowly with her up the stairs. "I discovered that our trunk has been taken up to my old apartments. We had best follow it and make good use of this short reprieve to be comfortable and refreshed, as the magistrate suggested."

They said no more until they reached Henry's rooms and were safely behind the closed door. Then Henry immediately wrapped his wife into a desperate embrace. "Oh, Catherine," he exclaimed, "You cannot imagine how I have longed to hold you like this ever since we learned what happened. It seems the whole world has gone mad! And yet if you are mine, it proves there is still some order and goodness to life."

"I feel the same way, Henry," cried Catherine, clinging to him just as urgently as they together swayed slightly back and forth, back and forth.

After several minutes, they at last released each other.

"Oh, but I have spoiled your gown," Henry said, quickly seeing the dark blotches on the pale pink fabric where the moisture from his wet attire had transferred to hers. "I should have had the self-control to wait with attacking you until I had dry clothes on." A mischievous glint – one Catherine by now knew very well – appeared in his eye. "Dear, me! What would Mrs. Allen say? You know she can never bear to see a good muslin ruined. I fear she will be very severe upon me when she hears of it."

Catherine laughed in spite of herself. "I believe you are safe, Henry. I no longer tell Mrs. Allen everything, you know, not since we married."

"Ah, that sets my mind greatly at ease. Then, you will not tell her about my disgraceful disregard for the safety of your gown?"

"No, I will not."

"Nor the people downstairs?"

"Nor the people downstairs."

"But they will know when they see you. The evidence will be before them in less than an hour. And they will immediately identify me as the guilty party, especially Sir Melvin. After all, I was the one with…"

"…*motive and opportunity!*" they said together, bursting into laughter again.

Presently, Catherine said, "I shall exchange this gown for something more comfortable before we return downstairs. Then there will be no evidence of a crime at all."

They became suddenly sober again, silent and looking earnestly at each other until Henry said what they were both thinking. "If only the other crime of the night could be so easily dealt with."

As Mr. Tilney began stripping off his wet tailcoat, Catherine asked with concern, "What will you tell Sir Melvin, Henry? He will say you had motive and opportunity to have murdered your father. Can anybody vouch for your whereabouts and activities during the hour in question?"

"Not all of it," Henry admitted. Then, tugging savagely at his cravat, he loudly expostulated. "Blast! This bloody thing feels like a noose about my neck."

Catherine immediately stepped forward, saying, "Leave it to me."

With another expostulation, Henry's arms fell to his side, surrendering the problem to more capable hands.

"It is the rain," Catherine continued soothingly as she worked the knot herself. "The cloth tightens and sticks together when it becomes wet, making it difficult to shift." Another minute and it was accomplished, however.

"Thank you, my love," he said, giving her a quick kiss. "And please forgive my violent outburst. I am not myself tonight."

"Of course. Your father has just died; it would be very shocking if you were not to show some sign of distress. But you did not answer my question, Henry. What *will* you tell Sir Melvin?"

"What can I tell him but the facts? I agree that it is not ideal, but there is no help for it. Certainly, if I had known I would be needing an alibi, I would have contrived something far better!"

"Perhaps you should invent an explanation for your absence that will allay suspicion. Say you went out riding to relieve your feelings over your father's behavior at the supper. Or say you and Jonathan were together. He may be as much in need of a solid alibi as you are."

Henry shook his head. "A lie would surely be found out, and then I would look twice as guilty. No, I can only tell the truth, Catherine. That is all any of us can do. We have to trust that it will be enough."

Catherine threw her hands in the air. "Oh, how I wish I had come with you when you went after your father! Then I could have sworn you never met with him at all."

"Or you may just as easily have fallen under suspicion yourself. You heard what Sir Melvin said; even a woman could have done it. Or it might look as if we had carried out the crime together. No, it is better this way. If suspicion falls on either one of us, let it be on me alone. I can bear anything if I know you are safe, you and Eleanor."

"Do not say that, Henry! Cannot you see that I will never be safe if you are in jeopardy? You are my life!" At this, Catherine burst into tears.

Henry held her again for a long time. Later, when she had quieted, he pulled away and affected a cheerful attitude. Looking down at her gown, now even more soaked than before, he said, "A few more embraces like that and I daresay *my* clothes shall be completely dry! But that is not the only reason for my cleaving so tightly to you, my dear. I need no excuses for that, as you well know by now." He pulled her tightly to himself again, this time in a different style of embrace, kissing her deeply. Afterward, he whispered in her ear. "Now, if only we had more time, we could make the changing of our clothes into something quite enjoyable."

"What a terrible tease you are, husband!" Catherine scolded in mock outrage, pulling away from him. "How dare you turn my mind to such a scandalous idea at a time like this... especially when it can go nowhere!"

"'Tis a pity, I agree, but if I have succeeded in turning your mind toward more pleasant thoughts, even for a moment, I am gratified. There is enormous satisfaction in learning one has been a good influence on another person. Do not you agree?"

Catherine laughed, and Henry was satisfied.

"Seriously, though," he added reluctantly, "we must get ourselves in order. The hour is melting away, and our brief respite will soon be over."

Catherine's smile faded at once.

11

TAKING INFORMATION

*W*hen the grim group reconvened in the small parlor shortly after four o'clock in the morning, the black of night was still holding out against the first hints that a new day was at hand. It would be a day in which few in the neighborhood of Northanger Abbey could take any joy, however.

Henry and Catherine sat close together on a settee to one side of the room, opposite Eleanor and her husband on the matching settee. The dead man's friends, General Courteney and the Marquis of Longtown, had taken the two armchairs at the back of the room, facing the door. Captain Tilney, a little apart from the others, chose to stand.

So they were all assembled and quiet when the magistrate came in accompanied by a constable, whose job, it soon became clear, was to keep his mouth shut and write down information. Sir Melvin took his stance just inside of the doorway with the constable beside him, as if to block any thoughts of escape.

"Glad to see you all remembered to return promptly," he said. "While you were taking your ease, I have been hard at work on your behalf, covering a lot of ground. You will be interested to know that all of the guests and most of the servants have already been interviewed and let go. Thus far, not one of them appears to have had sufficient motive to murder General Tilney, although that could always change. And several proved to be founts of helpful information. I now have a much clearer idea of what transpired here tonight.

"Next, I wish to say that this investigation will proceed most expeditiously if you can all give your information together in one room, corroborating or correcting each other on the spot. If someone gives information you know to be false, it is your duty to speak up! However, should any one of you have something to report that cannot be said in front of the others, I would be happy to step outside with you for a moment. The most important thing is that you do not hold back anything that could possibly be relevant. And as to what is relevant and what is not, *I* will be the judge." He paused to clear his throat. "Now then, suppose we begin at the beginning. Which of you was first to arrive?"

The Marquis of Longtown rose and said, "I believe I was, sir. My daughter and I were here well before the ball began."

"And why was that, sir?" the magistrate inquired.

"It was by the general's particular request. He wished to finalize the marriage arrangements so that the engagement could be announced at the supper tonight."

"I take it you were in favor of the match?"

"Yes, of course. General Tilney is… I mean, he was… one of my oldest and most trusted friends."

Sir Melvin dipped his chin and peered at the marquis over his spectacles. "Oldest, yes. If you don't mind my saying so, it strikes me that he was a bit too far past his prime to be marrying a girl of your daughter's tender age. As a young lady of rank, she could have been expected to take her pick amongst many highly eligible suitors."

"Perhaps, but the general was still a vigorous man with much to offer, and I was satisfied that it was for the best."

"Why exactly was that? I gather it was not a love match, at least not on her side."

Longtown glanced about uncomfortably.

"Come now, Lord Longtown," Sir Melvin prompted. "This is no time for false delicacy. We must all be prepared to give up some of our secrets tonight for the greater good. Or we can step outside if you prefer."

"No, that will not be necessary," said Longtown with all the dignity he could muster under the circumstances. "I suppose it is not much of a secret that my estate is heavily encumbered. So although Lady Charlotte is the daughter of a marquis, she has almost no fortune, something General Tilney did not quibble over. In fact, he offered to generously compensate me for the loss of my child."

"I see," said the magistrate with one eyebrow raised. He glanced at the constable's pad to be sure this fact was taken down.

"Come now, Sir Melvin," continued the marquis unapologetically. "You are a man of the world, and you understand these things. As you said a moment ago, we must all be prepared to make certain sacrifices for the greater good."

"Yes, I believe I *do* understand. But tell me this. Did your daughter agree with you? Was she prepared and pleased to make the necessary sacrifice for the sake of the family estate?"

Catherine recalled an uncomfortable Lady Charlotte sitting alongside General Tilney at the supper, and especially her countenance as the general announced their engagement. She truly had had the look of a lamb being led to the slaughter, one about to be sacrificed against her will.

"She knew her duty and was prepared to do it," answered the marquise sharply. "Nothing more need be said on that subject. And if you are looking for a motive to kill the general, you will find none here. I wanted my friend very much alive and healthy

– for my daughter's sake as well as my own. The benefits we hoped to derive from the match all died with the general."

"I see. So after you finalized your... your arrangements with General Tilney, what happened next?"

"My daughter and I retired to the rooms that had been assigned for our use and made ourselves ready for the ball. I assume the general did the same. The next time I saw him was when I came downstairs at the appointed hour. He was by then costumed as you found him, prepared to receive his guests, and with my daughter at his side."

"And how would you describe his state of mind?"

"He was quite cheerful – in anticipation of the evening to come, I assumed, and perhaps helped along a bit by wine."

"Cheerful, you say? Very well. As his close friend, did he ever confide to you that he feared for his safety, or did you have any reason to think he might take his own life? Consider carefully."

"There is nothing to consider. I can tell you absolutely that General Tilney never spoke of any threats. And, especially now, with his upcoming marriage, he had everything to live for."

"Quite so. Well I think that is all for now, Lord Longtown." As the marquis made ready to take his seat, Sir Melvin added, "Oh, one more thing."

Longtown froze in place, suspended midway down. "Yes?" he said, straightening again.

"For the record, where were you during the hour in question, the hour during which the crime took place?"

"After the supper, I adjourned to the billiard room with General Courteney. He can attest to that."

"And your daughter? Can you speak for Lady Charlotte's whereabouts?"

"She was a little... overwrought by some of the things General Tilney said at the supper. If you have talked to the other guests, Sir Melvin, you will know what I mean. In any case, she returned to her room to recover her composure, and she did not emerge again until after the body was found."

"Very good." The magistrate turned to the constable at his side, asking, "Did you get all of that?"

"Yes, sir, all the pertinent facts," the man said.

Looking at the marquise again, Sir Melvin said, "Thank you, Lord Longtown. You have been most helpful. Be advised that I will want to have a brief word with your daughter before you leave the premises, just to confirm what you have told me."

The marquise nodded curtly and resumed his seat at last, no doubt relieved to have his ordeal over. Not so for the rest of the group. They all waited in hushed anticipation, wondering who would be summoned to stand under the magistrate's harsh scrutiny next.

Sir Melvin soon turned his eye on General Courteney – a man with a fair complexion and a distinctive red moustache. "As long as your name has been raised, General, we may as well hear from you now."

"Very well," he said, standing and assuming the severely upright bearing of a military man at attention. "But I hardly know what help I can be, other than to confirm what Lord Longtown has already told you, that I was with him in the billiard room during the hour that most interests you."

"Did anybody else see the two of you there?"

"Not that I am aware of."

"Pity. It would have been useful to have a third person independently verify the fact, but never mind. What else can you tell me concerning the events of the night – motives, something you saw or heard perhaps?"

"Very little, as I said. Personally, I had no reason to want my friend dead, and I knew of no one else who did either. General Tilney was certainly a bit worse for the wine he had consumed, and he did succeed in insulting or otherwise upsetting many in the company. However, everybody seemed to either know him well enough to excuse his offenses, or they were at least prepared to overlook them for the sake of enjoying his excellent hospitality."

"No doubt. No doubt. One hesitates to look a gift horse in the mouth, after all."

"Quite."

"Now, General, what about the strange goings-on here tonight? I understand some of the guests were much alarmed by the storm, the candles blowing out in the midst of the ball, and some very odd noises heard overhead. Can you shed any light on that subject?"

"Well…" He ground to a halt without really ever getting his answer started.

"Come now, General," Sir Melvin said to encourage him. "This is no time to hold back. We must spread the facts out onto the table."

"As you say, then. It is my assumption that General Tilney himself was responsible for at least some of these effects. He told me beforehand that he intended to take advantage of the fact that it was All Hallows Eve to provide some 'special entertainment' for his guests. Although I suppose the storm was simply a happy coincidence. No one, not even a man of forceful will like Tilney, could have arranged thunder and lightening to arrive according to his timetable."

"I should think not, General. Well, if you are sure you have nothing else to add at this time, you may be seated. Do not hesitate to speak again, however, if anything else comes to mind." While the general resumed his seat, Sir Melvin examined the other faces. "What about the rest of you? Did you have any knowledge of these 'special entertainments' General Tilney may have been planning? I suppose that would include the unusual fireworks discovered on the roof."

"I did not," volunteered Captain Tilney, "but I would not put it past the man to try frightening his guests half out of their wits on top of offending them with his drunken diatribe."

"You refer to your father's comments at the supper, I presume," said the magistrate, to which he received an answering nod. "Then we may as well undertake that subject without further delay. I understand he threatened you quite openly, Captain. Can you elaborate?"

"As I am sure you already know," the captain said derisively, "my father threatened to disinherit me unless I married to please him – a threat he has made many times before, by the way. The new element on this occasion was that he boasted he was quite capable of raising up a new heir to take my place if necessary, no doubt anticipating the fact that he would soon have a young, presumably fertile new wife with whom to procreate."

"Here, now!" objected the marquise at once. "Have a care! There is no need to be vulgar, especially where my daughter is concerned. She is a respectable and still-unmarried lady."

"My apologies, Lord Longtown," said Tilney. "She is a very fine young woman, I am sure. Exactly the sort I was supposed to marry, but then my father decided to have her for himself, it seems."

"That will do, Captain," warned the magistrate. "Let us get back to the question at hand. Did you take your father's threat of disinheritance seriously?"

"Once again, I would not put such vindictive behavior past him. But I knew if I waited patiently, his threats would eventually come to naught."

"Indeed? How could you be so certain?"

"Is not it obvious? He could not live forever. Sooner or later the old man would pop off, and then I could do as I pleased."

"Yes," said the magistrate, disapprovingly. "But no doubt 'sooner' would have suited you much better than 'later.' Is not that so? The charming young lady who was with you earlier – Miss Holt? – she is hardly what your father had in mind for you, is she? And perhaps you did not want to keep her waiting another ten or fifteen years."

"If you are fishing for a motive, Sir Melvin," the captain said unflinchingly, "you may as well know that there was no love lost between my father and myself. That is hardly a secret either, so it would be pointless for me to lie and tell you I am very unhappy he is gone. But I did not kill him. What is more, I can prove it."

"Can you? Witnesses tell me you were absent from both the ballroom and the supper room between eleven and midnight, which gives you ample opportunity as well as an admitted motive."

"Sorry to disappoint you, Sir Melvin, but I have an unimpeachable alibi."

"Well? I am waiting to hear it."

"No," the captain firmly declared.

"Captain Tilney, what are you playing at? This is not a game, I warn you, and you *will* give me a full account of your whereabouts!"

"No," the captain repeated, "not in front of the others."

"You should have said so in the first place, sir, but my offer still stands. Shall we step out of the room for a moment?" It was an order, not a question, and everybody understood it as such.

Sir Melvin marched from the room with Captain Tilney and the constable on his heels. In their absence, the murmuring began.

"What do you think Frederick will tell the magistrate?" Catherine whispered in her husband's ear. "Do you suppose he really has an 'unimpeachable alibi,' as he says? And why will he not say what it is?"

"All I can think is that perhaps he is attempting to save his own neck without ruining Miss Holt's reputation," Henry whispered back.

"Do you mean that he may have been with her in... in some compromising situation?"

"It is possible. It is also possible that the idea simply creates a convenient and innocent – well, innocent of murder, that is – excuse for his absence. If he ends up on trial, however, his say-so will not be enough. Miss Holt would have to testify to their private assignation in open court to save him."

Catherine gave him a sharp look. "Henry, you speak as if you really believe he did it!"

"I do not like to think so ill of my own brother." Then he shook his head and continued with more conviction. "No, it is more than that. I *do not* think so ill of him! But, looking at the thing objectively, as would a disinterested party like Sir Melvin or a judge, it strikes me that no other likely suspect has emerged so far, nor is there likely to be one. Frederick certainly had the most to gain by my father's death, and he admits to not being fond of him. So he *needs* an unimpeachable alibi very much, and I truly hope he has one."

Catherine was silent, considering to herself the possibility of her brother-in-law's guilt with violently opposing feelings. On one hand, she should wish to spare Henry's family – now her own – any more pain and scandal than what must inevitably follow from such an event. On the other, anything would be far better than having Henry himself fall under suspicion. If it was to be one or the other, Catherine would not hesitate to throw Captain Tilney to the wolves. And she could not help wishing, therefore, that the unimpeachable alibi belonged to her husband instead.

The room quieted at once when the door opened, signaling the return of the magistrate, the constable, and Captain Tilney, who all resumed their former places.

Sir Melvin once again took control, saying, "I have heard Captain Tilney's alibi, which, presuming it is confirmed, will relieve him of suspicion. In the meantime, we shall move on. Perhaps we can hear from the ladies next. Mrs. Tilney?"

Catherine felt a stab of near panic at the sound of her name. Despite all the novels of crime and intrigue she had read, despite her thirst for tales of danger and mystery – still not completely done away with – she felt very ill-prepared to give evidence in a murder case, especially where so much was at stake for herself and those she held most dear. What if she said the wrong thing? What if her words accidentally implicated an innocent man? What if that innocent man were her husband? This was her greatest fear. Henry had been right. This was not one of the frightful stories she liked to read; this was quite real, and she was not finding the experience the least bit enjoyable – dreadfully spellbinding, yes, but not enjoyable.

Responding in an unsteady voice to the magistrate's call, she attempted to rise like the others had. "Yes?"

"Please, do remain seated, Mrs. Tilney," said the magistrate. "This is only a preliminary hearing; there truly is no need for witnesses to stand."

Catherine sank back down beside her husband, grateful for this small favor.

"Now, will you briefly explain your whereabouts during the hour in question and give any other information that may have a bearing on the case?"

"I… That is, Eleanor and I remained in the supper room the entire time, our husbands with us."

"Really? For the entire hour, the four of you together? That is not quite consistent with other reports I have received."

"Pardon me, sir. I should have made it clear that I meant Eleanor and I remained the entire hour, until we heard that poor girl scream. Our husbands were with us only part of that time."

"Yes, you *should* have made that clear," Sir Melvin said reproachfully, causing Mrs. Tilney's cheeks to color in mortification. He then continued. "So then, for which part of the hour were your husbands with you? To the best of your recollection, Mrs. Tilney, who left when, for what purpose, and for how long?"

"Oh, dear me!" said Catherine, even more disconcerted. "I had no timepiece to help me judge those sorts of details, sir. Perhaps you should ask Eleanor, I mean Lady Astley."

"I intend to, Mrs. Tilney, but first you must do the best you can."

"Very well," she said, taking a deep breath to steady her nerves. "Henry left the room first, perhaps ten minutes after his father did." Catherine glanced at her husband apologetically, feeling disloyal for what she must say. Henry gave her a nod, by way of assuring her she had his support and permission to continue. "He wished to speak to his father about..." She stopped again.

"There is no point in hiding the truth, Mrs. Tilney," said Sir Melvin. "I already know what the general said at the supper."

"Well, if you know, then you must know what Henry wished to speak to General Tilney about. But Henry returned perhaps forty-five minutes later, never having found his father. So you see, he had no opportunity to harm him. And anyway, Henry is not that sort of man! He could never..."

Sir Melvin interrupted this emotional plea, saying, "Mrs. Tilney, please keep your remarks confined to the facts. You cannot possibly testify to what your husband may or may not have done during the three quarters of an hour he was out of your sight. Now can you?"

"No... I suppose not."

"And Lord Astley? When did he depart and for what stated purpose?"

"Oh, that was perhaps another ten minutes after Henry. We heard those strange noises overhead that you mentioned before, and he felt obliged to go and investigate. I next saw him after we heard the screams."

"So he was absent a shorter length of time, but perhaps not too short to allow opportunity."

"I really cannot say as to that, sir."

"That was not a question, Mrs. Tilney. I was merely thinking aloud. One more thing, though. Are you aware of any cause for animosity, any ill-will the viscount may have held against General Tilney? Remember, we can step outside before you speak if that would make you more comfortable."

"I know nothing serious enough to require that sort of secrecy, Sir Melvin. The only offence I can imagine is what the rest of us have dealt with: the general trying to control his children's lives, especially when it comes to whom they may marry. As I understand it, the general had forbidden the marriage between Eleanor and Jonathan, even though they loved each other most sincerely. But that all changed when Jonathan acceded to his title. So whatever motive there once might have been in that was already done away with."

Sir Melvin took some minutes to verify Catherine's information with the viscount and viscountess. Yes, the timeline she had given seemed reasonably accurate. Jonathan had indeed been absent for somewhat more than half an hour as he searched without success for the source of the peculiar noises. No, he could not provide an iron-clad alibi for himself, but neither had he any imaginable reason for wanting to harm his father-in-law.

"I believe that is all for the time being," said Sir Melvin, apparently satisfied. He then, slowly and purposefully, redirected his scrutiny. Like a skilled marksman finally bringing his true quarry into his sights, the magistrate swung round to the other side of the room where his sharp focus settled on Henry. "It seems everybody else has fairly successfully acquitted themselves, Mr. Tilney. I wonder if you can you do the same."

"I will do my best, Sir Melvin." Despite Catherine's restraining hand and Sir Melvin's assurances that it was unnecessary, Mr. Tilney rose as the other men had done in their turns. "I am innocent, and I trust that the truth will win out in the end."

"A fine sentiment, sir. That is what we are after: the truth. Now, first of all, do you agree with the information given by your wife – that you followed your father from the supper room approximately ten minutes after he quit it, returning some forty-five minutes later?"

"Yes. Like her, I did not observe the time, but I believe that is a good estimate."

"And you sought him out to speak to him about what he said at the supper – that he intended to take your living from you and give it to another. Is that also accurate?"

"Yes. I knew it was possible he had no intention of following through on what he said, or that he might not even remember it the next day because of the great deal of wine he had consumed. I also doubted he would succeed in revoking the living even if he tried. Although I do not claim to understand all the intricacies of the law pertaining to such a case, I do know that the living was meant to be for life."

"Do you claim you were unconcerned about your father's threats, then?"

"On the contrary, Sir Melvin; I was very concerned. I was concerned for the possibility – however small it would prove to be – of losing my home and livelihood. I was concerned for my father's safety and his state of mind. I was concerned for how the things he said at the supper had embarrassed himself and the entire family. And I was especially concerned for my wife's happiness.

"So I decided that if there were any chance of an immediate resolution to the problem, of avoiding further unpleasantness altogether, it was my duty to make the attempt – not only for my own sake but for the others as well. I meant to apologize for displeasing him by my marriage and make peace if possible. I had little reason to expect success – my father could be a very obstinate man – but I felt I must at least try. Toward that end, I went all over this house in search of him. When I failed to discover him anywhere, I returned to my wife and sister in the supper room."

"'All over this house,' you say. Does that include the roof?"

"The roof? No! I had no reason to suppose I should find my father *there*."

"Can you provide any witnesses to verify your claim that you were never on the roof?"

"How can I be expected to prove where I was *not*? All I can say is that you will find no witnesses to say that I *was* on the roof. I encountered three of four servants in my search of the house." He paused a moment in thought. "Yes, four. It was four servants that I met with. Each one I asked if they had any idea of my father's whereabouts. Each one said no. You should be able to verify that much. That will prove I was not on the roof... at least not at those times."

"Three or four brief encounters in a span of forty-five minutes? That still leaves much time unaccounted for. You clearly had opportunity to have killed General Tilney, and the motive is clear for all to see as well. If you disposed of your father before he could speak to his attorney, you would be sure of keeping your living and your home. You would keep your wife happy too, which you have admitted is your primary object."

Catherine's anger flared at this. Oh, how she longed to tell Sir Melvin what she thought of him and of how he had twisted Henry's own words to suit his purposes. Inexcusable! A magistrate's job was to get at the truth; he himself had said so. It was not to build a case against an innocent man, and her Henry was so obviously innocent. Any person of sense should be able to see that was so! But even if Sir Melvin refused to act sensibly, she reminded herself that she must, for Henry's sake. That was the only thing that restrained her from leaping to her husband's defense. She knew that a violent outburst from her was more likely to harm than help his cause, so she bit her tongue in order to keep herself silent.

Henry, however, remained impressively calm, saying, "And yet the fact remains, sir, that I did not do it. I did not want my father dead. I do not solve my problems by violence; that is simply not my way. I would much rather be wronged and turn the other cheek than to violate all that I believe and my vows as a clergyman."

"A very pretty speech, Mr. Tilney," said Sir Melvin. "You sound quite earnest, I admit, and perhaps you are speaking the truth. However, I cannot afford to be swayed by sentiment. It is my job to discover the most logical suspect and remand him over for an inquest. I have to tell you that there is nothing so far that can exclude you and much that points in your direction as being that man. In truth, it is between you and your brother, and your brother claims to have an alibi."

At this, an involuntary cry finally escaped Catherine's lips. Henry reached for her hand but did not break eye contact with the magistrate. The magistrate himself continued as if he had not noticed.

"As to your profession, Mr. Tilney, you cannot hide behind that mantle. In my experience, some clergy are men of God in name only. And even one who is most sincere can sometimes be pushed beyond his breaking point. We are all sinners, as those in your line are particularly fond of reminding us."

Sir Melvin Whitmore briefly left them again. When he returned, he said, "Longtown, your daughter has given me the same account of events, so you may both go now. I will know where to find you if there are any more questions or should you be required to testify in any legal proceedings. The same applies to you, General. You said you can be reached at the Royal Arms at Bath?"

"That is correct, Sir Melvin. I plan to stay there until my regiment needs me again."

"You must be prepared to stay as long as *I* need you, sir. You are dismissed for now, but do not leave the vicinity without the permission of the courts." Turning to the viscount, the magistrate continued. "What about you, Astley? Where can you be located?"

The viscount first looked to his wife, who whispered something to him before he answered. "My wife and I will remain here at Northanger Abbey for the time being, in support of the family."

"Very well. That is good of you. This has been a severe blow, and I daresay there are difficult days ahead. The Tilney family will need their friends gathered round them. I have good news for you, Captain Tilney," Sir Melvin said, turning next to Frederick. "Your alibi has been confirmed."

Then, looking straight at Henry over the top of his spectacles, he added solemnly, "This is bad news for you, Mr. Tilney. As the only viable suspect remaining, I have no choice but to take you into custody. Hence, it is my duty to inform you that you are under arrest. You will be remanded over for an inquest to determine if there is enough evidence to try you for the crime of murdering your father."

12

SEPARATION

atherine felt her head began to spin at the magistrate's pronouncement, and instinctively she knew that, if ever there had been one, this was the exact right moment to swoon. Indeed, had she been the heroine of any one of the many Gothic tales she had read, she would surely have fainted dead away, demanding the worried attentions of all her friends.

For a moment, Catherine thought she might do just that. But then, much to her dismay, the spinning in her head subsided without accomplishing a thing. Now, on top of the shock of her husband's arrest, she would have to bear the shame that she was an heroine unworthy of him, for she remained disappointingly awake and alert through it all.

This is not to imply, dear reader, that Catherine did not feel her distress very keenly indeed. Nor was her attentiveness a true disappointment to her husband, for they only had a few minutes to say their good-byes before he was taken away.

"Have no fear, my dear Catherine," Henry told her. "The truth will win out, and then I will be free again. Find me a good lawyer. Frederick will be able to assist you with that. Then come visit me when you can. For now, though, promise not to worry and that you will get some sleep."

Before Catherine could even form a coherent sentence in reply, he took her face in both his hands and soundly kissed her, not caring who might be looking on.

"Come along now, Mr. Tilney," chided Sir Melvin before Henry had finished. "That will do for now, I'm sure." The magistrate took one of Henry's arms and the constable the other. "Since you are a gentleman, I trust no gyves will be necessary to ensure your cooperation."

In a sudden panic, Catherine remembered to ask, "Where are you taking him?"

"To the local gaol at Tetbury until an inquest can be convened there. Never fear, Mrs. Tilney, your husband will be humanely treated. Although he will be made far more comfortable if he is provided the necessary funds to have better food and drink brought in to him every day."

"I will see to that," said Captain Tilney, "and look out for Mrs. Tilney too. She must stay here, of course, with Eleanor and under my protection."

"Thank you, Frederick," Henry replied, giving his brother an earnest look. "I never thought to find myself in need of such manner of help."

"No. You never were much of one for getting into scrapes, were you? Not like I was."

Eleanor rushed forward at the last moment to kiss her brother on the cheek, and then he was led from the room. His weeping wife and somber siblings trailed after to see the prisoner loaded into Sir Melvin's carriage and driven away in the pale threads of the early dawn.

"I cannot believe it," Catherine said through her tears. "How can this have happened? No one who knows Henry could believe him capable of murder!"

"Of course not! It is all a terrible mistake," said Eleanor, coming to wrap her arms about her sister-in-law's shoulders. "My goodness, but you are freezing cold! And shivering too. It is the shock, I suppose. We must get you warm again. There is no use standing about out here in the weather any longer. Frederick, help me get Catherine inside and to a good fire."

Catherine was grateful for their supporting escort – one on either side – for she had no use for fainting belatedly. The moment for that had passed, and now there was too much to do, too much to think of: the getting of a lawyer, the organizing of a defense, and, most pressing of all, discovering the truth of what had happened. That was the surest way of seeing her husband completely out of danger. After all, Henry had only been arrested because a better suspect could not be found. Therefore, they simply must find one. No, not just a better suspect, but the real killer!

"Oh, there you are, Mrs. Brooks," said Eleanor in relief when they came into the house again. "Thank heavens. Mrs. Tilney is freezing cold and about to collapse, and I do not feel so very strong myself."

"I saw what happened," the housekeeper said, her voice quavering and her face red from crying. "I ordered the fires lit in your three rooms. They should be warm and toasty very soon, so you can go on up and get some sleep. I fear there's nothing else to be done for poor Master Henry tonight."

"Bless you, Mrs. Brooks. Would you see Mrs. Tilney to her room and into bed? And then you had best get some sleep yourself."

For confirmation, Mrs. Brooks looked to Captain Tilney, the heir presumptive to Northanger Abbey and therefore her new master.

"By all means, Mrs. Brooks," he said. "There will be much to do tomorrow, but first, some rest is in order for all of us."

As she was passed into Mrs. Brooks's care, Catherine gave

Eleanor a wan smile. By this time, the viscount had stepped forward to support his wife, so she was in good hands as well.

"Poor Master Henry," Mrs. Brooks was saying again, shaking her head sadly as she led Catherine up the stairs.

"Yes, it is a dreadful shock, Mrs. Brooks," was all Catherine could think to reply.

"Poor, poor Master Henry."

"You know, of course, that he did not do it."

"Of course, Mrs. Tilney! I've known the young man all his life, and he could no more commit murder than I could fly to the moon!"

"You are very fond of Henry, I understand, Mrs. Brooks."

"Yes. Forgive me if it sounds presumptuous, Mrs. Tilney, but he's like me own flesh and blood – the closest thing I ever had – or ever will have – to a son of my own. I love him for himself, right enough, but also for the sake of his sainted mother, God rest her soul. With her taken away so cruelly and not here to look after him anymore, I like to think I have done what I could in her place. Oh, poor Master Henry!"

Although it seemed a little odd to Catherine that she, Henry's own wife, should find herself called upon to comfort one seemingly at a greater distance from him and his predicament than herself, at the same time, this necessity gave her something useful to do. For the moment at least, it helped to prevent her falling into a state of helpless despair as well.

"I am certain you have been a friend to Henry in every way possible, Mrs. Brooks," Catherine said with conviction. "But I fear there is nothing much you can do for him now. That odious Sir Melvin is determined that Henry is to blame for General Tilney's death, and nothing will change his mind except if it can be proved that somebody else did it instead."

They continued up the stairs and then down the corridor in silence, except for the sound of the older woman's weeping. Catherine's mind was still at work, however, and when they reached the door to her bedchamber, she spoke again. "Mrs. Brooks, I expect that very little goes on in this house without your knowledge. Think, now. Think as hard as you can. Are you quite sure you neither saw nor heard anything last night that would point suspicion in a different direction? Henry's life may depend on it."

Mrs. Brooks broke down completely at this, clearly overcome by grief and unable to answer.

"Mrs. Brooks!" cried Catherine in some alarm. Laying a hand on the housekeeper's shoulder, she went on. "Oh, dear! You must forgive me for upsetting you so. I should not have asked. Of course you would help if you could! You care for Henry as much as the rest of us do. Do go to bed now and try not to worry. Something will turn up to prove his innocence. I feel somewhat recovered myself, and I can manage very well on my own from here."

With this permission from young Mrs. Tilney, Mrs. Brooks left her.

As Catherine entered her room and looked about herself, the chill of its bleakness was nearly too much for her to bear, especially after all that had come before. Yes, there was a glowing fire to support physical life and comfort. There was a fine bed where she could rest her head. But there was no Henry.

She trembled. Northanger Abbey without Henry was an unfriendly prospect indeed, one she never thought to encounter. And for a moment, she felt the strong impulse to fly back to her snug little home at Woodston, that is until it struck her that Henry would not be there either. Woodston without her husband might be even more unendurable – the cheery parlor without the source of her cheer, the marriage bed without her marriage partner. No, she would not go back there until Henry could return with her, not if she could help it.

Besides, Eleanor was here at Northanger, Catherine considered as she prepared herself for bed. Captain Tilney was here as well, and despite all her misgivings about him, she would need his help to free Henry. Most importantly, this was where the crime had taken place. Whatever clues might exist to what had really happened, they would most likely be found here. The key to the mystery was at Northanger, so at Northanger she must stay until the mystery was solved. Sir Melvin might be satisfied with what he had discovered so far, but Catherine was most decidedly not.

With such thoughts buzzing restlessly about in her brain, with such anguish of spirit as she suffered for Henry's sake, Catherine believed that sleep would long be kept at bay. In fact, she felt it her clear duty to remain awake in private testimony to her love for her husband and her determination to form a strategy to save him. However, Catherine underestimated her own exhaustion. She underestimated the body's powers of self preservation, by which it sometimes overrules the most resolute plans of the mind. Sleep was absolutely necessary, and so sleep soon claimed her, temporarily putting an end to her frets and worries, suspending her plans and scheming on Henry's behalf until she should awaken again.

FURTHER INVESTIGATION

*W*hen Catherine opened her eyes, a new fire had been laid and lit, and an unfamiliar young maid was just bringing a pot of chocolate in for her.

This was Northanger Abbey, not Woodston, Catherine realized with a fresh jolt to her nerves and a lurch of her stomach. A quick glance at the other half of the bed, which was cold and empty, confirmed that Henry was indeed missing. So it was not a dream; it was all too horribly real.

People always assure someone in distress that things will look brighter in the morning. "When you have had a good night's sleep," they say, "you will be more optimistic. You will see."

But as far as Catherine could judge, the fact that her husband had been arrested and charged with murder looked every bit as grim in the daylight hours as it had in the dark. The clear evidence that she had also failed in her heroic intention of lying awake all night on Henry's behalf only compounded her anguish.

"What time is it?" Catherine asked the maid, a waif-like creature who looked a few years younger than herself.

"Nearly one o'clock, Mrs. Tilney, ma'am."

"One o'clock! Oh, dear." Catherine immediately sat up and

stretched her arms high over her head in an effort to make herself more alert. "Are the others up?"

"Not Lady Astley – Miss Eleanor as was. But Captain Tilney were up hours ago. He breakfasted with the young lady and then went out to take her home."

"Miss Holt, do you mean?"

"Yes, ma'am. He is not yet returned."

"I see," said Catherine. What she saw was that there could be no need of her hurrying downstairs after all.

"I am to ask you, ma'am, do you want any help dressing or should I come back later?"

Catherine was about to send the girl away, preferring solitude and her own simple way of dressing herself, but then she reconsidered. Why should she waste this opportunity? There could be no better time than the present to begin making inquiries, she reasoned, and servants often knew more about what went on in a house than the family did. Despite her failure with Mrs. Brooks, Catherine remained undaunted. She was prepared to try again with somebody else. This girl, who was presumably not so emotionally entangled with the situation, might be the very one to help her.

"Yes, stay," Catherine said decisively. "What is your name, dear?"

"Patsy, ma'am."

"Thank you, Patsy. I would appreciate your help."

Catherine climbed out of bed and selected one of the spare gowns she had brought with her, which some servant – probably this very girl – had at one point or another efficiently unpacked from their trunk into the large, mahogany wardrobe. Henry's things were there too, of course. Seeing them sent another wave of grief washing over her. She wondered if he had been forced to sleep in the clothes he wore the night before. Had he been able to sleep at all in those strange and probably uncomfortable surroundings? At this, her conscience smote her, telling her once again that she should not have slept either. But such regrets were useless. She must simply be grateful for renewed energy to pursue her purpose, which was to find a way to free her husband.

Toward that end, Catherine began by asking the maid, "How long have you been in service here at Northanger, Patsy?"

"Oh, it must be coming on six years now, Mrs. Tilney. Me mum works in the kitchens under Mrs. O'Malley, and she got me the position. Lucky to have it, she says, but now I don't know how much longer it may last."

"Why do you say that?" asked Catherine, stepping out of her night dress.

"Well, with the master dying so unexpectedly and all, some are saying that nothing is sure, and that perhaps Captain Tilney will close up the house altogether, sending most of us away. When he is not with his regiment, he prefers London, they say. He never spends much time here at Northanger."

"Oh, yes, I see. Well, things will undoubtedly change with the general gone, but perhaps not in the way you think. Assuming he is master now, which seems all but certain, Captain Tilney may be more inclined to spend time here than before. As master, he can do as he pleases. That must be seen by him as an attractive prospect. He may even resign his commission and stay." Thinking of what she had lately observed of the captain with Miss Holt, Catherine added, "At his time of life, a man's mind turns to marriage and a family, especially when he has the means and a fine home to bring them into."

"Oh, I hadn't thought of that. That would be a fine thing, Mrs. Tilney, to have a mistress here again and young'uns round her skirts."

"Yes, in any case, nothing may be known for a time. The entire family is in upheaval at the moment." With the girl so willing to talk and the work of dressing proceeding but slowly, Catherine decided to try her luck at moving the conversation one step closer to her real objective. "Patsy, you have been here long enough to be at least a little familiar with my husband, I should think."

"Oh, yes, ma'am! It is a shocking thing that has happened to him. Not one of the servants believes he had anything to do with pushing General Tilney from the roof. They do say that the master's falling is a very bad business, to be sure, but how could that magistrate be so stupid as to take the wrong man into custody for it?"

"I agree with you that they have the wrong man, but I haven't any idea who the right one could be. Have you? What is the gossip among the servants?"

"Well…" she began, then stopped and resolutely shook her head. "No, ma'am, I mustn't say anything more. Mr. Hastings is very severe upon anybody he catches gossiping, especially about their betters."

"Please, Patsy. I must do my best to discover the truth in time to save my husband. I shudder to think what might become of him if he should be found guilty. He could be hung or transported for life!" And then she did shudder, quite involuntarily, from saying the words aloud. "If you know anything that could help him, I would be eternally grateful to hear it." Then Catherine had an inspiration. "You are worried about your position here, are you not? Well then, when all is set to rights again, I will be needing a lady's maid at Woodston. Is that something that would interest you?"

"Oh! To be sure, ma'am! That would be grand, and I should make you a very good lady's maid, I promise."

"That will only be possible, you understand, if my husband is released and we are allowed to return home to Woodston. Mr. Hastings's rule against gossiping is a good one, generally speaking, but this is a special case. There can be nothing wicked in helping an innocent man who has been wrongfully accused, now can there?"

Patsy considered this question for the time it took her to do up the back of Catherine's gown. When finished, she said, "Well, I can't say as I know anything for certain. It's just that the talk below stairs is that if the general was done in by one of his sons, odds are the magistrate laid hold of the wrong one."

This was not news to Catherine; she was entirely of the same opinion. Of course she could never say so, but it was interesting to hear that even the servants agreed.

Suddenly, a look of pure panic seized Patsy. "Oh, dear! You won't say anything to him, will you? Captain Tilney, I mean. That would be the end of me for sure, and maybe me mum as well! And like I said before, it's only gossip, after all."

"Never fear, Patsy," Catherine assured her. "I will not repeat a word; you may depend on it. But as you say, it is only gossip – nothing that can be proved, and so nothing that can help Mr. Tilney. Will you promise to tell me if you come across anything more useful? Keep your eyes and ears open. In your position, you will have access to people and parts of this house that I do not. Mr. Tilney and I will be very generous to whoever helps us in this time of great need." To underscore her willingness to reward loyal service, Catherine found a coin and slipped it into the girl's palm.

"Oh, thank you, ma'am!" she cried. "I will do my best for you. You can be sure of that."

When the maid had gone, Catherine tried to think what her next move should be. She was desperate to see Henry, of course, and she would have flown to him at once, had that been within her power. However, inconvenient though it was, reason told her a drive to Tetbury would probably have to wait until another family member was prepared to go with her.

In the meantime, she could not sit idly by, not while clues to the truth might remain in this house, just waiting to be discovered. No heroine she had ever heard of would do such a thing. And after all, with Captain Tilney away, this might be her best chance to have a private look about with no one the wiser. But where to start?

The roof. The answer was so obvious that Catherine could hardly believe it had not occurred to her at once. The roof had been the scene of the crime, if the magistrate's theory was correct. He and his men had already inspected the area, of course, but it had been dark then. It seemed entirely possible they had overlooked something – a button ripped from a coat in the struggle, a bit of the killer's hair or a scrap of torn fabric left behind. Who could say?

Catherine's heart began to race at the prospect of surreptitiously inspecting the murder scene and what she might find there. Every nerve felt suddenly alive. She recognized the feeling. It was uncomfortably reminiscent of the old thrill from when she had visited this ancient house before, when she had been determined to discover the unexplained circumstances of Mrs. Tilney's death.

That idea gave Catherine pause. That time, she had been caught in the act, and the result of her interference was nearly disastrous. She could have lost Henry forever had he not been so good natured and understanding, not to mention the ugly scene that surely would have transpired if it had been the general instead who had discovered her nosing about his house and his private affairs. He would not have been so forgiving!

Had she not vowed – to Henry and to herself – to put her fascination with unnatural beings and hideous crimes behind her? Had she not repented of her dangerous penchant for seeing corruption and intrigue round every corner?

This was quite a different case, however, Catherine reasoned. This crime was *not* imagined; something hideous had actually occurred. And, since she knew Henry could not be responsible, the question of the murderer's true identity still persisted. Her motives now were entirely different as well. Before, she embarked on her mission primarily for her own amusement, being so absurd as to believe she could solve a mystery that, as it evolved, never existed. But this *was* a true mystery, and she undertook to solve it primarily for Henry's sake, to prevent a tragic miscarriage of justice from sweeping him away forever. Surely that justified any necessary subterfuge on her part.

One final persuasive argument then weighed in. If she did not investigate further, who would? Sir Melvin Whitmore seemed perfectly content with his theory and satisfied he had the right man already in custody. And even though Henry had said Captain Tilney would help with hiring a good lawyer, could she really trust him to do everything possible to prove his brother's innocence? After all, the captain would not want to encourage suspicion being thrown back in his own direction, would he? Perhaps his supposed alibi would not withstand the glare of more intense scrutiny, and no doubt he would rather see anybody, even his brother, hung than himself.

Without further hesitation, Catherine added a shawl over top of her spencer and left her room, bound and determined to find whatever secrets the rooftop might reveal.

Catherine crept along the passageway, hoping not to awaken any creaky boards or otherwise attract unwanted attention. Fortunately, she saw no one on the way to the turret, which she knew housed the flight of steps that led to the roof.

Once there, though, she found that the entrance to the turret was barred by a heavy, antiquated door. It looked like something leftover from a century or more ago, with large rusty iron hinges that were sure to screech in complaint when disturbed. Then Catherine saw the equally unpromising keyhole, and her heart sank. It had not occurred to her that the door might be locked. With a quick whispered prayer (and fingers crossed for good measure), she tried the handle. She was instantly relieved when she heard the click of the latch and felt the heavy door give way. Luck was with her in that regard, but not with the hinges, which groaned alarmingly when the door was only six or seven inches ajar. Catherine froze, listened for any response, and then, hearing none, slipped through the narrow gap. Deciding it was worth the risk of a little extra noise, she closed the door behind her.

Leaning back against it, she took a deep breath and waited for her eyes to become accustomed to the dimness. Like the door itself, the turret interior was from another age. No modern improvements had insinuated themselves here, no effort made to soften the chiseled gray stone on every side. The main feature was, of course, the staircase itself, which wound upward in a spiral against the curved outer walls. For a moment, Catherine was tempted to believe she had somehow stepped into a medieval castle in the time of King Arthur, or at least the time of King Henry VIII. But this was no occasion for spinning romantic fantasies; she had serious work to do.

Catherine began climbing the worn stone treads on tiptoe, her heart in her throat, fully aware that she would have some very awkward explanations to make should she be discovered in this part of the house. Truly, there would be nothing at all she could say, no possible excuse to give other than the truth, which she did not care to admit to.

However, it was not only this horrifying idea that had her nerves strung tight as harp strings. It was that in these Gothic surroundings, other terrors – the kind she had been accustomed to dwelling on too much in the past – more easily sprang to mind. Vampires would probably be very much at home in the low light filtering in through the narrow slits that served as the only windows. No doubt disgruntled ghosts of past occupants would find the cold, dank, deserted stairwell a perfect haunt. They could so easily appear or retreat from sight round the curved walls when anybody did come that way. But then perhaps they could fly straight through the walls in any case.

Catherine shivered, and not entirely from the chill of the air. Even if there were no vampires, she had to consider the recent evidence of some kind of an unearthly presence. What about the strange noises and occurrences they had experienced the night before? Those had been largely forgot in the tumult that followed. General Courteney might think General Tilney himself was responsible, but there was no proof of that. Perhaps the reason no better human suspect than Henry could be found was because the murderer was not human at all! Catherine was not sure if a spirit could actually push a man from a roof, but she had certainly read tales where people had been so terrified by some horrible apparition that they ran into harm's way or even jumped to their deaths in their desperation to escape it.

"What would Henry say if he knew what you are thinking now?" Catherine asked herself by way of a scold. "He would say you have been reading too many novels again. Are you not ashamed of yourself?"

Catherine *was* ashamed, and yet that did little to quiet her imaginings. The bracing air that hit her full in the face as she stepped out onto the roof had a more sobering effect. It returned her mind to the task at hand. She had a job to do, one she wanted to complete as quickly but as thoroughly as possible. So off she scrambled towards the spot in question, holding her skirts high to avoid soiling them with the layers of soot and dirt everywhere present.

Several sets of recent footprints showed Catherine where to go. General Tilney himself and whoever sent him to his death may have been the first to leave their marks. Since then, however, Sir Melvin and the constables had trod the same path – over the rooftop, around chimneys, and then along the parapet – obliterating whatever might have been there to see before. Consequently, it seemed unlikely anybody would notice signs of her own passage along that way.

Catherine approached the actual scene more carefully. Fewer

feet had ventured there, but the prints she did see meant little to her. They were smudged and imperfect impressions, making it impossible to develop an accurate notion of what size or type of shoes had made them. However, it did appear to be, even to her untrained eye, the site of a struggle, as Sir Melvin had said. Along with the scrapes and scuff marks leading right to the edge, there was a broken wooden crate, its contents scattered, and a fractured piece of stone beside it. Catherine bent to pick up the shard, first turning it over in her hand and then stooping to fit it back to the place on the topmost edge of the parapet from whence it had apparently come.

From the looks of it, the crate had indeed carried fireworks, as Sir Melvin said. But how, wondered Catherine, had it come to be broken? Perhaps General Tilney had dropped it when surprised by his assailant. Or perhaps he had tripped over it – or attempted to stand on it – and as a result, tumbled over the edge. With the parapet wall well under three feet high at that point, it still did not seem to her impossible that the fall could have been an accident. She pictured in her mind what might have happened, first one way and then another, trying her best to make the pieces fit the evidence before her.

If Catherine had not been sunk so deep in concentration, she might have received some little warning, perhaps at least the sound of a footfall behind her or the prickling of the hairs on the back of her neck. As it was, the voice seemed to come out of nowhere.

CORNERED

"*W*hat do you do there?" the man's voice demanded. Catherine jumped in fright, and she could not immediately make sense of what she had heard. It had sounded so much like General Tilney himself that she thoroughly expected – and might have preferred – to see his ghost when she turned. Instead it was the menacing sight of Captain Tilney, not ten feet away, posed in a very good imitation of his father – hands on hips, feet apart, and face an angry scowl.

"Catherine?" he said with displeasure upon seeing who the intruder was. "I am astonished at you!" He moved towards her.

Catherine was so overcome that she could barely speak. "How... How did you know I was here?" she stuttered.

"I didn't. I was crossing from the stables when I saw movement on the roof. But never mind that. Explain yourself. What business have you here?" he demanded.

"I am very sorry if you are vexed with me, Captain," Catherine managed, "but I wanted to see the scene for myself. I hoped I might find something that could help Henry."

Captain Tilney came another step nearer until he loomed over Catherine, tall and forbidding. "You thought you could find some clue that trained officers of the law could not? You, a mere chit of a girl? You are grasping at straws."

In addition to his uncomfortable closeness, there was a teasing – no, it was more like mocking – tone in her brother-in-law's voice that Catherine could not like. Although she hated to give him the satisfaction of knowing how he intimidated her, her feet seemed to move backwards a pace of their own accord. "I must try," she said, hoping she sounded more sure of herself than she felt. "I will not sit idly by while my husband is sentenced for a murder he did not commit."

"My dear sister, is that head of yours filled with nothing but feathers? The law is the business of men. *I* will undertake the defense of my brother. I promise that I believe in his innocence as wholeheartedly as you can do. In fact, I think I am the very person uniquely situated to know with certainty that Henry did not kill my father." Once more, he closed the gap between them.

Catherine's left foot slid backwards again, only to be arrested by her heel running up against the base of the parapet wall. She could retreat no farther, and the captain effectively blocked the only way of escape. Though she counseled herself against it, she could not help glancing over her shoulder at the dramatic drop to the ground some thirty or forty feet below. It was then impossible not to think of General Tilney's downward plunge. It was then equally impossible not to imagine what it would feel like to be made to follow his example. Captain Tilney stood so close by... It would be nothing for him to send her over the edge if he so chose.

"Is something the matter, Catherine?" he asked in that same mocking tone. "I get the impression you do not entirely trust me... trust me to defend Henry, that is. What can it mean?"

Catherine hurried to reply. "No, I should be very glad of your assistance, Captain, I assure you," she said unsteadily. "Only please do allow me to pass. It is cold, and I wish to return to the house."

"My god! The look on your face, Mrs. Tilney!" he exclaimed with a derisive laugh. "I suppose you have it worked out in your mind that *I* am the killer. That is the only thing that can account for the absurd expression of terror distorting your otherwise comely countenance. Doubtless you are wondering if you will be next, eh?"

With her last ounce of courage, Catherine looked the captain in the eye and repeated her request, more insistently this time. "Allow me to pass, sir," she said.

Captain Tilney held his place a moment longer before smirking and stepping back out of Catherine's way. "Very well," he said, "I suppose I have had my fun... for now."

Catherine pushed past him, not stopping to look back when she heard his bellowing laugh. She hurried on even faster, retracing her steps to the turret as quickly as she could, fear dogging her heels as the sound of the captain's boots pounded a drum beat behind her.

"Hold up, there, Catherine," he called after her. "There is no need for you to run away like a frightened rabbit. You need not be in dread of me. Besides, we have important things to discuss."

But Catherine's perturbation was extreme. She barely heard the Captain's words, much less giving them consideration. Her only object was to retreat to the relative safety of her own room as rapidly as possible. There, she would lock the door behind her and collapse into the nearest chair until her heart should stop threatening to break out of her chest. Only then could she hope to assess what to do next.

Catherine flew down the turret stairs, flung the creaky door at the bottom wide, and kept running clear along the passageway to her bedchamber, where another surprise awaited her.

"There you are, Catherine," said Eleanor. "I was –"

Catherine did not wait for explanations. She caught Eleanor's hand, pulled her through the door into the room, then slammed and locked it.

"Catherine!" exclaimed Eleanor. "What on earth is the matter?"

Catherine's chest heaved once, twice, three times more before she recovered her breath enough to speak at all. "I think... I think your brother may be a... a murderer after all!"

"Henry?" Eleanor said, incredulous.

"No! No, of course not. I speak of Frederick!"

"Oh, I see. Well, do come and sit, Catherine. Calm yourself and tell me what has happened to so unnerve you. What suddenly makes you so sure Frederick is the villain?"

Catherine allowed herself to be led to the settee, where she explained to her friend what had just occurred on the roof.

"...So you see why I suspect him." Catherine finished, nearly as agitated as before for having relived all the horror of the experience in the faithful retelling of it.

"I suspect him too," said Eleanor, patting her companion's hand, "but not in the same way. My dearest friend, I know my brother better than you do, and I suspect Frederick of toying with you for his own amusement, nothing more. When he found you on the roof, I imagine he could not resist the chance of playing upon your guilt and fear at being discovered there. He is a cad and a rascal, but I do not believe Frederick murdered anybody. Nor do I believe he had any intention of doing more than teasing you half out of your wits. I expect he will apologize directly for being so successful at it. And in the meantime, allow me to speak in his place. Catherine, I am very sorry Frederick should have given you such a fright!"

"So you do not think he could have killed your father?"

"No, I do not. As unscrupulous as he appears sometimes, as questionable his behavior and manner, I cannot believe that of him. Besides, he has an alibi, remember?"

"Yes, but I thought perhaps Miss Holt – if she really is his alibi – might be only saying she was with Frederick to save him. Perhaps she loves him quite desperately and he has promised to marry her. Of course I would never wish Frederick or anybody you and Henry care for should be guilty of such a crime as murder. And he is my own brother now as well. But dear Eleanor, if not Frederick, then who?"

Eleanor sighed and shook her head. "I wish I knew, or better still, I wish it would be found out that it was an accident after all. Father dying is hard enough. I hate to think that any person of our acquaintance could be responsible for it."

Just then, Catherine perceived the sound of someone attempting to turn the door knob. She could not help a little gasp at the thought that it might be Captain Tilney.

Observing this, Eleanor called out, "Who is there?"

There was a pause, and then a female voice said, "Miss Tilney? Is that you? Your ladyship, I mean."

Eleanor rose. "'Tis only one of the maids," she told Catherine. Unlocking and opening the door a few inches, she said, "Yes, Beth, what is it?"

"Pardon me, ma'am, but Captain Tilney says as you're wanted downstairs, you and Mrs. Tilney."

Eleanor cast a look of concern in Catherine's direction before responding. "Did Captain Tilney say why, Beth?"

"I believe it is on account of a Mr. Wilcox, who is just arrived from town. The captain requires both you young ladies to join them in the library at once, he says."

Eleanor thanked the maid and closed the door again.

"Father's lawyer!" she exclaimed, throwing her hands in the air. "With all that has occurred, it completely slipped my mind that Father told us Mr. Wilcox was coming today. Apparently, at least that much of what he said was true. Well, I suppose we had best go down without delay, Catherine. There is nothing else to be done."

"Oh, but Eleanor! How shall I be able to face Captain Tilney? If I have been wrong about him, how unforgivable!" To herself she added *and how much worse if I have been right.*

Eleanor came to help her sister-in-law to her feet. "Courage, dearest," she said. "Ten to one Frederick has already forgot about the incident on the roof. And if he has not, you must act as if *you* have. My guess, though, is that if you do not mention it, he never will either. Besides, there are more important things to think of now. We must do what we can for Henry."

"Yes, Henry! Oh, Eleanor, when I think of what he must be suffering, imprisoned and alone… I must go to him as soon as possible! I was only waiting until you and the viscount might go with me. At least I hoped you might."

"I wish to see my brother as much as you do, and we should be more than happy to take you thither. In fact, that is why I came looking for you just now. It appears we must put up with one more delay first, however. And you know, it may be worthwhile in the end. Perhaps Mr. Wilcox will be of some help in giving advice for Henry's defense."

MR. WILCOX

*D*espite Eleanor's assurances, Catherine felt her cheeks grow hot when she entered the library, and she could not meet Captain Tilney's eye. The viscount was already there with him as well, as was a thin man of middling height and years, who was Mr. Wilcox, of course. After Captain Tilney made the necessary introductions, they all sat down. Catherine took a seat next to Eleanor, who had her husband on her other side.

"I have just now apprised Mr. Wilcox of what has happened," Frederick explained, sitting behind his father's desk. "The general's death and Henry's arrest have naturally come as quite a shock to him."

"They have indeed!" Mr. Wilcox confirmed. "Allow me to express my sincere condolences to you all."

"Thank you, Mr. Wilcox," said Frederick, who clearly intended to take charge of the proceedings in his new role as presumptive head of the family. "There is nothing that any of us can do for the general, of course, so all our efforts are now directed towards protecting my brother from a gross miscarriage of justice. Perhaps you might be of some assistance to us there, Mr. Wilcox."

The solicitor hesitated. "I cannot say as to that, sir. For one thing, I am not your brother's solicitor, though I was your father's. My main responsibility to *him* now is to be certain his estate is settled properly. Of course if I can be of assistance in seeing the man who killed him hung..."

Catherine cried out in dismay at this, and Eleanor took her hand.

"Have a care, sir!" exclaimed the viscount.

Realizing his mistake, Mr. Wilcox said, "Oh, please do excuse me, Mrs. Tilney! That was unforgivably tactless."

When she had recovered herself a little, Catherine answered, "I am sure we all want the guilty person brought to justice, Mr. Wilcox, although I can hardly bear to think of anybody being hung. But the wrong man is currently accused of the crime. My husband is innocent!"

Mr. Wilcox continued, still looking greatly disconcerted. "Again, you must forgive me, Mrs. Tilney, but that is something I would have no means of knowing, one way or the other."

"Mr. Wilcox," said Captain Tilney stridently. "Allow me to return our discussion to things you *do* have knowledge of." After Mr. Wilcox composed himself and nodded, the captain resumed. "At the ball last night..."

At this, Catherine was momentarily distracted. Had it really been only the night before that she and Henry were dancing together without a care in the world? It seemed impossible. It seemed more like a lifetime ago... or another life entirely, for everything had changed since, and not for the better.

"...my father, who had consumed a great deal of wine," the captain continued, "said some rather outrageous things. Most importantly, he proclaimed to the entire company his contempt for his two sons."

"Oh, dear me. How unfortunate," said the solicitor.

"Quite," agreed the captain. "In short, sir, he threatened to disinherit us both, Henry at once and me if I did not capitulate to his demands as regards to my choice of wife. He said in fact that *that* would be your primary business in coming here today – to amend his will to these effects. The magistrate has made out that this must have been Henry's motive for murder and the justification for accusing him of the crime. Although I agree that you cannot divine my brother's guilt or innocence, you can at least enlighten us as to whether or not changing his will was my father's reason for summoning you here."

All eyes turned on Mr. Wilcox, who squirmed uncomfortably in his chair. "Well, sir, by rights, I should not divulge your father's private business even to you, though you are his son and heir..." Mr. Wilcox paused, and everybody else held their collective breath to hear what he would say next. "...Under the circumstances, however, I cannot see that it would do your father any harm. For your information, then, this is the first serious talk I have heard about disinheritance. I was told there were a couple of items – estate business – needing my attention, but the only thing concerning the will was adding a provision for the general's intended bride."

There was a joint sigh of relief from the family.

"I suppose the latter will no longer be needed," Mr. Wilcox added introspectively. "How unfortunate... uh... for them both. I thought it such a good sign that General Tilney intended to marry again. A young wife might be expected to do wonders for a man in his middle years. Why, I myself have sometimes thought..."

"Nevertheless, Mr. Wilcox," said the captain, calling him back into the desired line. "What you say is good news, for Henry and for all of us. It seems likely, then, that the general's threats grew out of some passion of the moment, helped on by drink, rather than a considered and decided plan. That is as I suspected. Are you willing to testify to this information at the inquest, sir... and at a trial if necessary?"

"Of course. If… if I am called upon, I will do my duty. I will tell the truth of what I know in the interest of justice. But you will need to hire a barrister for your brother as well, Captain Tilney. I am not qualified to serve in that capacity and would never presume to put myself forward."

"Thank you for your candor, sir. I intend to do just that. In fact, I have already sent an express off this morning to Mr. Cogsgrove of the Inner Temples to retain his services for Henry."

Catherine leant forward. "You have?" she said in a tone she instantly recognized as sounding too much like disbelief to be polite.

"Yes, my dear sister-in-law," the captain returned patronizingly. "It might interest you to know that while you slept and then crept about the place, *I* was at work on behalf of your husband. I have seen him, paid for his keep, and hired him the best lawyer I could find."

Catherine sank back into her chair feeling properly chastened, even grateful to the captain for undertaking these measures so swiftly. Although none of this proved absolutely that he was not the real murderer himself, it did speak more of a concerned brother than a guilty man glad to have suspicion thrown on somebody else. Perhaps she had misjudged him after all. "Thank you," Catherine said meekly.

He nodded and then turned back to the solicitor. "Now, Mr. Wilcox, are you acquainted with this Mr. Cogsgrove?"

"Not acquainted with the man himself, but I am with his reputation! You could not have chosen better, Captain. If you can persuade Mr. Cogsgrove to take an interest in the case, your brother will be in very good hands."

Shortly thereafter, Mr. Wilcox stood to take his leave, saying he would stop off in Tetbury to give a statement of evidence for the inquest before returning to London to begin work on the disposition of General Tilney's estate.

Catherine was mightily relieved that the meeting had been

brief, thus preserving the possibility of seeing her husband before the day was out. Not only that, however. She hoped she might now be released from the discomfort of Captain Tilney's presence as well. Luck was with her and her desires immediately answered. The viscount announced his intention of taking his wife and sister-in-law into Tetbury just as soon as could be. And the captain, having been there only a few hours before, declined to join them.

They delayed just long enough for Catherine to assemble Henry's clothing. There was so little that all fit neatly into a modest-sized port-manteau that Eleanor provided her. These few things would have to do either until Henry was released or until she could have more sent from Woodston, whichever came first. *Pray, let it be the former,* she silently pleaded.

As Catherine prepared to close the case, something caught her eye. There was a place where the lining had become a little loose, giving access to the cavity beneath. It was not much of a tear, but it was enough to start an idea spinning in Catherine's brain.

More than once she had read in a novel how the heroine had smuggled some means of escape to her wrongfully imprisoned lover. *Margarita,* she remembered, had hidden a metal file up her sleeve. Under the guard's very nose, she had managed to discreetly pass the tool to Miguel when he bent to kiss her hand through the cold iron bars. After he worked silently and tirelessly for two days and nights to cut his way to freedom, they had run off together to be married and happily live out their lives abroad. It was all terribly romantic. Perhaps she could do likewise for Henry. Perhaps she could conceal a file beneath the lining…

A rap at the door interrupted Catherine's reverie.

"Mrs. Tilney?" said Patsy, coming in. "Do you need any help?"

Catherine vigorously shook her head, more to straighten out her thoughts than to answer the maid. "Thank you, Pasty, but I am finished. Perhaps you could give me a hand carrying this case down, though." Catherine closed and latched the port-manteau at once.

It had been a tempting but entirely impractical scheme, she decided. Even if she were successful in her part of such a wild plan, she was sure her husband was far too principled to go along with it. He would probably sooner go to his death, wrongfully convicted, than to be known to have evaded punishment by dishonorable means. Besides, she was not sure she could leave everything she knew behind to live permanently abroad. Much as she might like to see such exotic places as Morocco, Antigua, and the Alhambra of Spain, she could not quite imagine making a home anywhere outside of England. No, it would never do, and it had been foolish of her to even consider it.

It was this place, she concluded as she proceeded past the ancient tapestries lining the passageway and then down the massive stone staircase. No matter how sensible she resolved on behaving, Northanger Abbey seemed to always awaken in her slumbering ideas of dark mystery and latent thoughts of unlikely heroics. She needed Henry to settle her and plant her feet firmly back on solid ground. She needed him to tell her that he loved her and that everything would sort itself out rightly in the end. She simply needed Henry. She was not at all the same person without him. How would she ever survive if the worst should happen? A strangled sob escaped her lips at this horrible thought.

Eleanor stepped forward to meet Catherine at the bottom of the stairs. "There, now," she said. "You will feel much better once you have seen Henry."

- 16 -

VISITING HENRY

*H*enry had garnered little sleep. It was not that his bed was uncomfortable or even that his worries kept him awake. It was the separation from Catherine that disturbed him, even more than he had expected. Although he had slept alone for all of his life until recently, it had only taken a few short weeks with the warmth of his young wife at his side to completely spoil him, to turn him against ever wanting a solitary bed again. Now her first visit was all he could think of. *Please, God, let it be soon.* That was as much of a prayer as Henry's mind could construct at the moment.

Frederick had come already, of course, which was good of him, Henry acknowledged. But his brother brought comforts of a purely practical nature. Only Catherine could supply the extravagant affection Henry required to counteract the current bleakness of his situation. He sat in gloom, and she would bring the sunshine.

"Oh, Henry! How I have missed you! Are you well?" These things Catherine cried out in rapid succession as she flew into her husband's arms the moment the gaoler closed the door after admitting her. Henry was not allowed to answer, however. Such kisses as stopped his mouth, such passionate embraces and other demonstrations of affection as followed were worthy of marking the end of a lovers' separation of at least a twelve-month instead of a separation much closer to twelve hours. (But as to details, here the reader must use his own imagination, for I should blush to describe such things too minutely, even if I had been so rude as to watch Catherine and Henry's reunion myself.)

When at last the pair's hunger for one another was sated enough to once again allow for the exercise of speech, Henry proclaimed, "I declare the small inconvenience of my arrest is made entirely worthwhile by such an enthusiastic greeting from you, my beloved Catherine." Another kiss followed as further justification of his statement.

Although neither one could bear to release the other even then, Catherine did rouse herself sufficiently to look about from the safe confines of her husband's arms. After taking in the surroundings, she blinked in some surprise. She had unconsciously expected a moldy dungeon – an uncomfortable chamber of torment if not torture – such as were commonplace to the stories that had so long nourished her imagination. Instead, she saw a small but commodious room serviceably furnished.

"You see now that I am well looked after," Henry said. "I am not at all ill treated here. I have the best room in the place and the best food money can buy. Frederick has seen to that."

"Yes, so he told me. He has sent for an excellent barrister as well – a Mr. Cogsgrove of the Inner Temples. Oh, and Mr. Wilcox came. He is… he *was* your father's solicitor, but I suppose you knew that already. Anyway, he said your father had made no mention to him of revoking your living at Woodston. He was summoned on more ordinary business, and he will give testimony to that fact. Is not that good news? If the general had no true intention of disinheriting you, then you had no true motive for killing him. Anybody can see that!"

After thinking a moment, Henry relinquished all but Catherine's hand, motioning for her to take the plain but sturdy chair while he sat on the bed next to her. "Yes, my dear. It is good news, although perhaps more for my peace of mind than for any legal ramifications. I would be greatly relieved to know that my father had not been so displeased by our marriage as to make him plot the most painful way to punish me. But as to removing my supposed motive, this information comes too late. Any competent prosecutor will argue that what I believed at the time is all that matters, and as you know, my father put on a very convincing show last night with many witnesses. I was not sure myself but what he meant every word of his threats."

"Oh, Henry!" Catherine cried out in disappointment. "But you must never admit to that. You must say that you knew your father too well to believe his threats. Say you went in search of him for a different reason. Or, perhaps you were not looking for him at all. Perhaps you were doing something else entirely. I know you do not hold with telling falsehoods, but you are not obliged to help the court to convict you either."

"That is true enough. Now, tell me what else you have been doing. Did you get any sleep? You looked quite done in when I left you."

"When you left me? Henry, you make it sound as if you had gone off on business of your own accord instead of being dragged away as surely as if you had been in chains! I shall never forget that horrible sight. I nearly fainted dead away!"

"I am sorry for your distress, Catherine, truly I am. But I am proud of you for resisting the temptation to faint."

"Are you indeed?"

"Certainly! It is far more heroic to keep one's head under duress than to lose it."

"I had not thought of it that way," Catherine admitted, suddenly feeling much better about her performance the night before. "Would the same apply to sleeping, Henry? I must say that I felt a little guilty about not staying awake the *whole* night on your account as I had intended, though I was very worried, I assure you."

"The very same principle, my dear. Keeping one's head in a crisis means getting the food and rest one needs in order to continue the fight. So you did sleep?"

"Yes, some, and then when I awoke, I spoke to Patsy, the maid. She promised to keep her ears and eyes open below stairs, in case any of the servants should know anything."

"That was good thinking."

"Also, I went up to the roof." Catherine had not meant to tell him this last, especially since the misadventure had achieved nothing except her own humiliation, but she found she had no ability to withhold a single thought from her husband after all.

"The roof! What on earth did you expect to find there?"

"I hardly know. Perhaps some evidence overlooked in the dark the night before. In any case, I found nothing useful. Then Captain Tilney discovered me there and gave me quite a scare, as if he intended to throw *me* off next. But Eleanor assures me it must have been his idea of a tease. Do you think so, Henry?"

"I daresay it was," he answered slowly. "He did not actually lay a hand on you, did he?"

"Oh, no! Not even so much as one finger. He only said some things that made me nervous and then seemed to block my way. I suppose it was only teasing after all. You and Eleanor know him better than I do. If you both say I have nothing to fear from your brother, I must believe you. Oh! Speaking of Eleanor reminds me that she is here to see you as well, she and Jonathan. They were so good as to bring me in their carriage and to insist that I should come in first. One visitor at a time, you know."

"Yes. Of course I shall be glad to see them both as well, but not just yet. Stay with me a little longer, won't you? You have a way of cheering me as no one else can."

Catherine's cheeks glowed with pleasure. Other than saying that he was free to come home with her, there was scarcely anything her husband could have told her that would have delighted her more. It gave her courage, in fact, to confess her foolish idea of smuggling in a file to promote his escape, thinking he might find the story diverting.

Henry laughed heartily upon hearing it. "A plot from one of your novels, no doubt!"

"It is true. It succeeded for Miguel and Margarita."

"And made them quite notorious, I daresay!"

"Yes, so much so that they had to quickly leave the country and never return. They seemed not to mind, but I did not think that would suit either of us, so I gave up on the idea."

"Very sensible, Catherine. We shall hold that plan in reserve in case it is needed later. For now, however, I think we should pursue more customary channels for winning my release."

They spoke of many other things. Henry told Catherine what she must expect in the days to come – what the coroner's inquest would entail and the likelihood that he would then be remanded over for a full trial afterward. "We must not be overly dismayed if that should happen, my love," he said. "It does not mean they believe me guilty, only that there is enough evidence to refer the matter on to the higher courts." He also instructed her to send messages to Woodston to inform the curate of the parish, as well as the servants at the parsonage, what had happened. "Perhaps you should send Mr. Peabody home with the news," he suggested, "if you think you can do without the carriage for now. Yes, that would probably be best."

At last the couple said their adieus, consoled only by the fact that there was nothing preventing the visit being repeated in a day or two. Eleanor was allowed in next and finally Jonathan for only a few minutes each before the party was obliged to leave Henry behind and return to Northanger.

"He seems well," said Eleanor, when they were underway. "Not at all uncomfortable or despondent. That is a good sign, I think. He must believe he will be exonerated in the end."

"An innocent man has nothing to fear from the law," said the viscount.

"True enough," Catherine agreed, and yet in her heart of hearts she could not be quite so sanguine. An innocent man *should* have nothing to fear from the law, but the reality was somewhat different, she believed. She had certainly read novels where the wrong man had been convicted while the murderer went free, at least until the very last moment. She didn't think she could bear it if something similar happened to Henry. If his exoneration did not come until he was climbing the gallows, Catherine was quite sure she herself should expire from fright, though he be saved.

The same three repeated the visit two days later with Captain Tilney accompanying them, riding his own horse. It seemed he intended to meet with Mr. Cogsgrove there in Tetbury while the others saw Henry. When Catherine learned of it, she requested the chance to be present for their conference as well.

"There is no need," Captain Tilney told her firmly. "I am fully acquainted with the facts of the case and will require no assistance making Mr. Cogsgrove familiar with them as well. Then he will want to speak to Henry himself. So you had much better get your visit with him beforehand."

It was another variation of what he had told her before: the law was the business of men, and she would be allowed no part in it. For the moment, Catherine could not conjure a successful argument by which to attack his reasoning, and her brother-in-law was correct about one thing. Seeing Henry had to be her highest priority. There, at least, she could do some good. She knew nothing about the law, but, according to Henry himself, she was the one person singularly qualified to cheer him. Thus it was that Catherine had not spoken even one word to the man on whom her husband's life might well depend before seeing him later that week at the coroner's inquest.

17

CORONER'S INQUEST

wo coaches came from Northanger Abbey for the inquest that day – one carrying the family and the other for the servants who either wanted or needed to be there. Upon arrival in Tetbury, Catherine was helped into a large room above the inn (which had been designated to serve for the purpose) on the arm of her brother-in-law Captain Tilney, Eleanor and Jonathan with them. Catherine scanned the room, which was already half full, for Henry's face. Instead, she saw a distinguished man at the front, tall and thin and in his prime, who bowed his head in their direction as a sign of recognition.

"That is Mr. Thomas Cogsgrove," Captain Tilney explained. "Now, here are chairs, four together. Let us be seated."

They took the chairs – the two ladies sitting between the two gentlemen – and soon counted themselves fortunate to have found them, for the room was rapidly filling with a noisy mix of what looked to be random locals as well as other more particularly interested parties. Since murder was a rare occurrence, no doubt it had been some time since a case of such import – an entertainment so worthy of their time and attention – had been offered in their midst. Nobody who could help it would have missed it.

However, the almost-festive atmosphere did not sit well with Catherine, who was amazed that so many of those gathered there seemed unaware of the seriousness of the proceedings about to begin. "Do not they understand what has happened and what is at stake?" she whispered to Eleanor. "A man has died and another man's fate – Henry's fate! – hangs in the balance. And yet they behave as if it were some sort of carnival put on for their amusement. It is, above all things, disgusting to me!"

"Never mind, dearest," Eleanor answered, threading her arm through Catherine's. "They do not know Henry as we do. They probably expect to see a murderer, and him sent to his just punishment. Still not an occasion for frivolity, I agree, but it makes their behavior more understandable."

The merriment presently died down somewhat, as Henry himself entered, escorted between two guards to a seat at the front by Mr. Cogsgrove. Every head turned for a first look at the accused. In Catherine's hearing, a man nearby said to his friend, "By gaw, he looks guilty as sin, does that one. I can al'ays tell. It's in t' eyes."

Eleanor squeezed Catherine's arm tightly. "That uncouth fellow is nothing but a foolish braggart," she whispered. "His opinion is immaterial. We must not dignify it with a response of any kind."

Catherine nodded and, with great difficulty, held her tongue. She focused all her energy on Henry instead, willing him to turn and see her. She could not speak to him, but she felt that if only their eyes could meet, even for a moment, they would both be much comforted. "Look at me, Henry," she urged him under her breath. "Look at me."

He did not find her in the sea of faces before him, however, and soon there was more to think of. Someone called for quiet as the coroner, who was introduced as the Honorable Maxim

Renwell, entered. Everybody present silenced themselves and rose in unison. Renwell acknowledged the men of the jury and then took his seat, allowing everybody else to be seated again also. The coroner's chair was quite naturally the one of most consequence, both in size, style, and place, situated as it was behind a table at the center of a raised platform, with the chairs of the other court officials arranged on either side. The only person amongst them that Catherine recognized was the offensive magistrate, Sir Melvin Whitmore.

The jury was administered an oath, and then the coroner addressed his sober instructions to them.

"Gentlemen, as most if not all of you have served in this same capacity before, I will make this brief. You are here to listen carefully to the evidence offered and to subsequently render your considered opinion on the cause of death of one General Albert Tilney of Northanger Abbey, which occurred the last night of October. This is not a criminal trial. Your responsibility is confined to the following. You are to decide if the unfortunate gentleman met his end by accident, by suicide, or by homicide. Then, if the evidence convinces you of homicide, you must further determine if it clearly suggests to you the killer's identity. Any person you so name, whether the man currently held or another, will be committed for trial at the next assize court in Gloucester. Otherwise, you may rule it was murder by a person or persons unknown."

Catherine, upon hearing this last phrase, immediately clutched hold of it as Henry's best hope in the current action. Even if the jury decided for murder rather than accident or suicide, that was no reason they had to point the finger at her husband as the one who had done it. They had the option to say they did not know, that the evidence had not convinced them, which indeed was where the thing stood in her mind. She was willing to believe it was murder, if that is what all the experts persisted in testifying, but she was by no means sure who had done the deed, only that it could not have been Henry.

As the proceedings wore on, however, that hope faded. There were no surprise witnesses called by the coroner. Instead, it was a fair repeat of those persons Sir Melvin had relied upon to establish *his* vision of the facts: General Courteney and the Marquis of Longtown to set the stage, the maid who had discovered the body as well as the doctor who examined it, Sir Melvin himself and one of the constables who had accompanied him that night.

The family had been assured that none of them would be summoned to the witness box – none other than Henry, that is – since there was nothing they might contribute that could not be established by other means, including what Henry himself was willing to stipulate under oath.

Catherine was glad for herself and for Eleanor that they would be spared, especially spared from saying anything that would unwillingly cast aspersions on Henry's innocence. And yet, she would like to have been allowed to do something useful in his defense. In addition, she secretly wished that Captain Tilney, the menacing presence beside her, would be required to give information. She wished to see how well he would be able to acquit himself under scrutiny. She would have liked for the jury to at least set eyes on him, to hear him speak of his father, to have been able to picture him as an alternative suspect, one with more to gain from his father's death than Henry. How were they to consider that it could have been somebody else when they were given only one choice?

Just as there were no surprise witnesses, there was almost no new evidence brought forward either, only a recounting of Sir Melvin's discoveries and theories. Everybody agreed that, although the general was allowed to have been in liquor, it could not have been an accidental fall. Everybody said that suicide was out of the question, since General Tilney had everything to live for. Sir Melvin explained how he had come to settle on his chief suspect in the crime. And then it was Henry's turn to swear the oath and testify.

"Mr. Tilney," said the coroner, "You have heard the magistrate's conclusion that you are the most logical suspect in this crime, and furthermore that you indeed had strong motive and undeniable opportunity to have taken your father's life. Can you refute with facts any of the evidence against you?"

At that moment, Catherine squeezed her eyes tight and silently prayer more fervently than she ever had in her life before. She prayed Henry would think of something to say that would clear his name, that the jury would see his honest character and believe in him, that the nightmare would soon be over.

"Unfortunately, I cannot," Henry said clearly, his head held high. "I can only say what I have said before. I did not hate my father, even after the things he said that night. I did not seek him out in anger with murder on my mind. If I had found him, I meant to try to reason with him, to ask him to return to the party and make some apology for the scene he had created and the feelings he had wounded. But I had no opportunity for that or for any other discussion with him, because I did not in fact see my father again after he left the dinner until his body was found."

"So you did not go up to the roof?"

"No, I did not."

"And yet, no one can corroborate that contention, I understand."

"None that I am aware of, sir. Others saw me elsewhere throughout the house, but no one can account for all of my time away from the group. Besides God, who knows all things, I suppose the only one alive who knows with certainty that I was *not* there would be the person who *was* with my father on the roof that night. The real killer knows the truth of the matter."

"Indeed. But if you are innocent as you say, Mr. Tilney, can you suggest who this 'real killer' might be?"

Henry hesitated only a moment. "No sir, I cannot. My father

was not a kind or generous man, and he had offended any number of people, that night and before. But it is not my place to judge him nor to speculate about who may have actually wanted to see him dead. I will not bear false witness against my neighbor, sir. I will not slander another to save myself. I must trust to God and to the wisdom of the courts to vindicate me."

It was a very moving speech, and Catherine was not the only one to think so, for, upon hearing a muffled sob, she turned to see a woman with a hanky pressed to her eyes sitting several chairs down and a row behind. It was Mrs. Brooks, Catherine then realized. Mrs. Brooks, who loved Henry like a son, must feel much as Catherine herself did at that moment – proud for how honorably he had comported himself under difficult circumstances, but wishing all the same that he had named someone (anyone!) else to divert suspicion from himself. Catching the housekeeper's eye, Catherine gave her a sad smile of commiseration. Then the coroner's voice claimed their attention again.

He addressed the jury. "Gentlemen, Mr. Tilney is our final witness. Do you have any further questions for him or for any other of those whom you have heard from today?" He paused. "Hearing none, I suggest you retire to the antechamber to consider your verdict."

As the jury did so, murmurings broke out all over the room. Catherine herself grew quite restless and distressed, worrying aloud to her friends. "Oh, why did not they call Mr. Wilcox to give evidence, to say that the general did not mean to disinherit Henry? Why did not Mr. Cogsgrove argue for Henry's innocence? How can the jurors be expected to fairly judge when they were told only one side of the story? That odious Sir Melvin made sure they heard just what he wanted them to hear and no more! And who are these men anyway, these jurors, that they should decide Henry's fate?"

"Calm yourself, my dear," said Eleanor. "It is natural that you should be distressed, but you will not help Henry by allowing him to see that you have worked yourself into such an agitated state. Be strong, for his sake as well as your own."

From Catherine's other side, the captain spoke firmly. "Eleanor is correct. You *must* exert yourself, Catherine, and not cry out if the jury should rule that Henry is to stand trial, as I fully expect they will. *Then* will come Henry's chance to prove his innocence. *Then* will be the time that Mr. Cogsgrove can bring in his witnesses and put forth his own theories. We must be patient and allow the judicial process to work as it is designed to do."

Although Catherine cared little what anybody else thought, she *would* be strong for Henry. She would do what she could for him. Through a small gap between the heads in front of her, she could see that he was looking over the room, probably for her, she realized. But he would never spot her in the crowd of people who all seemed to sit taller than she, not unless she did something about it. So she simply stood where she was, saying nothing but waiting for Henry's eyes to alight upon her. They did so almost immediately and held her gaze for a long, fortifying minute. For that space of time, the distance between them and the noise of the raucous crowd faded away to insignificance. There was only Henry and Catherine, and all was right with the world.

Then the jury returned.

18

A FOREGONE CONCLUSION

*I*t seemed to Catherine that, just for that brief moment, she had been suspended far above the fray by a cord made up of two threads – one being that precious sightline to Henry and the other the feverish hope that he would not be bound over for trial. But the first of those cords was cruelly cut as soon as the jury returned. The room was called to order once more and everybody told to resume their seats. Catherine had no choice but to comply, painfully curtailing that short, exquisite communion with her husband.

Our fair heroine was then left to dangle precariously in a fitting agony of suspense on what was left to her, the slim thread of hope for Henry's acquittal. Catherine's suspense was mercifully short, however, and the outcome just what the captain had predicted. The jury ruled that the manner of General Tilney's death was murder and that they believed his younger son to have dealt the fatal blow, as alleged. Henry would be soon transferred to the county prison at Gloucester, there to await a trial for his life at the next assizes.

It was the shock of Henry's arrest all over again, alarmingly real and impossibly nightmarish at the same time. And once again Catherine was lost between the competing temptations to either faint dead away or to stand as an unassailable tower of strength for her husband. Either one, in the proper light, could have been seen as the action of a true heroine. But in the end she failed at both, landing somewhere betwixt the two, comforted by her friends as she slumped down into an undignified posture in her chair upon the jury's pronouncement and the coroner's subsequent orders. She had at least, by a Herculean effort, successfully stifled her urge to cry out at the injustice of the news. There was much honor in that.

"Mrs. Tilney, I presume," heard Catherine then. "Allow me to introduce myself; I am Mr. Thomas Cogsgrove, at your service."

Catherine looked up to find the distinguished man, whom her brother-in-law had identified earlier, neatly bowing before her. Rallying her remaining stores of strength, she straightened and attempted to rise.

"No, no," said Mr. Cogsgrove. "Please do remain as you were, Mrs. Tilney. I only wished to make myself known to you and to reassure you that, despite today's verdict, your husband's situation is far from hopeless."

Captain Tilney then spoke up. "Indeed, Mr. Cogsgrove, I was saying much the same to my sister-in-law only a moment ago." The captain then completed the introductions by formally presenting the viscount and the viscountess to the barrister.

"I am pleased to make the acquaintance of you all," said Mr. Cogsgrove. "I only wish it might have come under more favorable conditions. Now, in consideration of the lateness of the hour and the fatigues of the day, I will be brief. Mr. Tilney is this moment being returned to his place of confinement, where you may see him if you wish. In any case, he will not be transferred to Gloucester until Friday, so there will be time. Tomorrow begins my work in earnest. There will be just over two weeks to prepare for trial, and I do not intend to waste one moment of it.

So if it is not inconvenient to you all, I shall propose myself your visitor at Northanger Abbey to arrive in the morning. I will wish to see for myself the place where this unfortunate incident occurred and to interview all parties concerned. Sir Melvin has offered one interpretation of events, but in my experience, there is always more than a single explanation possible for a set of circumstances. We shall be after a better alternative."

"By all means," said Captain Tilney. "Northanger Abbey and its inhabitants shall be put completely at your disposal, Mr. Cogsgrove, and you may stay as long as you find necessary. Achieving my brother's release is the highest priority for us all."

By the time Catherine applied for admittance to her husband's cell, she had tolerably composed herself. Still, despite all her earnest vows of being strong for his sake, when the door opened she could not prevent herself flying headlong into Henry's arms with a mighty sob. Upon the whole, however, discovering what an amorous reception it earned her, she really could not regret it. Henry held her very tight and showered her with kisses, with most particular attention to a favorite patch of soft skin just below her left ear. Such felicity was worth nearly anything! That wild thought had just taken hold in Catherine's head, when her husband's ministrations came to an abrupt end.

"My love," he said, reluctantly loosening their embrace. "We must remember where we are."

"I care not, Henry," Catherine gasped. "Truly. Do carry on!"

Henry's laugh rumbled low in his chest. "Why Mrs. Tilney, you continue to surprise me – surprise and delight. What a good bargain I made when I married you. Most men are not so fortu- nate in their life's partner, to find a woman who is so... so... shall we say eager?"

But the spell was broken and Catherine returned to solid

ground. "On the contrary, Henry; I fear you made a very *bad* bargain when you married me," she whined. "You would not be here in this awful fix except for that. You would have done much better to have married somebody else, somebody of whom your father approved. Then even that horrid Sir Melvin could not think you had a motive for murder."

"My dear Catherine," he said, gently corralling a wisp of her hair that had come loose, "marrying some other woman does not even bear contemplation. I would not exchange these last few months together for anything in the world." Catherine intended to protest, but he stopped her with a finger to her lips. "And before you say a word, I assure you that I depend on many, many more years of the same, once we put this obstacle behind us. Now, have you met Mr. Cogsgrove?"

"Yes, but…"

"Good sort of fellow, is not he? I like him very much and expect he will serve me well."

"He is to come to Northanger tomorrow to continue his investigations on your behalf."

"Yes. He told me as much. Remember, today was merely a small setback. The verdict was to be expected, really – a forgone conclusion. It would have been a great surprise, in fact, if it had been something otherwise."

"That is what your brother said too. Oh, but Henry! I had so hoped for exactly that: something otherwise. The jury might have said they were not convinced of murder, or that if it was murder they could not say who had done it. I do not know how anybody could be certain only by what they heard today."

"They were only certain enough to recommend a trial; that was all that was required of *this* jury. At the trial itself, the standard will be much different and the prosecution's burden of proof a great deal higher. It is much less likely the next jury will be so easily convinced of my guilt; Mr. Cogsgrove will see to that. In the meantime, we must bear these inconveniences. We have endured separation before, and we will this one just as well."

All too soon, Catherine was forced to take leave of the prisoner and join the others in the carriage for the drive back to Northanger. No one seemed in a talkative mood, which was perfectly understandable and as Catherine would have wished it. There was nothing any of her fellow travelers could say that would have added to her comfort. Neither could she think of anything that would meaningfully augment theirs. They were all four, presumably, united in their mutual misery on their own and Henry's behalf. They were all left primarily to the company of their own thoughts, the counsel of their own consciences.

She hoped Captain Tilney's conscience troubled him severely. Most probably it did not, however, not because he was innocent, but because she understood some men learned to silence that inner voice when convenient. Perhaps that was especially true of those who were trained as soldiers. After all, they had to be able to kill and still go on about their business. They had to be able to kill and still look their neighbors and their own reflections in the eye.

A chill ran up Catherine's spine as she once more pictured her brother-in-law pushing his own father to his death, a cruel snarl upon his lips. The captain, who once again sat only inches from her, radiated an air of malevolence, of which no one but herself seemed to be cognizant.

At that moment, the carriage wheel hit a rut, pitching Catherine full against her companion. She pulled back at once, saying, "Pardon me, Captain." In the waning light, she saw his leering smile as he looked down at her.

"I don't mind in the least your throwing yourself at me. We need not tell your husband."

"Really, Frederick," Eleanor protested wearily.

Catherine schooled her countenance into a mask of passive composure and said nothing. It would be safest if the captain did not see her revulsion, could not sense how much his mere presence intimidated her.

For the moment, there was nothing Catherine could do with her persistent suspicions about Captain Tilney, but she would not keep silent forever. At the very least, she would be sure to find a chance to drop a hint... No, nothing so subtle. She was determined that at her very first opportunity she would insist that Mr. Cogsgrove check the captain's alibi more thoroughly. There was a time for polite respect and then there was a time for speaking out.

Meanwhile, she distracted her troubled mind with something else entirely, something Henry had said: that they had successfully endured separation before. She knew he meant the time spent waiting for General Tilney's grudging consent to their marriage, without the decent appearance of which Catherine's own parents would not give theirs. The lovers thus had parted with a strong understanding between themselves but nearly despairing of the necessary change in the general's position ever taking place. Henry had returned to Woodston to hope and to pray and to pursue improvements to his domestic situation for Catherine's sake. Catherine remained at Fullerton to pine and to cry and to watch for the letter from Henry she felt their unofficial engagement would justify.

In the mode of the true romantic heroine, Catherine had secretly intercepted her lover's initial correspondence, thereafter always keeping it concealed on her person and close to her heart, and faithfully reading the missive through several times a day, despite the tears of exquisite torture it invariably drew from her already red-rimmed eyes. Fortunately, however, having committed the entire contents to memory, she soon had no need of worrying the paper parcel any further, for indeed it was at the point of falling to bits where the pages had been folded and unfolded an hundred times or more. She could instead call every touching passage to mind at will anytime she chose during those difficult months of waiting. Even now, she could still remember.

Catherine looked out of the carriage window. The route was familiar to her – and to the horses and driver too, she hoped, for the light was indeed fading fast. Inside, she could barely make out the faces across from her. So she closed her eyes instead. Then, as an exercise of duty, as a testimony to her unfailing constancy to her husband, who had written that exceptional letter, and as a reminder that seemingly impossible situations do sometimes come right in the end, Catherine allowed her mind's eye to travel across those long-cherished pages again, silently reciting the words once more but hearing them in Henry's voice.

My Dearest Catherine,

May I presume to call you mine, though I cannot yet fully possess you? I dare to hope that I may, for when I look into my mind, into my heart, and into my imagination, I find you already resident there, a warm and vital part of me. In these three seats of my affection, there is no one but you, Catherine. In truth, there never was and never will be another. You have captured me altogether, and I ache with longing until our union can at last be made complete.

Do I shock you, my darling, by the force of my affection, with the strength of these sentiments? Indeed, I shock myself. You have been used to hearing only lightness and teasing from me, only joviality and laughter. That is always my preferred way. But I find that I am, after all, capable of much more serious reflections when hard pressed, as I now am by this separation. I find it is difficult to speak lightly when my heart is heavy.

And yet I do not despair at our situation. Although there currently seems no reasonable basis for hope of an early solution, I remain ever hopeful. I refuse to be reasonable if being reasonable means I must consign myself to a world where the contrariness of one stubborn gentleman should overrule all that is good, right, and fitting. If my father will be obstinate in his position, I will hold even more tenaciously to mine. I can even be patient if necessary, because I am convinced that, with right on our side, we will prevail in the end, you and I. I also believe that the reward – the deep satisfaction we may expect to find in our marriage – will be well worth waiting for. But I dare not say more on that subject here.

So I entreat you to join me in this belief, my dearest, fairest Catherine. Do let me hear from you soon to confirm your love and faithfulness, as I do now confirm mine for you. Tell me you will wait as long as it may take for our happiness to be fulfilled.

I remain ever yours, body and soul,

Henry

Catherine was glad for the relative darkness of the carriage, for she felt her cheeks grow hot at the review of these passionate sentiments… and especially with the thought of how their implied promise had been more than amply fulfilled since their marriage.

She knew Henry was right; she must take courage from the lessons of the past. She must put her faith in the justness of their cause and in their ultimate success. They could endure this separation as they had that other one, with eyes looking to the reward that would, if God be merciful, surely follow. Absence made the heart grow fonder. Likewise, a period of forced separation no doubt would make their coming together again all the sweeter. Catherine resolved to hold fast to these truths.

19

INTERVIEWS

*M*r. Cogsgrove arrived early the next day, just as he had said he would, and he set about his work without delay. He was first shown the relevant rooms of the house by Captain Tilney, including the roof and the place where the general's body had been found. Then he asked to address the family in the common drawing room.

"Thank you for receiving me so graciously," the barrister began when they had gathered. "I will endeavor to incommode you and this household as little as possible while I remain, but I will need to speak to each one of you in private, and as many of the servants as possible. I know it will be going over the same ground as Sir Melvin has covered before, but I will be looking from a different perspective – not to accuse but to exonerate. I often find that new information – perhaps even a thing of great import – turns up upon a second perusal. That is what I am counting on in my efforts to free Mr. Tilney. Therefore, I ask your indulgence in this."

"Of course," said the captain, joined by the rest with similar words of accord.

"What of the others?" asked the viscount, "I am thinking of

the Marquis of Longtown, his daughter, General Courteney, and so forth. I do not like to tell you your business, Mr. Cogsgrove, but it is my personal opinion that the answers you seek are not in this household and neither is the killer."

"You may be right, Lord Astley. Time will tell. I have formed no firm opinions as to those things yet; I prefer to keep an open mind, especially in the beginning. That being said, I always start with those closest to the victim. I will by no means finish there, however. I have Sir Melvin's list from that night and will not be merely taking his word for ruling each person in or out of suspicion. Besides my own efforts, I have set my best assistant on the case – a doggedly tireless investigator. You may be sure that between the two of us we will leave no stone unturned. I hope that sets your mind at ease."

"It does, Mr. Cogsgrove," said the viscount. "Thank you."

"Not at all. Now, I will require a place to work whilst I am here, a room where I can conduct my interviews and compile my notes undisturbed."

"Certainly, sir," said Captain Tilney, rising to his feet. "Might I suggest the library? It is just across the way. And I will take the first interview with you myself." He then softened his tone to add, "That is, if it is all the same to you. I have an appointment later in the village that I wish to keep if possible."

"Whether I speak to you first or last makes no difference to me," said Mr. Cogsgrove. Turning to the others, he added, "Is that agreeable to the rest of you."

"We are entirely at your disposal, sir," said the viscount, the ladies agreeing with him.

"Very well, then. Let us get on with it, Captain."

When they had gone, Catherine looked at her two remaining companions and said, "I wonder what Mr. Cogsgrove expects to discover."

"I do not know," answered Eleanor. "I have nothing new or useful to tell him, unfortunately. Do you, Jonathan?" Her husband only shook his head. "For Henry's sake, I dearly wish I had," continued Eleanor. "I have thought and thought, and still I have no idea what really happened that night, except that I would prefer to believe it had all been a terrible accident. It seems no one supports me in that opinion, however."

"I would prefer that explanation as well," said Catherine with feeling. "But I no longer can truly believe it."

Eleanor sighed heavily. "I suppose if I am honest, I cannot either."

"Mr. Cogsgrove is a highly trained and experienced man," said the viscount. "No doubt he is skilled at eliciting information from all types of characters, even the forgetful and uncooperative sorts. I should think it would be next to impossible to pass off a lie as truth to him. And with judicious questions, he may often prompt the brain, sparking something in the memory that a person had forgot was there, something overlooked before and helpful to the case. I place great store by that kind of investigative work."

"I hope you are right," said Catherine. "Something *must* have been overlooked, forgot, or deliberately hidden, because so far a lie has been believed."

Soon becoming restless, Catherine abandoned her comfortable chair near the fire to move to the window. As she leant close for a more comprehensive view from that elevated vantage point, she could feel the chill of the cold day penetrating through the glazing. Patches of frost still persisted in protected areas, she noticed, giving further confirmation of the fact that winter was at hand. The sky was a clear blue, however, and very few reminders of the recent storm remained – only the occasional broken branch fallen at the margins of the vast grassy meadow far below. Even those remnants would soon be gone, she surmised from the presence of a cart and two workers, who appeared to be clearing away the bits and pieces.

If only the other consequences of that stormy night could be dealt with so quickly and straightforwardly! But no, the disarray over General Tilney's death was likely to take weeks, possibly months, to be resolved. Even then – even after Henry was exonerated, which she had to believe he would be – things would never be the same again. How could any of them ever approach the entrance to Northanger Abbey without their eyes involuntarily drifting to the side, to the place General Tilney had come to rest, and picturing his corpse lying there? Although he had more than once proved he was not her friend, he was Henry's father, and as such he deserved her respect and pity.

Catherine hugged herself and rubbed her arms to keep from shivering. Her own good sense, when augmented by Eleanor's injunction to "come away from the window," decided her. She returned to the fire, more grateful for its warmth than before.

After being closeted with Mr. Cogsgrove for about thirty-five minutes, the captain returned from the library for a few parting words. Pulling on his riding gloves, he said, "Cogsgrove is asking for you next, Eleanor. I am off now, but I will return before dark."

"Where are you going, Frederick?" his sister asked.

"As I said before," the captain replied a little testily, "I have an appointment in the village. Nothing that concerns you, Eleanor."

Her curiosity left unsatisfied, Eleanor let her brother go and likewise disappeared – in her case, for her interview with Mr. Cogsgrove. She was gone a similar length of time, returning to send her husband to the library after her. "I am sorry you are to be kept waiting until last, Catherine," she said.

"It makes no difference to me; I have nothing else of importance to do." Catherine looked a little closer at her sister-in-law and did not like what she saw. "You are unwell, Eleanor. Were Mr. Cogsgrove's questions *very* grueling?"

"Oh, no, not really. A little fatiguing perhaps, because I

wanted so much to be of use. Now that it is done, however, I must admit I am weary indeed."

"Then you must by all means rest yourself. There is nothing more you can do. I am perfectly well here on my own, and I will tell Jonathan when he comes that you have gone up to your rooms to lie down."

"Are you quite sure?"

"Quite."

"Very well, then. I am glad to do as you say, dear, kind Catherine. I will just summon Mrs. Brooks first, though. Mr. Cogsgrove said he would see her after you."

When Mrs. Brooks reported to the common drawing room, she had already commenced wringing her hands, as was her habit when anxious. Seeing Catherine there also, she said, distractedly, "Oh, good day, Mrs. Tilney. What do you suppose that man wants with me? I could ill be spared from my duties to answer questions I have answered three times before, let alone to stand by awaitin' the privilege."

"No need to fret, Mrs. Brooks. This work supercedes anything else you might have been doing. And Mr. Cogsgrove is our friend. Since he is looking for something to help Henry, we must be entirely cooperative with his questions. Who knows but what something you say may turn out to be the key to solving the puzzle of General Tilney's death? Now, do please sit down." Catherine motioned towards a gold colored paisley damask upholstered chair, the mate to her own.

Mrs. Brooks resolutely shook her head and remained where she was. "It don't seem right. What would the young master say to find the housekeeper taking her ease on his fine furniture?"

"Come now, Mrs. Brooks, I insist. Captain Tilney is away at present. And besides, I have given you permission."

With that, Mrs. Brooks looked about the room and finally settled on a straight-backed chair, perching on the very edge of it like a nervous hen.

"Today is a special case," Catherine then continued. "We are all here to do our best for Mr. Tilney. Is not that so?"

"By all means, Mrs. Tilney," agreed Mrs. Brooks. "Poor boy. Yes, by all means. I... I suppose this Mr. Cogsgrove will be about finding who the real murderer is."

"He is looking for anything that will help, but discovering the real killer would certainly be the best way to show Henry had nothing to do with it. Otherwise, I cannot bear to think..." Catherine's voice faltered, and she stopped until she had regained her composure. "Forgive me, Mrs. Brooks. I do not mean to distress you. I know you care for my husband too. I meant to thank you for your support at the inquest. When I spoke to Henry afterward, I made sure he knew you had been there."

Mrs. Brooks seemed too overcome to do more than nod her acknowledgement before the two women lapsed into silence.

At last it was Catherine's turn to be summoned to the library. Mr. Cogsgrove met her at the door, saying, "Thank you for your patience, Mrs. Tilney. These things take time, as I am sure you can appreciate. Now, please do make yourself comfortable." He gestured her to a chair, closed the door securely, and then took the seat on the opposite side of the heavy desk at the center of the room.

Although Catherine had schooled herself to be calm and dignified, in her anxiety she attacked the man as soon as he was seated, saying, "Oh, Mr. Cogsgrove, forgive me. I know you are meant to ask the questions and I to answer them, but I cannot wait another minute. I must know if you have discovered anything yet that can help my husband. Have you? You cannot imagine how worried I have been for Henry and how much we all depend on you to save him. Do you think you can? Oh, sorry! I did not mean to imply that I doubted your abilities, only that... Dear me. This is not how I meant to behave at all."

Mr. Cogsgrove smiled benignly and answered without even a hint of irritation. "That is quite all right, Mrs. Tilney. Your questions and concerns are only natural in your current situation."

"But I did not mean to offend you, and at the very outset of our acquaintance too."

"I am not the least offended, good lady, I do assure you. I regret that I cannot answer your questions satisfactorily at present, however. We are still very early in the process."

"Is there nothing you can tell me, though? Nothing at all?"

"Only that my investigation is proceeding as well as can be expected, and I remain very hopeful of a good outcome. Now it is your turn to answer questions, agreed?"

"Yes, of course, Mr. Cogsgrove. Do proceed. I promise to behave myself and answer to the best of my ability."

"Thank you. And do be as candid as possible, Mrs. Tilney. What you say to me will not be repeated to anyone, even to your husband, without your consent. Do you understand?"

"Yes, of course."

Mr. Cogsgrove slowly and methodically reviewed with Catherine how she came to be a Tilney in the first place, and then the particulars of that night – where she was and when; what she did, saw, heard, and said; what she recalled of the activities and words of others in attendance.

Catherine held nothing back. Often in long and rambling narrative fashion, she offered the barrister every detail she could remember, whether it seemed important or not, in the hope that something she said might prove to be the key that unlocked the mystery of General Tilney's death, just as she had suggested to Mrs. Brooks. For his part, Mr. Cogsgrove listened attentively, making notes from time to time in the log book before him.

"And are you perfectly satisfied, Mrs. Tilney, that your husband is innocent of these charges?" he asked after Catherine had finished giving her account. "You have known him for a relatively brief time, after all. Perhaps you married in haste, before you understood his character. Remember, your reply will remain between the two of us, and I am bound to defend Mr. Tilney to the best of my ability either way."

For a moment, Catherine could make no answer; she only looked at Mr. Cogsgrove askance. When she realized that her mouth had fallen open, she closed it, swallowed, and replied with conviction. "Mr. Cogsgrove, I suppose you must ask such questions, so I will try not to think ill of you for it. But I assure you that I am as certain as a person can be that my husband is entirely innocent. There is no violence or malice in him. I daresay his character is as irreproachable as that of any man in England. As his wife, I would know. He did not do this thing of which he is accused, and I cannot image how anybody who has ever met him could think that he did!"

"I am very glad to hear it, Mrs. Tilney, and do please forgive what must have seemed an impertinence. Now, I believe we are almost finished. Before you go, though, I would like to hear anything else you think might have a bearing on this case, anything at all that we have not already covered. Do you have a theory for what really happened that night, for example, perhaps a suspicion about who might actually be responsible for General Tilney's demise? This is your opportunity to relate whatever you like."

Catherine knew this was the chance she had been waiting for. And yet she hesitated, feeling it in some way dishonorable or underhanded, a disloyalty to her adopted family and perhaps even to Henry himself. Still, it must be said. "As a matter of fact, Mr. Cogsgrove, there is something…"

"Do continue, Mrs. Tilney. Please. It may be important."

"Very well, Mr. Cogsgrove, but do keep this to yourself. I would not like even my husband to know what I am about to mention. It needs to be said, however, and perhaps I am the only one who will tell you. It is just that, as sorry as I am to have to say it, it would be far worse *not* to say it and Henry pay the price. Do you see what I mean?"

"Of course, Mrs. Tilney. That is, I am sure I shall, just as soon as you tell me what it is," he clarified. "Please proceed."

"It is this, Mr. Cogsgrove. Although I do not like to slander my brother-in-law, I cannot shake the conviction that he – Captain Tilney, I mean – is a much more likely candidate for this murder. His motive was greater, and it is more in his nature to be resentful. Plus, he is a soldier, and as such, he must, at least under the right circumstances, be capable of violence. Of course I have no proof, but please, *please*, do check his alibi very rigorously. It was the only thing that kept him from being arrested instead of Henry, you understand. Henry and Eleanor do not suspect him, and it is difficult to believe that any man would knowingly see his brother charged in his place, still..."

"Yes, I see," Mr. Cogsgrove said gravely. "Thank you, Mrs. Tilney."

Suddenly, Catherine's eyes grew wide and she gasped, her hand flying up to cover her mouth involuntarily.

"What is it, Mrs. Tilney?" asked her distinguished companion. "Has something happened to distress you?"

"I have just remembered something, Mr. Cogsgrove. It was Captain Tilney who engaged your services. He is the one who is paying you, and that no doubt makes you beholden to *him*! Now I have told what I suspect, what is to keep you from reporting it directly to him? Good heavens, I am such a fool! I should never have said a word. He will resent me more than ever now. I am afraid I shall never be safe in this house again!"

"Calm yourself, Mrs. Tilney," said Mr. Cogsgrove. "You are in no danger, at least not from me, I assure you. Regardless who engaged my services, my only loyalty is to the man I will represent in court: your husband, Mr. Tilney. If it comes to that, I am perfectly capable of biting the hand that feeds me, so to speak. If

I discover that Captain Tilney is the true murderer, I will have no qualms in revealing that fact to the authorities for the sake of justice. And should that occur, no one need ever know that it was you who gave me the clue to check a little deeper into that line of investigation. Either way, our conversation will remain confidential, as I said before. You have my solemn promise on that, and also that I will diligently follow up on what you have told me. Every man should pay for his own crimes, after all."

COMMUNICATION, INTENTIONAL AND OTHERWISE

*C*atherine was a little relieved for having unburdened herself to Mr. Cogsgrove and for receiving his promise to attend to her concerns. Still, when she sat down to dinner that night across from Captain Tilney, and she chanced to meet his eye for a moment over the soup, she had the uncomfortable sensation that he knew all about it. If Mr. Cogsgrove had not told him, then perhaps he had divined it for himself.

So far as Catherine knew, she had never successfully deceived anybody. On those rare occasions when she had attempted a lie to one of her parents, it had been found out at once. "You *are* a daft little creature if you expect me to believe that," Mrs. Morland had said the time Catherine had tried to shift blame from herself to her brother for a broken pitcher. "Why, the truth of the matter is as plain as the nose on your face! Now confess what really happened, clean up this mess, and perhaps nothing much more need be said about it." Catherine's capitulation had been immediate, her mild punishment entirely just, and her mortification sufficient to long remind her not to indulge in falsehoods again.

Her face was far too open; that was the trouble. And now she was persuaded that her current betrayal was just as clearly written in her countenance for her brother-in-law to read. In *his* visage she deciphered what seemed to be resentment or even malice. What was worse, if her suspicions about him were correct, he was the sort of man who had, at least once before, *acted* on such malice. There would be very little to prevent him doing so again if he should take the notion, least of all the meager efforts of one as powerless as herself.

Other than Mr. Cogsgrove, who had already finished his work and gone, there was no one Catherine could confide in, no one to whom she could turn for protection except Captain Tilney himself. But who would protect her from *him*? Eleanor had already dismissed Catherine's fears about her elder brother, and Catherine could not bring herself to distress Henry further. In any case, he was locked up miles away; he was in no position to defend her against a threat here at Northanger. If a genuine emergency arose, she would have to turn to the viscount, Catherine decided. Surely, as a man of honor, Jonathan would act first to ensure her safety and sort the rest out later. Of course, if it turned out another one of her infamous blunders, she would feel a great fool and never be able to face Henry's family again.

All things considered, Catherine could have wished herself miles away from Northanger at that moment. Although she should have been sorry to give up Eleanor's company, otherwise she could not regret anything she would leave behind. And it no longer seemed likely she should discover useful clues at the abbey, as she had once hoped. That idea had been only the most recent page in her annals of folly, only another example of how too many novels had led her reason astray. To think that she had imagined herself a detective of sorts now seemed laughable. She had accomplished nothing and must instead depend on Mr. Cogsgrove's investigation to save Henry.

Oh, to return to the comfort of her snug parsonage home! She would have felt altogether safer away from Captain Tilney's dark looks and unknown intentions, with familiar things about to comfort her: her favorite rooms, the garden views, Henry's dogs. But that was out of the question. Her last vestige of independence had gone when she sent Mr. Peabody and her carriage away. Now she was entirely reliant upon others and under the control of her intimidating host.

"You are very quiet tonight," said Captain Tilney. "Something on your mind, sister?"

Thus roused, Catherine lifted her eyes to find that it was to herself and not Eleanor that her brother-in-law's dry remarks were addressed. He had broken off eating and was looking straight at her with raised eyebrows. And once again, Catherine had the disquieting impression that he could read her thoughts, that he knew exactly what it was she had that moment been contemplating.

"Oh! My goodness, no," said Catherine hastily. "Pardon me, but I am sure I was not thinking of anything at all, Captain. Nothing in particular, in any case. Certainly nothing that would be of interest to you… or to anybody else… Really, it was nothing at all." She could feel her face burning.

Captain Tilney studied her a moment more. "That is not the way it appeared to me. Your brow was furrowed as deep as a river gorge. You must take care that it does not stay that way. Most unbecoming in a young lady."

"Oh, Frederick," sighed Eleanor, wearily. "Do leave poor Catherine alone. You will distress her, for she does not understand your style of teasing."

"Very well," Tilney said with a sigh. "My apologies, sister, dear. My apologies to you all. I was merely trying to enliven the conversation a little. We are grown very silent and dull this evening."

"This is hardly a fit occasion for frivolity, sir, with Henry's fate so uncertain," said the viscount with stately authority. "This may be your house and your table, but in my opinion, Mrs.

Tilney has every right to keep her own counsel if she chooses, without being accused of dullness."

"I stand corrected, Jonathan," Captain Tilney said with a dignified nod, "and properly chastened, too. Catherine, feel free to be as silent as you please. You will suffer no more attacks from me tonight."

Catherine thanked the captain for these assurances, and then smiled her appreciation to her other brother-in-law. Seeing how Jonathan had risen to her defense in such a trifling matter confirmed for her that she could trust him if she came under a more serious attack. There was some comfort in that.

Nevertheless, the primary problem persisted. Whilst Henry remained in peril, Catherine could never be entirely easy. Her own personal safety would be little comfort if Henry should be convicted of murder. And perhaps there was still something more she could do. Several days had elapsed since she had spoken of the matter to Patsy, her spy amongst the servants, and so Catherine decided she would try once more to elicit some useful information from the girl, if there was any at all to be had.

"I'm sorry, Mrs. Tilney," Patsy said in response to the question that night, "but I have nothing to tell you. I would not have waited to be asked if I had."

Catherine dropped into a chair, her thin hope of an affirmative answer, which had supported her until that moment, now gone. "Yes, I supposed as much. It was just, with Mr. Cogsgrove being here today, I thought perhaps it would have got the servants talking on the subject again."

"I wish it had, but everybody is being quite tight lipped about it. You know of Mr. Hastings's rule against gossip. And Mrs. Brooks told everybody under her that if we had any information for Mr. Cogsgrove, we should tell her instead. She would report to the barrister herself so the rest of us would be spared an interrogation."

"That was kind of her," said Catherine.

"Very kind, because some of the younger maids and such like were shaking in their shoes at the thought of being locked in an interview with an important man like Mr. Cogsgrove. Not me, though; I would have been ready. And I did try to ask around a bit, kind of cagey like, but nobody was talking."

"Do you think some of them had things to tell but would not, or that nobody knew anything in any case? The two are very different matters."

"Don't rightly know, ma'am. Could be either one or t'other. Mostly the second, I expect. Not too many what has brains enough to be that secretive, if you ask me, not when the natural inclination is to boast and embellish what little they do happen to know."

"I suppose you are right," said Catherine with a sigh. She rose to her feet, turned, and allowed Patsy to finally set about helping her off with her gown in preparation for bed. "Very well then. I appreciate that you tried, and I beg you would keep alert to whatever might yet come in your way. I fear we are running out of time, though."

The family was able to accomplish one more visit to Henry before he was moved to Gloucester, where the increased distance would make any repetition vastly more difficult. During Catherine's time, she found very little to say to her husband that she had not already said before, very little of her worries that she could share without risk of distressing him – on her account or his own. Henry suffered under similar constraints, wanting Catherine to be reassured but unable to provide her any tangible reason that she should be.

Catherine had asked, "Has Mr. Cogsgrove told you nothing about his investigation, then, no new information that he has unearthed?"

To which Henry had only replied, "At the moment, I am nearly as much in the dark as you appear to be, my dear. Still, I have every confidence in him. My brother would not have hired Mr. Cogsgrove for me if he had not been the very best man available. I expect to hear a report of his progress when I see him tomorrow."

After this comparatively meager intercourse at the beginning, Henry and Catherine spent the last few of their limited minutes together in a rather desperate effort to make up for it, to adequately convey by word and touch their mutual and abiding affection. The astute reader may well imagine the scene. "I love you" was pronounced by the one and echoed by the other so many times as could not be counted, the rapid succession only interrupted enough to admit the equally essential embraces and kisses of their leave-taking ceremony. In the end, the gaoler had to threaten to have Mrs. Tilney forcibly removed in order to gain her cooperation so that he might finally lock the door and go home to his supper.

Then there followed a stretch of days to be got through with no news, no visits to Henry, and little to do. With Eleanor, Catherine spent the chief of her time, walking about the grounds whenever weather permitted and pacing the halls of the house when it did not. She was much too restless to sit and do nothing, and the idea of setting her hand to any kind of tedious needle-work was insupportable.

Meanwhile, Henry Tilney remained perfectly ignorant of his wife's tortures of mind and lost in some of his own. He sat alone at Gloucester in a single room secured by a bolted door with very little to occupy his time. In the first days of his residency there, he had with him only his Bible and his prayers – no small comfort for a man of serious reflections, and yet Henry Tilney was not accustomed or well suited to the monastic life. He could not convince himself that his cell was a cloister he inhabited by choice. For his religion was not one of solitary faith but one lived out in community with likeminded others, others he was now deprived of.

Mr. Cogsgrove (his only visitor) proved his temporary deliverance by supplying other civilized comforts: books (in the first instance, a copy of *Tom Jones*), paper and pen for writing letters, and at least a few minutes of intelligent conversation each day. This was meager fare, however, which Mr. Tilney made every effort to supplement through the only other source possible – the two gaolers who by turns brought him his meals.

Henry quickly apprehended that the one called Webster would be perfectly useless to him. No effort of cunning or wit could elicit from the man either a smile or more than a monosyllable of speech. The other showed more promise, though, and Henry's spirits always rose when McLean appeared instead, for then there was hope of a minute or two of ordinary talk to break up the long hours of solitude.

"How is your wife?" Henry asked McLean on the second day, after learning on the first that such a person existed and was ill.

"Thank you kindly for asking, sir. She is on the mend but still a mite poorly," the man said, depositing a full tin plate and cup on the small table before preparing to take away the empty vessels. "It's the damp that hangs about the place, y' see."

"Well, I am sorry to hear it. No, no, don't go yet, my good fellow! I wanted to ask you a question – a favor really. I was wondering if there might be any chance of acquiring a chess board and perhaps your company in a match."

McLean confessed that he did not know the game, but he promised to look out a deck of cards for Mr. Tilney. That was the best he could do. But what good would cards be with no partner for a game?

Henry took up his pen.

·   ·   ·

My dearest Catherine,

I know I should be strong for your sake, and yet I confess that my spirits are ebbing low. It is mere days since I saw you last, and yet it seems an age. No good news reaches me here. Do send an encouraging word soon. I depend on you so...

Henry read what he had set down, tore it asunder, and put his pen aside until such time as he was in a fit humor to write something more cheerful. Nevertheless, though he had not asked, an encouraging letter from his wife did soon arrive to put him in a better humor to write one of his own.

Although hours of unrestricted communication with such a friend as Eleanor would normally have been a delight, Catherine's head was too full of Henry's plight to take much pleasure in anything at all, even her dear sister-in-law's company. There was a sense of restraint between them for the first time, just as Catherine had felt with her husband. Each was sensible of protecting the feelings of the other in regards to Henry's dire situation, and yet neither could think of anything else. Consequently, much of their time together was kept in mutual silence.

With her own family, Catherine felt no such need for circumspection. She poured out her uncensored fears and sorrows to her parents in a lengthy letter that she had begun on the eve of the disastrous inquest – what had happened to General Tilney, how Henry had been wrongfully accused, and her own trials of mind and spirit since. Day by day, Catherine's agitated feelings streamed forth onto the page until she finally thought it best to bring her extended opus to a close as follows:

. . .

...My dear mother and father, knowing you as I do, I feel secure of your doing so without my even suggesting it, but I must ask in any case. Please pray for us as often as you can spare a moment or a thought from your other duties. And pray for Mr. Cogsgrove to discover a way to convince the world of Henry's innocence. Be so good as to enlist the assistance in this endeavor of all my brothers and sisters, and indeed, anybody else you would trust with this information. I will write again when there is something more to tell. I will only add what you must already know to be true. If anything were to happen to my beloved husband, I am certain I should perish as well. Love to you all,

Your ever devoted daughter,
Catherine Tilney

Perhaps Catherine should have exercised more restraint after all. Perhaps she might have taken into account the effect such frank sentiments from a cherished child were bound to have upon a set of loving parents. One cannot help but imagine the extreme distress to them both at being suddenly overtaken by such shocking information. Surely an average mother must have fainted on the occasion. The blow must have done the average father a serious injury.

Fortunately, however, the Morlands were nothing so useless as only average. They were both very stout of physical constitution and even sounder of mind. Be assured that they were able to weather the arrival of Catherine's alarming missive with appropriate soberness but also with the mutual faith – a faith confirmed many times over the course of the years – that things would sort themselves out right in the end.

Catherine solemnly sealed her letter and carried it downstairs to see that it was posted as soon as possible. Before she could entrust her parcel to Mr. Hastings, however, she came across Captain Tilney in the passageway.

"Ah, Catherine." His eyes traveled to her hand. "What do you have there? A letter?"

Catherine stopped short and examined the article tightly gripped between her fingers, as if surprised to see it there. "Oh, this?" she asked.

"Yes, that. It looks very much like a letter to me."

"It... it is, in fact. I have written to my parents at Fullerton. I was going to see Hastings about getting it to the post."

Captain Tilney extended his hand. "Give it to me, and I will see to it myself. I am bound for the village shortly, in any case."

Catherine hesitated. "Oh... thank you, Captain, but I would not wish to trouble you. The letter can very easily wait for one of the servants."

"Don't be silly," he said with a note of impatience. "It is no trouble. Now, give it here."

His open hand waited, and Catherine had no choice but to comply. She then watched as her missive, carrying all her personal thoughts and feelings, disappeared into her brother-in-law's waistcoat pocket.

"I will offer you another in exchange," he said, giving her a much less corpulent packet.

Taking it eagerly, Catherine noticed at once that the seal had been broken. "But it has been opened," she said, disappointedly.

"Has it? Oh, yes, I see what you mean. A mere oversight. I found it mixed in amongst my own letters. I must have begun to open it before I consulted the direction and saw your name. No harm done. Well, I must be off. See you at dinner."

With that, Captain Tilney was gone, leaving Catherine to wonder at another uncomfortable encounter with her host. But soon the new letter claimed her full attention. Taking it to the light of the nearest window, she hurriedly opened it for herself.

She did not recognize the hand, but the contents quickly revealed the sender of the brief note to be Mr. Cogsgrove.

Mrs. Tilney,

I thought you would wish to know as soon as possible that I have done as you asked. I have investigated Captain Tilney's alibi for myself. While I agree with you that it was a logical line of inquiry, it has yielded no helpful information. The lady who vouched for your brother-in-law's whereabouts before is standing most resolutely by what she told Sir Melvin. She insists that the captain was with her for the entirety of the hour in question and that she would willingly testify to that fact in court if necessary.

Moreover, when I suggested to your husband that alluding to his brother in court as an alternative suspect for the crime, even without any proof, could be of use in creating the required reasonable doubt in the minds of the jurors, he would not hear of it. Although I admire him for his principles, I fear that in this case, they do him no good service. Mr. Tilney has now expressly forbidden me from using such a tactic. So there is an end to it, for I am obliged to abide by his wishes.

Nevertheless, you must not despair, Mrs. Tilney. I am by no means conceding the campaign. The tide is bound to turn in our favor soon.

Your humble servant, etc.
Thomas E. Cogsgrove, Esq.

After returning to her own room, Catherine read the letter through a second time, intending to discover some morsel of encouragement that she must have overlooked in her rapid first perusal. There was nothing, however – nothing to justify the prospect of an early reprieve, nothing to even indicate progress in a line of defense for Henry's trial. Neither could Catherine put much store by Mr. Cogsgrove's stated confidence that the tide would soon turn. It sounded very much like the sort of thing one said as a blind to cover the real hopelessness of a situation, like something one might call out to a drowning man already going down for the third time. "Have no fear; help is on the way."

Perfectly useless if it came too late.

REMOVING THE BLINKERS

*C*atherine sighed as she refolded the letter. Until that moment, she had not realized how much she had been depending on a different answer, how much she had counted on Mr. Cogsgrove to overturn Captain Tilney's alibi. In truth, all her hopes for saving Henry had been pinned on that one idea. Now the pin had been plucked from the wall and her hopes had plummeted to the floor, where they lay forlorn and irretrievable.

Catherine dropped Mr. Cogsgrove's note on the bedside table before thinking better of it and tossing it into the fire instead. She had no further need of it, and it would not due to have a nosey servant reading what was written there, especially about her suspicions of Captain Tilney.

Then her heart gave a great lurch at the still more awful prospect of Captain Tilney himself reading it. Indeed, what if he already had! Had he not admitted to 'accidentally' opening the letter? Suppose he had done more than that. Once the seal was broken, there would have been absolutely nothing preventing him from examining the contents. Any person with an average amount of curiosity would have been sorely tempted to at least sneak a quick look, and even the first few lines were enough to condemn her. Her accusations against her brother-in-law were plain; Mr. Cogsgrove had documented them in black and white.

The suspense was something dreadful, the weight of worrying about when consequences might strike, almost unbearable. Catherine would have preferred being flung from the house that minute, as she had been once before and survived, to not knowing if or when the blow would fall.

Captain Tilney, she realized, would not feel obliged to consult her wishes in the matter. If he had read her letter, he would consider only his own ideas of justice when dealing with the offender: herself. Perhaps Captain Tilney preferred something less direct but more severe, and her current discomfiture was part of her penalty. Perhaps he preferred to exact his retribution slowly, dealing the final blow, whatever that might be, at a time she least expected.

Is that why he smiled at her across the dinner table instead of glowering as she had expected? Is that why he seemed to be making more of an effort than usual at polite conversation? Or dare she hope he did not know of her treachery?

She could hope, of course. But all the same, she was careful to lock the door to her bedchamber that night, taking the extra precaution of sliding her trunk over against it as well. Whether these measures foiled a nefarious person's midnight attempt or not, Catherine would never know. They did, however, succeed in preventing the entry of the servant who would otherwise have lit the fire without waking her the next morning... and the several mornings after that.

The floor was particularly glacial this time when Catherine of necessity hurriedly crossed the room to unbar the door for the servant. Then back she skipped, bounding onto the bed and under her cozy covers again until the fire could do its work. In the meantime, Catherine attempted to fix her attention on the pages of a book she had borrowed from the library downstairs.

Other than repeatedly perusing the two letters that had

arrived from Henry since their parting, there had been so little for her to do during the long days of waiting that she naturally turned to her best refuge: reading. The Northanger Abbey library had proved a cruel disappointment, however. Eleanor's books must have all gone with her after she married, and if Henry's mother had been fond of novels, none of them remained. Catherine could find nothing to suit a lady's taste.

Still, remembering Henry had often said that a wider range of reading was desirable for improving the mind, she had determined to make an attempt at a volume of history. By an effort of sheer will and fortitude, she had eventually conquered chapter one. But now, lying in bed and endeavoring to get on in chapter two, after staring for fully ten minutes at the first page without any comprehension, Catherine discovered the book to be an insipid thing not worth one's time. She snapped it shut and tossed it aside.

Catherine suspected, however, that not even Mrs. Radcliffe could have held her attention at that moment. With mere days left until Henry's trial, it was impossible to think of anything else. There still had been no definitive news from Mr. Cogsgrove about what he intended to offer as Henry's defense, no news of any breakthroughs in the case that would exonerate him.

"We must be patient and allow the judicial process to work as it is designed to do," her brother-in-law had said at the inquest. Henry's own words – in person and more recently by his letters from Gloucester – echoed the same, along with the admonition to entrust all things to God in prayer. And then there was Mr. Cogsgrove's line about the tide soon turning in their favor. But time and tide were running out, and Catherine's faith in God and the judicial system were no longer absolute. With Henry under lock and key whilst General Tilney's true killer still roamed free, she could now imagine very well that innocent men might sometimes be convicted – convicted and hung.

For Catherine, the worst part was knowing that the tragedy

might play out in front of her eyes without her having any power to prevent it. As in so many nightmares where one is powerless to speak or act, she would sit in court as an observer, not a participant. No one would solicit her opinion. No one would allow her to testify to Henry's noble character and steady temperament. No one would listen if she tried to cry out in protest against an obvious miscarriage of justice. Indeed, if she did not remain quiet, if she created a disturbance of any kind, she probably would be removed from the courtroom altogether, as if she too were a dangerous criminal element that must be eliminated.

Catherine violently threw herself from her side onto her back, staring at the ceiling as if the answers she sought might be found there when viewed with a discerning eye.

If only she had some proof of Henry's innocence! Then they would have to listen to her. Was not that so? Proof could save Henry because proof would speak louder than mere words alone. Even the hateful Sir Melvin and all those like him must pay attention to anyone who could show clear evidence that the crime had occurred another way, that somebody else had done it. But where was such evidence to be obtained? She had been all over this house, as had the magistrate and his men. She had racked her brain for ideas, and then Mr. Cogsgrove had applied his expertise to the problem as well. Still, they had missed something, apparently. They had *all* missed something, but what?

Think! she commanded herself. *For Henry's sake, think like you never have before.* Catherine closed her eyes and pressed her hands against her forehead, as if that might help her mind to better organize its thoughts, to keep anything valuable from leaking out at the corners or crevices.

It made sense that the truth must be there in her brain somewhere, if only she could discover it, if only she could remember! Was it something she had heard or observed? Perhaps the key was right in front of her. No, that could not be so, for when she looked straight ahead, like a horse with blinkers on, all she had ever been able to see was Captain Tilney and the reasons he made a much more likely suspect than Henry. But that strategy had got her nowhere except run up against a solid brick wall again and again. Surely only a fool would continue to beat her head against it. Surely only a fool would fail to learn by that repeated mistake.

Catherine suddenly sat up in bed and gave her head a good shake to clear her vision. It was time to take the blinkers off and consider that she might actually have been wrong about Captain Tilney. After all, having a questionable character did not necessarily make a person a murderer. Appearances could be deceiving, too. She supposed not everything that at first gave the impression of being an oily, slithering serpent would prove so in the end.

With time running out, she could no longer afford to close her mind to other possibilities. For Henry's sake, every prospect needed to be reexamined, every idea tried again. The truth was out there; she was certain of it. Perhaps she had only missed seeing it before because she had been always looking in the wrong place, focusing all her attention on the wrong person.

Catherine closed her eyes again and turned back the clock to that dreadful night. Starting at the very beginning, she reviewed events minute by minute and conversations word by word, reliving them in her memory and trying to recall every detail, even things that seemed perfectly irrelevant.

The awful thunderstorm had been brewing before they arrived at Northanger that night, she recalled, perhaps contributing to the sense of foreboding she felt at the time. But then dear Eleanor met them just inside the door, soon joined by her husband Jonathan. All was friendship and goodwill there, at least until they had been obliged to approach and exchange words with General Tilney in his impressive costume. He had not been exactly cordial, but there was nothing particularly menacing in his manner either, nothing to give any alarm. She remembered he had alluded to some sort of entertainment his guests would not soon forget. Then he had introduced them to Lady Charlotte Penninger, whom they would later learn the general intended to make his bride.

Only after Catherine was satisfied that she had thoroughly canvassed every aspect of that scene did she move ahead to what followed: coming across Mrs. Brooks on their way to the ball-room. That meeting with the housekeeper was still clear to her – the words exchanged, the warmth between Henry and his self-proclaimed surrogate mother, and how it had been abruptly cut short by General Tilney's rebuke. "Mrs. Brooks! You forget yourself. It is not your place to annoy the guests. My sons do not consort with servants." Those were his very words on the occasion, or at least some of them. Poor Mrs. Brooks.

Next they had taken in the spectacle of the ballroom, which had so impressed her with its air of grandeur augmented by the agreeable influence of great age. Catherine examined the picture again in her mind's eye: the high ceilings, the glittering chandeliers, and finally the people, all in elegant fancy dress. They had exchanged a few words with Captain Tilney – just the standard pleasantries – and then he had introduced Miss Holt. Nothing remarkable in any of that, even the not unexpected little awkwardness she had felt. She remembered being relieved when Eleanor came to claim her.

While Henry remained with his brother, Eleanor had taken the ladies – herself and Miss Holt – to be introduced to some people of note. There was the disgruntled neighbor Mr. Oberton, the Marquis of Longtown, General Courtney, and... She had met at least one other person as they had made their circuit of the room under Eleanor's care. Catherine was sure of it. Then she remembered who; it was that delightful creature, Lady Melanie Rice.

Had there been any clue in those encounters, any hint of trouble? One by one, Catherine reviewed those conversations to the best of her recollection.

Suddenly, Catherine gasped, threw off her covers, and ran for the bell. Then, without waiting for Patsy, she began to hurriedly dress herself.

"Here, let me help you with that," said Patsy a minute later, coming to Catherine's aid.

"Yes, but please do hurry. I must see the others at once! Do you know if Captain Tilney, the viscount, and Lady Astley are awake and at home?"

"I saw the master going into the billiard room only a moment ago, but the other two drove out in their carriage quite early this morning. That is all I know."

This news was a blow indeed, but it could not be helped. "Then I suppose I shall have to speak to Captain Tilney alone. There is not a moment to lose!"

- 22 -

A NEW THEORY

"I t is Mr. Oberton!" Catherine cried out as she burst into the billiard room.

Unperturbed, Captain Tilney took his shot, skillfully sinking a red ball in a corner pocket before turning to see what the disturbance was. "Ah, Catherine," he said, affecting an air of boredom. "To what do I owe the pleasure of this unexpected visit?"

Catching a breath first, Catherine repeated her declaration. "It is Mr. Oberton. He is your father's killer. I am certain of it!"

Captain Tilney rested back against the table and crossed his arms. "That is quite a bold accusation you make, sister. I admit I am quite intrigued. But have you any proof of your wild assertion, or does it result from a sudden gift of clairvoyance?"

Catherine ignored his slighting remarks and, in her agitation, tumbled her words out rapidly. "Neither, sir. I have no absolute proof it is true, but the idea is more than something wild… or clairvoyance either. No, it all makes perfect sense! I am sure you will agree… I only wonder I did not see it before. Or Eleanor! For she was there as well. She will support me, in case you are inclined to disbelieve my account. Oh, how unlucky that she should be away just when she is most needed! Where have she and the viscount gone, do you know? And when will they return? There is not a moment to lose!"

Giving up his game as irretrievable, Captain Tilney laid his cue aside, took his sister-in-law by the arm, and led her to a chair. "Never mind all that now," he said. "I can see you are quite overwrought. Sit down here, calm yourself, and organize your thoughts. Then start once more from the beginning." The captain then sat down as well.

Under ordinary circumstances, Catherine might have been expected to resent his condescending attitude. But she considered her own feelings unimportant where Henry's fate was at stake. Consequently, she forced herself to do as the captain said. She had no choice, for she needed his help. After taking two deep breaths, she tried again. "Mr. Oberton, your neighbor at Compton Court."

"Yes, of course, I *know* who he is."

"Well, I did not until I was introduced to him by Eleanor at the beginning of the ball that night. I was very much surprised by how he spoke to me of your father, especially since I was a member of the general's own family – calling him a 'hard-hearted schemer' and pitying me my 'unfortunate connection' to such a man."

"It is no more than he has said to the general's face... nor is it any worse abuse than what he has endured himself at my father's hands. Their longstanding feud was no secret."

"Yes, so Henry explained to me, and I thought no more about it then."

"Quarrels over boundary lines are common enough. There is no proof of murder in that."

"No proof, but you must agree there is at least some motive in it. Henry said your father had had the surveyor out more than once and that he had threatened charges over poaching and... Oh, I do not remember what else. In any case, a proud man could not but resent such slander, if slander it was. And if were true, even worse." Catherine paused before adding, "And there is more."

"Well then, let us get to it, for as yet I have heard nothing to warrant all this perturbation, nothing I did not know before."

Catherine leant a little closer. "Later that night – after your father's unfortunate comments at supper and after he and Henry and the viscount and you yourself were all gone from us – Eleanor and I were walking about the supper room when Mr. Oberton burst in. He made out that he was glad to have accidentally come upon us, but I do not believe that was true. He was in quite a state – disheveled and drenched from some obvious exertion – and in a great hurry to get away.

"We believed at the time that he had just come from the dancing, but what if it was something else? What if instead he had just come from an altercation with the general? This was during the hour when your father is supposed to have met his end, you understand. And then Mr. Oberton left Northanger immediately thereafter, before the crime was discovered. So he was gone when Sir Melvin and the constables arrived. I do not believe he was ever questioned or considered for a possible suspect, and I did not think of it myself until this morning!"

Here Catherine's words ran out, and here she waited to see what effect they made on her brother-in-law. Surely, this new theory must ring true and inspire him to action. For Henry's sake, it *must* be the answer to the mystery! Captain Tilney said nothing, however; he only got to his feet and slowly crossed the room, his hand worrying his chin.

"You must now see the likelihood of Mr. Oberton's involvement in the crime," Catherine added at last. "It makes perfect sense, as I said before."

Still Tilney made no reply; he only paced in silence. When Catherine thought she could bear the suspense no longer, he abruptly turned and purposefully strode back to her.

"So you have told no one but me of this theory?" he asked.

"That is correct."

"And Eleanor. What makes you believe she has not thought of it either?"

"We have often talked together about that night, looking for an explanation that would exonerate Henry. She surely would have spoken to me of Mr. Oberton if she had any thoughts of him."

"Well, yes, I expect she would have indeed, just as you say."

"We must send for Mr. Cogsgrove at once!" urged Catherine, jumping to her feet again.

"There is no time. Even if he were to set out immediately upon receiving our summons, he should never reach us, conclude his business here, and be back in court by the appointed hour. That would mean certain disaster for Henry. No, I will dash off a quick note to him, but I believe we must deal with this ourselves."

"How do you mean?"

"We must confront Mr. Oberton at once. Perhaps he will surrender when he knows the truth is come out. If not, then will be the time to send for the authorities. Sir Melvin and his men can be at our service soon enough, sooner than Mr. Cogsgrove. Can you be ready to set out for Compton Court within this half hour?"

Catherine was immediately taken aback. The thought of a volatile face-to-face confrontation with their neighbor – a man whose character she had no very good opinion of – gave Catherine significant qualms, not to mention the idea of Captain Tilney being her only friend and defender in such an enterprise. No doubt he was a capable man, but would he have her well-being at heart?

"Surely we should wait for Eleanor and the viscount," she said, "or perhaps send for Sir Melvin first. It seems to me that Mr. Oberton is far more likely to surrender to him than to you."

Captain Tilney's grim aspect and heavy sigh evinced his

impatience. "Look here, Catherine. You have just convinced me of the urgency in the case, and as a military man, I am not one to sit on my hands and wait for others when there is a clear course of action before me. I am surely going to Compton Court at once. Are you coming with me or not? That is your only choice in the matter."

"I suppose I may at least bring a maid along. I am certain Patsy could be…"

Captain Tilney interrupted. "No, my scatter-brained little sister-in-law. No maid. As we are brother and sister, there is no issue of propriety at stake here, and there will be room for only two in my gig. I refuse to take anything larger. Light and fast – that is the vehicle we require since time is of the essence if we are to save Henry. So are you coming?"

Those words brought the question onto sharper focus. To save Henry, Catherine would do anything – face any unpleasantness, inconvenience, or even danger.

"I will be ready in five minutes," she said.

There was no time to think, only to act.

Catherine at once dashed off to her room to fetch her warmest cloak for the expedition. Then, true to her word, she was back downstairs and out of the door with Captain Tilney within five minutes. She needn't have rushed quite so much because the gig was by no means ready as quickly as were its intended occupants. Still, they were underway in very short order, headed for Compton Court and the momentous confrontation with Mr. Oberton.

As her companion whipped the horse into a rapid clip, Catherine pulled her cloak tighter about herself against the cold wind that clawed at her face and neck. She would not complain, though. Instead, to cheer herself, Catherine thought of Henry.

How she longed to tell him of this positive turn of events, that there might at last be good news on the horizon. She imagined him sitting in quiet resignation, having nearly lost hope of a reprieve. How happy it would make him when he heard that help was on the way, and how proud that she had been the one to solve the puzzle that would bring about his release!

If all went well today, Henry would soon be coming home, and not just to Northanger Abbey but to Woodston Cottage. With all that had happened since, it seemed an age since they had left their happy home. She could think of no sweeter or more complete felicity than the two of them being restored to it again and to their simple, quiet life there.

Despite her trepidation for what lay ahead, it felt good to be doing something at last after so many days and hours of waiting and hoping in vain for a solution from another quarter. As long as she was counting her blessings, Catherine decided to be thankful for Captain Tilney's assistance too. She could have done nothing alone, and he was a formidable man to have fighting on her side. Regardless of her personal sentiments about him, Catherine felt it only fair to give him his due. And fortunately, it had not been as difficult as she had anticipated to convince him of the merit of her latest theory. Of course, conceding merit was not necessarily the same thing as being fully convinced.

"So do you really think I am correct about Mr. Oberton, Captain?" she presently asked him.

He gave the reins a sharp slap. "I do. As you said, it makes perfect sense – both that he could have done it and that he could have escaped detection until now. You have quite convinced me." A few moments later, he added with a sideways look, "Besides, I like this new theory of yours much better than your previous one."

Catherine hoped the color she felt suffuse her cheeks at that moment would be attributed to the chaffing of the wind. "I'm sure I do not know what you mean, Captain" she said as lightly as she could.

Catherine kept her eyes straight ahead, aware all the while that he was watching her. A hint of panic now stirred within her breast and began creeping up into her throat.

THE TABLES TURN... AGAIN

*C*atherine's mind buzzed with equal parts fear and self-recrimination, leaping quickly from one thought to the next.

She wondered how it could possibly have happened again. How could she have allowed herself to be...? No, it was worse than that. She had done this to herself! She had once again blundered into trouble by depending on her own questionable powers of deductive reasoning, so sure of her mad theories and conclusions that she charged ahead without proper precaution. Since initially setting eyes on Northanger Abbey and letting her imagination run wild, it seemed she had learnt nothing at all.

First she had been absolutely convinced of Captain Tilney's guilt. Then, as of this morning, she had been equally convinced she was mistaken and that the villain was Mr. Oberton instead. But now that it was too late, she had to consider she might have been mistaken about being mistaken! What if her first conclusion had been correct after all, in which case she had now placed herself in grave danger. She was alone with a murderer! She was under his power, and worse still, nobody knew it. She had told no one where she was going and with whom. As far as she was aware, nobody at Northanger had even seen her leave with Captain Tilney. So when she could not be found, it would be as if she had simply wandered off into the woods on her own and got lost.

Perhaps, if Captain Tilney knew about her accusations against him, which seemed all but certain now, he had only been held back from acting against her before by the chance of being discovered. Now she had played right into his hands. She might easily disappear forever into a gully choked with brambles – exactly like the one she remembered passing a few minutes before – and wild animals would disperse her bones far and wide. Now there ran a rushing river beside the road they traveled. What a convenience! With very little trouble, a man bent on murder might tip her in, allowing the turbulent waters to carry the evidence of his crime away to the sea. No one would be the wiser.

Captain Tilney was a highly capable man, as she had just been thinking only moments ago, and he was strong. It would be nothing at all for him to overpower a small woman and dispose of her body somewhere along this road. He probably would not even disturb his hair or soil his immaculate clothing in the process. She would stand no chance against him, of course, and if she should scream, who would hear her in this lonely place?

There would be some sort of search undertaken when she was missed. She believed Eleanor at least cared enough to insist on that. But they might have no idea where to start. In all likelihood, there had been no note dispatched to Mr. Cogsgrove about Mr. Oberton before they left, and for all she knew, this might not even be the road to Compton Court. Besides, Captain Tilney would have some clever story prepared so he could deny any knowledge of what had happened to his 'scatter-brained little sister-in-law.'

The greatest heartbreak was that poor Henry would never know what had become of her. Then, with no one to save him, he would go to the gallows in his brother's place. All was lost indeed! The only thing either of them could look forward to was being reunited on the other side of that great divide. Catherine choked back a sob. It was every bit as tragic as any novel she had ever read!

Captain Tilney slowed the gig to turn onto the bridge that had come up on the right. Catherine peered down at the icy water below. She knew at once that this was the moment, the ideal opportunity the captain had been waiting for. She only hoped he would be mercifully quick about it.

Imagine her surprise, then, when he urged his horse on again without stopping. Its hooves briefly rang out on the heavy planks of the bridge before once more pounding the hardened earth of the road on the other side.

Catherine looked at her captor, her supposed nemesis, amazed to see him as calm and composed as if he were sitting in his own drawing room, no murderous leer in evidence.

"Almost there," he said, glancing her way. Then something about his female companion drew his closer scrutiny. "Good god, but you are become dreadfully pale, Catherine. One would think you had just seen a ghost. I hope you are not losing your nerve, or it would have been better if you had stayed at home and left this to me."

Catherine's mouth was so dry that she could not immediately answer him. "Not at all," she managed a few moments later. "I am perfectly well."

And Catherine Tilney remained well. *None* of the drama she had lately been predicting actually transpired that day. Even the visit to Compton Court failed to live up to reasonable expectations.

Catherine and the captain arrived safely and in good time. They found their quarry – Mr. Oberton – at home and pleased to see them. In fact, he was highly diverted to discover the purpose of their visit, once Captain Tilney had explained it to him.

"Oh, my goodness!" he exclaimed. "How delightful! I cannot tell you how flattered I am to have been thought worthy of your suspicions. I do not deny, Captain, that I have plotted your father's demise many a time over the years, and if thoughts alone could force a man to throw himself off a roof, you might have a case against me. But I do not believe thinking of murder is a prosecutable offense. I would never have had the nerve to carry through with it, you understand.

"As for my disheveled appearance that night, Mrs. Tilney, it truly was the dancing responsible, I assure you. Many people can vouch for how I carried on as if I were pretending to be a youth of nineteen or twenty again. I eventually worked myself into such a state that I felt quite unwell. When I saw you and your lovely sister-in-law, I was in a great hurry to make my escape before I disgraced myself still further.

"You see, I had been determined to take full advantage of my host's unusual hospitality, to cost him as much as possible by my over consumption. The general did not fare at all well that night, of course, but I ended by paying a high price of my own. Excesses of rich food, drink, and dancing should not all be indulged in one night, I discovered, at least not at my age. I was violently ill even before I reached home and for days afterward. I have since taken a vow of moderation in all things."

Further discussion revealed that the magistrate, acting on some information of his own, had already made inquiries of Mr. Oberton, checking and confirming with named witnesses his presence amongst the dancers for the greater part of the hour in question.

"I was so sure," a deflated Catherine said when she and Captain Tilney had returned to the gig and departed. "How is it we never were told all this before?"

"No doubt it was simply because we never thought to ask,"

the captain answered. "If Sir Melvin's inquiry had unearthed anything useful, we surely should have heard. Since it did not, there was nothing worth reporting to the family."

They rode along, mostly in silence, traveling at a slower pace, now that there was no longer any urgency. Captain Tilney made one detour for the purpose of seeing Sir Melvin to confirm what Mr. Oberton had told them. Not that there had been much doubt; Mr. Oberton had not appeared to be behaving deceptively, and he would have known his story would be easy enough to verify.

"I am as disappointed as you are, Catherine," said Captain Tilney when they were once more bound for home, "especially for Henry's sake, of course. I truly thought you had been on the right track this time."

"I am a very poor detective, it seems, Captain."

A pensive pause later, he said matter-of-factly, "Perhaps now your suspicions will fall back upon me again."

Catherine was too emotionally spent to pretend incomprehension... or even surprise. She only looked her companion full in the face and frowned. "So you *did* read Mr. Cogsgrove's letter. I thought so."

He shrugged. "The temptation was irresistible. And besides, I thought it my right to know what goes on under my own roof. Of course, what the letter revealed was nothing new to me. I had long understood that you favored me for the crime. Do you still?"

A direct question seemed to demand an equally direct if unsatisfactory answer. "I scarcely know what to think anymore," said Catherine. "I am sorry, though, if in my zeal for Henry I have wronged you."

"Yes... Well, perhaps you will not think it unreasonable, then, that I have resented you for it. Still, I can hardly fault your logic. As a betting man, I would have laid heavy odds on somebody exactly like me for the culprit. As it happens, though, I am no murderer either, at least no more than Mr. Oberton. I nurtured homicidal thoughts against my father, I raged and threatened, but I did not do the deed. And I have that one great advantage over my brother. He may be the better man, at least by some people's reckoning, but I am the *luckier*, for I happen to have a genuine alibi.

"God bless Miss Holt. When this nightmare is finally over, I believe I should have married the dear girl just for that – for risking her reputation to admit she was with me that night. Fortunately, I had in mind marrying her even before, so it will be no sacrifice. It will be making myself happy as well as her. Does that sound conceited? I only repeat what she tells me. For some unfathomable reason, Miss Holt believes I am worth caring about. I suppose the explanation is what I said before; I am a lucky man, and sometimes it is better to be lucky than good."

They lapsed into silence again, leaving Catherine alone with her thoughts as the gig rolled and bumped along. She was satisfied with the truth of Mr. Oberton's explanations, much as she had wanted to believe otherwise. And she was a good deal reassured about her brother-in-law also. She still could not like him very well, but she began to be less afraid of him, even considering it possible that she might one day learn to sleep at Northanger with her door unbarred by furniture.

As soon as they arrived at home, Catherine gladly exchanged the company of Captain Tilney for his sister's. Taking Eleanor aside, Catherine related the substance of the day's misadventures, minus any mention of her wild imaginings regarding the captain.

"Oh, Catherine," said Eleanor. "I am sorry you and Frederick should have gone to such trouble, only to have your hopes dashed at the last. Still, it was a very reasonable hypothesis. Remembering how Mr. Oberton looked and behaved, I should have come to the same conclusion if ever I had considered it. Not that I like to think any of our neighbors a murderer. Still, better it had been Mr. Oberton than Henry to stand trial."

"Better anybody at all than Henry," Catherine agreed.

Yet the most troublesome question remained. If neither Mr. Oberton nor Captain Tilney had done it, then who? She had no more viable suspects. Without an answer and soon, Henry would take the blame for his father's death, paying with his life! Although quite capable of gross errors in judgment – as lately proved once again – Catherine was very much afraid she would be all too correct about that.

DINNER INTERRUPTIONS

*A*s they were all proceeding to dinner the next night, Mrs. Brooks tentatively approached and addressed the captain.

"Begging your pardon, sir, but might I have a moment of your time?"

Clearly annoyed, Captain Tilney said, "Did not you hear dinner announced, Mrs. Brooks? Surely whatever it is can wait."

"I'm afraid it cannot, sir," she said, beginning to wring her hands. "I must ask your permission to travel with your party to Gloucester tomorrow. I wish to be present for the trial. Master Henry is like family to me, and I know he would want me there."

"I can see no occasion for that, Mrs. Brooks. Mr. Tilney will have his *real* family present to support him; he needs no other. Besides, there will be no room in the carriage, and I will not send a second for the sole purpose of transporting one servant, no matter how devoted you claim to be. You had much better stay here and attend your duties. *That* is how you serve this family best."

As Captain Tilney swept past and continued on to dinner, Catherine paused for a moment. Laying a hand on the housekeeper's shoulder, she whispered close to her ear, "Do not fret, Mrs. Brooks. I will speak to him."

Catherine meant to do just that, yet as the first course finished and the second began, still she hesitated, hoping for either a sign that her brother-in-law's mood had improved or for a propitious opening in the conversation. During the fish course, her prayers were answered... at least as to this one specific item.

The butler, holding a silver salver, appeared at the door of the dining parlor and discreetly cleared his throat so that Captain Tilney was forced to look up and acknowledge his presence. "Yes, Hastings," he said impatiently, "what is it?"

"Pardon me, sir," said the butler from his position at the doorway, "but this letter has just arrived by express. I thought you might wish to see it without delay."

The captain motioned with his hand. "Very well. Bring it here, then. Clearly, I was not meant to dine in peace tonight." When the captain had taken the letter from the salver, he asked, "Is the messenger waiting for a reply?"

"No, sir."

"Then you may go."

"Very good, sir," said Hastings, retreating at once.

"What is it, Frederick?" asked Eleanor.

Before answering, Captain Tilney broke the seal and gave a silent, cursory inspection of the contents, his expression darkening as he read. Next, he dismissed the rest of the servants from the room. When the door was closed and only the family remained, he announced rather grimly, "It is from Mr. Cogsgrove, and it contains no very good news."

Catherine drew a sharp breath and covered her mouth. Eleanor reached for her husband's hand. The viscount spoke for them all, saying, "Well, sir, do not keep the ladies in this awful suspense. Tell us the news, whatever it is. What does your brother's barrister have to say?"

Captain Tilney sighed. "As we are all gathered and dinner is

ruined already, I suppose I may as well read it out to you. Cogsgrove sends us the standard greetings and compliments, and then
we get to the heart of the matter." Looking at the missive again,
he read,

*...I feel I have failed you all, most particularly your brother,
since I have been unable to turn up any solid evidence of either
his innocence or another's guilt, though not for lack of trying, I
assure you. I do not mean to say that all is lost, only to warn you
that the task has become more difficult and the outcome far from
certain. I am going into battle with very little ammunition, but
nevertheless, I am prepared to fight, tooth and nail, with everything at my disposal.*

*Your brother's defense will of necessity rely on three factors.
First, while I can give no absolute proof of his innocence, I will
be quick to point out that there is likewise no real proof of his
guilt either. In theory, that should be enough to win an acquittal.
Unfortunately, lack of sound evidence does not always prevent a
jury from convicting. Where a crime has been committed, people
like to see someone held accountable. They tend to assume the
accused must have been remanded for trial for good reason, and
they may be willing to overlook the weakness of the prosecutor's
case if he tells them a plausible tale.*

*Next, my strategy will be to remind the jury of how many
other people may have had motive and opportunity – the fact that
the general had made many enemies, some of whom were
amongst those present that night. Here again, I am somewhat
handicapped, for I have no specific alternative suspects to offer.
However, I will endeavor to paint a picture for the jury of the
multitude of guests and servants coming and going, the whereabouts of many of them having never been absolutely
ascertained.*

Finally, we must depend heavily upon establishing Mr.

Tilney's unimpeachable character as firmly as possible. Toward this end, I have summoned several people who may be called on to vouch in court for his peaceable nature and integrity. You must all be prepared to testify as well if needed, although juries tend to dismiss family members as biased. The average man will be more inclined to credit the word of a trustworthy servant, and Mr. Tilney has suggested Mrs. Brooks as one such, since I understand she has known him nearly all his life. Therefore, you must insist that she accompany you when you come…

Captain Tilney looked up, adding dryly, "So it seems Mrs. Brooks will have her way after all, and we shall be forced to make room for her somewhere. I suppose she might ride on the box with the driver."

"At this time of year?" exclaimed Eleanor. "Oh, Frederick, you cannot be serious."

"Perfectly serious. She is a servant after all, same as the driver. She is not entitled to – nor indeed accustomed to – the same comforts we are."

"After all her years of loyal service to this family, she is entitled to better treatment than this," rejoined Eleanor, "especially when she is being asked to come to the aid of our brother."

Then Catherine spoke up. "She may ride with me. I shall have room."

"With you?" Eleanor inquired. "But my dearest sister, are not we four traveling together in one carriage?"

Catherine colored. "With all that has been on my mind, perhaps I forgot to mention it before, but I have sent for my own carriage to take me to Gloucester."

"Why on earth would you do that?" challenged the captain. "You would be much more comfortable in mine than in that old rattletrap Henry keeps. And despite what Eleanor says, the box will do very well for Mrs. Brooks."

"I was not thinking of Mrs. Brooks when I sent to Woodston for the carriage."

"What then?"

Catherine's eyes dropped. "While I daresay we four could have traveled comfortably in one carriage, sir, you forget that, God willing, we will be five upon our return. And I do not mean Mrs. Brooks."

"Of course!" gasped Eleanor. "Dear Henry! I had not thought that far ahead. At times like this, it is all one can do to make it through the day. Bless you, Catherine, for keeping your wits about you!"

"Yes, well, I was thinking," said Catherine, "that especially after his long confinement in strange surroundings, Henry deserved to enjoy the familiar, roomy ease of his own equipage for the journey home."

A brief, awkward silence followed, during which some at the table were thinking what I daresay many of my readers are as well – that, according to the implications of Mr. Cogsgrove's letter, there was every chance the extra space on their return would not be needed for anybody but Mrs. Brooks, that Henry might not be making the trip with them after all. But I trust that you, like the others, will be too polite to voice such an unpleasant thought aloud, especially over dinner.

The viscount broke the silence. "It seems it is all commodiously arranged," he suggested with affected cheer.

"Oh, very well, Catherine," said the captain. "Mrs. Brooks may ride with you to Gloucester if you wish it... and Henry on the way back, of course. Now, if that is settled, may we at long last return our attention to dinner?"

After the close of the meal, Catherine retrieved Mr. Cogsgrove's letter, which the captain had left lying on the table. She carefully refolded it, meaning to tuck it away among her things, although she could hardly have articulated why. It contained no good news to treasure or any information she needed to retain. Its value derived solely from serving as the most recent connection back to her beloved husband. For that alone, it must be worth something to her.

Her dinner companions had all disappeared somewhere or other, but finding the housekeeper hovering nearby, Catherine hastened to give her the good news. "You are to come with us after all, Mrs. Brooks," she said, briefly squeezing the older woman's hand.

"Oh, thank you, Mrs. Tilney!" she said. "I am very grateful to you for using your influence with the master. He would not have listened to me."

"I am glad for you, Mrs. Brooks, but in truth, you need not thank me. As it came about, I have had no part in the business. A letter from Mr. Cogsgrove has worked the alteration. It seems Henry has asked for you most particularly."

"Master Henry wants to see me?"

"Why should you be surprised? As you yourself have said, you are like family to him. But it is more than that; Henry has named you to serve as a character witness for him in court. You are to testify to his... his *peaceable nature and integrity*. I believe those were Mr. Cogsgrove's words. In any case, you understand, and I knew you would be eager to do whatever you could for him." But Catherine noticed at once that Mrs. Brooks looked far from eager at the news. In fact, she had blanched alarmingly. "Why Mrs. Brook, what is the matter?"

"Naturally I should be glad to do what I can for Master Henry, ma'am, but oh, dear!" She clasped her hands together to stop them trembling. "To testify in court... in front of all those people. And with Master Henry's fate on the line. I am sure I shall swoon."

Catherine laid a firm hand on the woman's arm and looked her in the eye. "You shall do no such thing, Mrs. Brooks. Henry needs you, and when the time comes, you will not think of your nerves. You will think of him and do what is necessary."

The housekeeper drew a shaky breath. "Yes, of course you are right. I would do anything for Master Henry," she finished tearfully.

"Just the same as if you were his mother," Catherine added to extend the thought one measure further. "Isn't that right?"

Mrs. Brooks nodded her agreement before moving off, but Catherine was far from sanguine. To imagine that Henry's fate might hang on that lady's testimony... Well, it did not bear thinking of. No matter how devoted Mrs. Brooks claimed to be, she did not look like someone a jury would readily believe, unsure and trembling as she was. And this while she was still at home! What would become of her under the scrutiny of the court? Catherine began to doubt Mrs. Brooks's ability to convince a jury of her *own* innocence in the case, let alone Henry's.

That now-familiar sensation overtook her again – the twist in her belly, as if unseen hands were wringing her out like so much wash on laundry day. "Oh, Henry! How shall I bear it if anything should happen to you?"

"Nothing will happen to Henry."

Unaware that she had spoken aloud, Catherine was surprised to have received an answer to her question. It was Eleanor, who immediately enfolded her sister-in-law into a much appreciated embrace.

"We must pray and have faith, Catherine. I know things look grim at the moment, but I truly believe all will turn out well."

"Truly? Do you?"

Eleanor released her to arm's length. "Surprising as it may seem, I do. I cannot explain it other than to say that Henry himself has convinced me. Remember what he said in his last letter."

"Perhaps I should read it again."

"Yes, do, Catherine. I believe it will give you the courage to face what lies ahead, to be brave and confident for Henry's sake."

Catherine knew the part Eleanor meant. She had read the letter, arrived three days earlier, often enough, and yet never received anything like the serenity her sister had obviously derived from it.

Back in her room at the end of the day, Catherine drew out the missive once more. Since it had been addressed to the entire family, it lacked the special intimacy that must have otherwise been expected in more private communications between husband and wife. And yet there was some comfort in merely seeing Henry's familiar handwriting again, in then imagining his face and voice present with her, as if he had no need to write at all.

...For the world, I would not trouble you with this before, but I have been to the depths and back in my lonely contemplations since I reached Gloucester. However, now at last my fears are laid to rest. My fate is in God's hands, and therein lies my peace, come what may. And yet, I am firmly convinced within myself that I will be exonerated and returned to the bosom of my home and family. Take courage in this also...

Although Catherine was somewhat comforted in knowing that Henry suffered no more torment over what might await him, his faith went only so far in soothing her own fears. Henry might have emerged to see the green pastures and still waters ahead, but for Catherine, the shadows of the valley still obstructed her view.

TRAVELING TO GLOUCESTER

*C*atherine spent a fitful night interrupted by worrisome dreams, only to be awakened in the midst of one the next morning.

Pardon me, ma'am," said Patsy, "but this is the time you said I should call you."

Catherine frowned and rubbed her eyes in confusion. Then a moment later, comprehension struck, landing like a great weight upon her chest. Today they traveled to Gloucester, and tomorrow was Henry's trial. She drew a long, shuddering breath and then exhaled. "Yes, of course," she said.

Mrs. Tilney dragged herself out of bed only because she knew she had no choice. She accepted the maid's assistance dressing with hardly a word. Also with Patsy's help, she packed her few necessary items in a portmanteau, stumbling about as if still half asleep. It was not the dream she had lately awakened from that oppressed her. It was the real nightmare she was living, which seemed to go on and on.

Perhaps sensing her mistress's mood, Patsy said, "You will see your husband today, I hope."

Yes, realized Catherine. When they arrived in Gloucester, she would see Henry! That was the thing to hold onto. That thought would carry her forward through the difficulties of the day. "Yes, it must be so!" she replied. "It would be too cruel to keep me from him, and yet I hardly know what is allowed and what is not in these unfamiliar circumstances."

"As you say, ma'am. Now, is there anything else I can do for you?"

Catherine roused herself from her troubles to regard the girl beside her. "I wish there were, Patsy, but I thank you sincerely just the same. You have been very good to me through these difficult weeks, and I will not forget your kindness."

"I only wish I could have been of more help, that I might have discovered something useful, as you asked me to do."

"I know you did your best. We both did, and it is not for lack of trying that we have nothing to show for our efforts. Nevertheless, I shall remember your goodness to me, whatever happens in Gloucester."

Catherine gave the maid a quick embrace and hastily left the room. She breakfasted with the family, and then it was time to depart.

"Do you mind if I travel a while with you and Mrs. Brooks?" Eleanor asked Catherine. "I will leave the men to their tedious talk of guns and dogs and politics. Perhaps they will have worn themselves out with it before I rejoin them later."

So, for the first leg of their journey, it was the two men in one carriage and the three women in the other. Of her own accord, Mrs. Brooks took a backward-facing seat, leaving the preferred forward-facing seats for the two young ladies, who at first occupied themselves only with staring out of the windows at a day too fine for their somber errand, or talking between themselves of the little nothings that must pass for polite conversation at such a time. Later, though, they succeeded onto a topic to which Mrs. Brooks was the chief expert: the old days in the nursery.

"...Oh, you remember the one I mean, Mrs. Brooks," said

Eleanor. "What was that yarn you spun to keep us children in line? I doubt it worked with Frederick, but I know I was terrified to misbehave ever after."

"You mean the one about the Fairy Beasts, ma'am."

"Yes! That was it – how they would visit disobedient children, tucked up in their beds at night, and nibble off their fingers and toes. Ghastly! You cannot imagine what a fright it gave me, Mrs. Brooks."

"That is an old, old tale, Miss Eleanor, told by governesses and nursery maids over the centuries, I should think."

"Were you ever told it, Catherine?"

"Oh, dear me, no! But then I never had a nursery maid or a governess."

"Well, Mrs. Brooks told the tale to great effect," continued Eleanor, "at least in my case. Whenever I might think of some scheme for making mischief, I would remember the story of the Fairy Beasts and give up my plan straightaway."

"A very useful tool for wee ones of a certain disposition," agreed Mrs. Brooks. "You were just tender enough to be susceptible to its influence. My stories were completely useless on your brothers, though. Frederick was too full of his own importance to believe anything could happen to him. And Henry..." She laughed. "Henry argued with me about it. 'If such things as Fairy Beasts exist,' he would say, 'why do I not see dozens and dozens of people about, all missing fingers and toes? For surely there are plenty of disobedient children, some now grown up.' I remember telling him that a great many people indeed *are* missing toes at the very least. 'They are so ashamed of themselves,' I said, 'that they never let their feet be seen.'"

Eleanor laughed. "I can just imagine Henry reasoning his way through the problem like that. It was quick thinking on your part, Mrs. Brooks, to come up with a rational explanation."

"It was enough to make Master Henry wonder if there might not be some truth to the tale after all. And then one day – I shall never forget – we were at the market in Tetbury and he caught sight of an old woman with only three fingers on one hand. He said not a word, but I saw his eyes grow big as saucers as he stared." Mrs. Brooks wagged her head back and forth. "You can be sure I had myself a good chuckle over that later. But then Master Henry weren't ever any real trouble. He were such a bonny little lad."

Catherine, who had been a very interested observer to this exchange, further observed Mrs. Brooks's smile fade and a tear slide down the woman's cheek. "Take heart, Mrs. Brooks," she said. "Henry will soon be back among us again."

"Yes, ma'am. Yes, of course."

In like manner passed the interval until a stop at a coaching inn for refreshment and for the changing of horses, after which Eleanor left them for the other carriage and the company of her husband and brother. Then on they traveled, Catherine and Mrs. Brooks now alone together and having very little left to say to one another. Mrs. Brooks seemed to have exhausted all her stories about Henry earlier, and Catherine hated to distress her traveling companion with her own gloomy contemplations. And yet, distressed Mrs. Brooks clearly was.

Catherine, feeling it her duty to keep up the woman's spirits if possible, as well as hopefully her own, said brightly, "I suppose you are thinking of Henry again, Mrs. Brooks. But you mustn't despair. Things will turn out right in the end."

"I never had any doubt of that, Mrs. Tilney, that after this season of trouble, things would indeed be set right again. An innocent man has nothing to fear from the law, after all. It is just that it pains me dreadfully to think that Master Henry must endure these false accusations, even for a little while. Yet I knew he would do so with fortitude and emerge none the worse for it."

"Then you are of the same mind as Henry himself. He is convinced he will be fully exonerated." Here Catherine's false cheerfulness failed her. "Although I must admit Mr. Cogsgrove's letter was considerably less optimistic."

"Oh, dear! Was he not confident of an acquittal, Mrs. Tilney?"

"Far from it, I'm afraid." Then, seeing the markedly increased anxiety this news awakened in her companion, Catherine went on. "Never mind me, Mrs. Brooks; I would have done much better to have kept such pessimistic ideas to myself. Forgive me."

"Not at all, Mrs. Tilney, but now I must know the truth at once! Master Henry's fate is of vital importance to me, more so than you can possibly imagine. So tell me, what did Mr. Cogsgrove write?"

"Very well. I suppose you may as well hear it now as later. Wait, I have the letter here with me." Catherine foraged in her reticule until she found it. "As you are nearly family, Mrs. Brooks, I can see no reason you may not read his remarks instead of hearing my poor interpretation of them. Mr. Cogsgrove will speak much better for himself, I daresay. This is the part right here," she added, pointing.

Taking the missive with tremulous fingers, Mrs. Brooks read the pertinent portion aloud. "*I feel I have failed you all, most particularly your brother, since I have been unable to turn up any solid evidence of either his innocence or another's guilt, though not for lack of trying, I assure you. I do not mean to say that all is lost, only to warn you that the task has become more difficult and the outcome far from certain. I am going into battle with very little ammunition, but nevertheless, I am prepared to fight, tooth and nail, with everything at my disposal...*

"Oh! I had not imagined the situation could be as bad as this!" Mrs. Brooks continued. "What has this Mr. Cogsgrove been about to let things come to such a pass? It is his clear responsibility to prove Master Henry innocent. Since everybody with any sense knows that to be the case, it should not be too difficult for a lawyer of his stature. If he cannot, he has failed us all indeed. He has failed Master Henry!"

Catherine was surprised at the violence of her complaint. "I am severely disappointed as well, Mrs. Brooks, and hardly able to conceal it. Yet I am sure Mr. Cogsgrove has done – and will continue to do – everything humanly possible. We can only hope it will be enough, and, as Henry has repeatedly told me, we must trust to God for the rest."

"Beggin' your pardon, Mrs. Tilney," her companion said somewhat indignantly, "but there's no need to be bringin' God into this. My feelings about *Him* are none too cordial at the moment either, to think that He might allow such an injustice to stand."

Since Catherine had no idea what answer she should make to this, she could only look on with some bewilderment, waiting to see what surprising thing Mrs. Brooks might say next. Catherine had not long to wait.

Mrs. Brooks raised the letter in the air and shook it. "I depended on this Mr. Cogsgrove to free Master Henry!" Allowing her hand and its contents to fall into her lap again, she presently went on miserably. "Now what are we to do? Is there no chance?"

"The situation is far from hopeless." Taking the letter back, Catherine said, "See here, Mrs. Brooks. Mr. Cogsgrove describes how he intends to defend Henry. That is where you come in too. In this paragraph, he explains how important your testimony about Henry's fine character will be towards convincing the jurors..." Catherine trailed off.

Mrs. Brooks, now staring out of the carriage window, seemed to be paying no heed in any case. "Poor Master Henry!" she rambled on distractedly. "My own darling boy. There never were a finer creature born to man nor beast, and I could not love you more if you were my own son. I daresay you have never harmed a soul in your life, and there you sit, accused of murdering your father – a man not worth regretting."

"Have a care, Mrs. Brooks," Catherine said in gentle admonition. "Any loss of life must be considered regrettable."

Turning back, Mrs. Brooks seemed surprised, and not a little displeased, to see Catherine sitting there. Then her countenance cleared and she drew herself up a bit taller. "Forgive me for saying so, Mrs. Tilney, but I knew the man better than you did. For years, I had to watch as he browbeat his own family – especially poor Mrs. Tilney – and I have endured much at his hands myself. Then that nasty business at the ball... Well, the truth of the matter is this. The general was a bad-tempered old sod with a heart of stone. To my way of thinking, whoever it was that *did* send him off the roof did us all a great favor. Such a person deserves a reward, not punishment."

Catherine straightened her spine to match the woman across from her, adopting the unfamiliar authority of a person of superior position, despite her inferior size. "Mrs. Brooks, you forget yourself!" she declared. "Because I understand that you are suffering considerable distress on Henry's account, I will report none of your disrespect to the Tilneys. But neither will I listen to any more of it myself. Is that clear?"

Mrs. Brooks's mouth drew into a hard line, but she curtly nodded once and said no more. Indeed, neither of the women spoke a word for fully half an hour. While Mrs. Brooks watched out of the window, Catherine surreptitiously watched her. The one probably had no idea as to how far the recent, passionate exchange would go towards enlightening the other, how much of character and motivation she had inadvertently revealed.

REVELATIONS

*W*e have, all of us, done it. Can you deny it? Everybody hides behind a mask at times, and very glad we are that others cannot see what would ill bear public scrutiny – uncharitable thoughts, greedy or malicious aspirations, guilty secrets.

Mrs. Brooks was no exception. She had concealed her secret well. But excess emotion had made her careless, and now what she had so painstakingly sought to hide had begun to leak out, bit by bit, through the cracks in her façade, like shafts of sunlight breaking through gaps in the clouds. A word, a tone of voice, a gesture, an expression of the eye: although each in itself would have been insufficient to attract attention, the cumulative effect was to shine enough light on the truth that the dark reaches of her companion's active mind were suddenly illuminated.

Catherine gasped, and before she could think whether or not it was wise, she uttered aloud, "It was you!"

Mrs. Brooks slowly turned, and for a long moment the two women stared at one another, as if frozen there, unable to speak or act. Still, Catherine could see at once that Mrs. Brooks understood her. No pretense at incomprehension and no immediate denial left only one possibility. This time Catherine actually *was* trapped alone in a carriage with a murderer.

Her heart raced and so did her mind. What should she do? Was she, too, in mortal danger? Having already killed once, a murderer had very little to lose by killing a second time. So she had always read.

Catherine instantly acknowledged Mrs. Brooks to be the larger woman, and, having worked hard all her life, strong for her age, no doubt – strong enough, apparently, to push a man in his prime from a rooftop! Catherine would have no way to defend herself from a physical attack if one should come. She could only hope to attract the coachman's attention for help. Should she scream? Should she attempt to stop the coach at once? All these thoughts and questions raced through her mind in that one brief moment of indecision, waiting to see how a murderer would react to being found out and half expecting Mrs. Brooks to lunge at her throat.

When Mrs. Brooks did indeed lunge at Catherine, however, it was not an attack of murderous rage; it was an attack of conscience and tears. She clutched young Catherine's hands tightly in her own, bowing her head low over them and wailing, "Oh, Mrs. Tilney, have mercy, I beg you! For I confess, it is all too true. You have found me out. But I swear to you, it were only an accident! Or mostly so. I were too afraid of what might happen to me to speak of it before, you must understand."

Catherine threw off Mrs. Brooks and cried indignantly, "What might happen to *you*! What of Henry? Did you never once think of him?"

"Mercy! I have thought of nothing else since!" she sobbed. "And I would never have let him be punished in my place, I swear to you. I would sacrifice my own life to save his. Whatever else you may think of me, you must believe that, Mrs. Tilney."

When Catherine said nothing, Mrs. Brooks hurried on.

"I never dreamt it would go this far, you see! Until today, when you showed me that letter, I never believed there were any real danger to him. Like I said before, since Master Henry is innocent, I expected Mr. Cogsgrove to have very little difficulty proving it. Then there would have been no need for me to speak up at all. Indeed, there still may not be. Oh, Mrs. Tilney, you may imagine how severely my conscience has troubled me for what Master Henry has suffered on my account, but still I could not speak. You will say I am a great coward, and so I am. I simply could not bear the thought of being locked away forever while there were any chance of avoiding it. God forgive me my weakness!" So saying, she buried her face in her hands and cried all the louder.

Catherine, although no longer in fear for her life, was no less at a loss for what to do next. Mrs. Brooks in her current state made a pitiful sight, one which could not fail to excite a certain degree of compassion in the tender-hearted Mrs. Tilney, at least until she again thought of her husband. Then anger on his behalf flared up in at least equal measure. Oh, how she wished Henry had been there to tell her what was right, for this was certainly his area of expertise, not hers. In matters of law and justice, sin and forgiveness, his understanding infinitely surpassed her own. His years and his profession gave him that advantage.

For now, Catherine decided, she would learn what more there was to know before she was forced to choose the best course of action. "Sit back and compose yourself, Mrs. Brooks," she said firmly. "Then start at the beginning and tell me exactly what transpired that terrible night."

Mrs. Brooks made no remonstration, and after several minutes had passed and she was tolerably calm again, she began her story.

"You say to start at the beginning. Well, that means going back farther than that one night. I am sorry if it pains you, Mrs.

Tilney, but the general had been in an especially foul temper ever since your marriage to Master Henry. He counted it a moment of weakness that made him give his permission in the first place, or that he had somehow been tricked into doing it. I daresay the more he thought about it afterward, the more resentful he became, until he could bear it no longer. So he cooked up his nasty scheme to punish you and everybody else he could get his hooks into."

Catherine could not hide her astonishment.

"Oh, you may well be amazed at my knowing so much about what the general had on his mind," Mrs. Brooks continued, "me being only a servant and all. But you would be surprised to discover how freely men like General Tilney talk when they think nobody is listening. And make no mistake about it; servants count as 'nobody.' Or maybe it was more that his ego demanded an audience who could not disagree with him. Either way, I heard more than I cared to. He meant the ball to be a chance to impress his friends and embarrass or intimidate those who had or might displease him."

"That much seems clear, Mrs. Brooks, but do you think he really meant *all* of what he said at the dinner? Or did he say more than he intended because of excess drink?"

"That I do not know... nor ever will, I suppose. I did ask him a question like that myself... But I am running ahead. You see, I heard his performance that night at dinner, and even I, who knew what he was, were shocked by it. Then afterward, he catches sight of me and insists I help him with something. I had many other duties that demanded my attention on such an occasion, I can tell you, but he would not be denied. 'Mrs. Brooks,' he says. 'I am master here, and you will do as I say!' which was entirely typical of him. 'Come with me,' he says, and so I went... right on up to the roof."

Catherine's already rapt attention grew even sharper at the

mention of 'the roof,' drawing her back to the day of her own explorations there – her thoughts of a ghostly presence as she climbed the dark spiral staircase, the tangle of footprints and signs of a struggle at the spot where the crime occurred, and her terrifying backward glance over the edge when confronted by Captain Tilney. The sights and sounds and feelings came flooding back.

Catherine cleared her throat and said, "Yes, the roof. Do go on, Mrs. Brooks."

"Well, first the general amuses himself with pushing and shoving things about, toppling things over with my help – anything he could contrive to make noise enough to be heard from downstairs, and laughing heartily at his success. Then he takes me to the spot where he had left the crates of fireworks. While he sets to work making the final preparations for the spectacle he has planned, I asks him that question we talked about before. 'You're not really going to disinherit poor Henry, are you sir?' I says. And I will never forget what he answered me. He says, real cold like, 'Oh, no? Just you watch me!' Then he asks me to hand him the next crate..."

Catherine, afraid that the ensuing silence meant an end without a proper finish, gently but firmly encouraged the other woman. "Yes, Mrs. Brooks? Please continue. You must tell me the rest as well."

"I wish I could, but I don't rightly know m'self, Mrs. Tilney. All I remember is that I were angry, and that I had to really put me back into it to shift that great, heavy box. So maybe I were off my balance when I turned to give it to General Tilney, or maybe he were when he took it from my hands. Or maybe, God forgive me, I gave it an extra shove. In any case, when I saw that the weight of the thing was about to carry him over the edge, I tried to pull him back. But the only thing I succeeded in getting hold of were the crate of fireworks. It fell and smashed to pieces, and when I looked up again, the general were gone."

She paused, the look on her face evidence that she had relived the horror of that moment as she told it. Catherine could only imagine that it was for the hundredth time or more.

"So you see, Mrs. Tilney, it weren't no murder at all: it were an accident." She scratched her head and then slowly wagged it back and forth, now looking less sure. "It must have been an accident, for I would never have done such a thing on purpose... especially not to him."

Catherine thought this an unlikely sentiment. "Except earlier you said the general's death should not be regretted and that the one who brought it about deserved a reward. That is not quite consistent with your claim now that you wished the general no harm. You must see the contradiction, as would any court of law."

"Oh, yes, but then feelings are often complicated and even contradictory things, Mrs. Tilney. Have you never noticed? Oftentimes it is not simply one way or the other, love or hate. One can despise a scoundrel for all the harm he has done and yet not wish him dead. One can even hate such a man, truly believe the world would be better off without him, and at the same time love him to distraction. I cried as much as anybody when the general died – more than most, I daresay." In remembrance, more tears flowed from her eyes.

Now Catherine was thoroughly confused. "I thought your tears were for Henry!"

"And so they were... but not only for him."

"What are you telling me, Mrs. Brooks? What are you saying, that you were secretly in love with General Tilney?"

Through her tears, Mrs. Brooks laughed sardonically. "I was not *in* love with him, not in the way you mean. But I did love him after a fashion, in the manner of family affection, for he were my own flesh and blood. No one was meant to know it, of course. These things are always hushed up as well as possible. And yet me mother told me the truth afore she died. Now all those who might have been harmed by the knowledge are dead, so I don't suppose it matters anymore. The plain truth is this, Mrs. Tilney. Your father-in-law, General Tilney, were my own brother."

NIGHT AT THE INN

*M*rs. Brooks's last revelation had been as shocking as the discovery that she was the killer. "I cannot believe it," Catherine said presently.

"Nevertheless, it is the truth, Mrs. Tilney, as sure as God is my witness. General Tilney were my brother, right enough – my brother by half blood, that is. Years ago, my mother were a pretty young chambermaid at Northanger, and his, the lady of the house. But the general's father and mine were one and the same man. So you see, Mrs. Tilney, Master Henry is my nephew and the closest thing I will ever have to a son. I would never allow anything to happen to him as long as there were some way in my power to prevent it. If it becomes genuinely necessary, I will confess what I done. But otherwise, you mustn't tell, I beg you. I know Master Henry would not want you to do that. He would not want to see me put in prison if it can be helped."

There. That was the heart of the question, Catherine surmised. What would Henry want her to do – report the woman at once or hold off in the hope it would not be necessary? With it supposedly being little more than an accident, and with Mrs.

Brooks being such a favorite of his... perhaps actually his aunt! "Does Henry know of this?" she asked. "Your... your parentage, I mean."

"I don't expect he does, ma'am, not by my information, in any case. I had no wish to impose on him."

There was no time to pursue the matter further. Catherine had been distractedly observing the increasing signs of civilization outside of her window, and now suddenly the carriage was drawing to a halt at their destination. But what on earth was she to do about Mrs. Brooks? Some kind of decision was required and without delay.

Mrs. Brooks looked equally distressed. She leant forward, pleading, "Please, Mrs. Tilney, ma'am! I don't mind you knowing, but don't tell anybody else what I done! Not yet anyway."

"Your secret is safe with me for now, Mrs. Brooks," Catherine found herself saying a moment before the footman opened the door. "See to it that you give me no cause to change my mind until I have more time to consider what is best to be done."

She must see Henry. That was what Catherine was thinking. Now that they had actually arrived in Gloucester and he was somewhere nearby, nothing else seemed to matter. If she could but see him, be held in his arms again, hear his voice telling her all would be well, then surely she would finally stop shaking. Surely things would become clear, and together they would decide what to do about Mrs. Brooks.

As Catherine stepped from the carriage in front of the inn, she was forcibly struck by another fact – a singularly sublime fact! – that had all but escaped her during the commotion of Mrs. Brooks's revelations. Henry would go free! The danger was over, now that the true culprit had been discovered.

The rest of the party – Eleanor, the viscount, and Captain Tilney – were at the same time exiting the other carriage and looking about themselves.

Catherine could not stop smiling. Although as yet she could tell no one why, it was enough that she now knew the truth would come out and Henry would be exonerated. She pictured them home together at Woodston Cottage again, resuming their quiet, ordinary lives – Henry about the business of the parish, she managing their modest household, and both making plans for the future together.

Oh, for the bliss of the commonplace, for the comfort of a predictably pleasant routine! To regain the comfortable proportions of her parsonage home, she would give up the luxury of Northanger Abbey in an instant. The romance of the ancient edifice, the massive scale of the rooms, the sumptuous food and drink, the expensive furnishings, the liveried army of servants: these things meant nothing to her now that she had learnt by painful experience what was truly important.

While Henry was with her and a roof over their heads, she would ask for nothing else. She would be content to never roam again, and she should never even *think* of desiring another adventure... outside the safety of a book, that is.

Eleanor drew alongside her, taking her arm and saying, "You look as if you passed the second half of the journey pleasantly, Catherine. Did you and Mrs. Brooks find enough to talk about?"

Catherine stifled a laugh and only nodded. Oh, yes, they had found plenty to talk about! Eleanor would have been quite amazed if she had known but the half of it.

Captain Tilney, who had entered the inn at once, now returned to direct the servants and relate what he had discovered there. Mr. Cogsgrove had indeed secured lodgings for the entire party, including Mrs. Brooks, as had been the prior arrangement. He had also bespoken a meal for them all in a private dining room, where he would be joining them shortly.

"See your rooms," the captain instructed them, "and take care of only your most necessary business. Then presently we will reassemble below to hear what Mr. Cogsgrove has to tell us."

As she made her way upstairs, Catherine's only thought was a passionate desire that she might get through the coming hour quickly and soon be taken to Henry.

Catherine's hopes were soon dashed, however, when the question uppermost in her mind was asked and answered at the first possible moment.

"No, I am sorry, Mrs. Tilney," said Mr. Cogsgrove. "I anticipated your request, but unfortunately I was unable to obtain permission for your husband to have visitors tonight. Never fear, though; there will be opportunity enough in the morning, since his is not the first trial on tomorrow's docket. Now let us all sit down together. You must be tired from your long journey and greatly in need of refreshment."

Mr. Cogsgrove did most of the talking over dinner, eating little himself whilst explaining at length what they were to expect on the morrow – the who, where, when, and how of Henry's day in court. Before the trial began, however, one or two of them might visit Henry, as he had said earlier. When all the others deferred in Catherine's favor, agreeing that she should be allotted the full time, she was most grateful... grateful and relieved. It was imperative that she saw her husband as soon as possible and for more than a minute or two – both for her own peace of mind, but also to relate to him the new information about Mrs. Brooks and to hear his wishes in the case. Whatever he advised – whether to report Mrs. Brooks at once or wait in the hopes she might be saved, and what to tell Mr. Cogsgrove if anything – Catherine was prepared to do.

"...I have written each of you a summons," Mr. Cogsgrove continued. "Although at this time I have no intention of calling anybody to testify except you, Mrs. Brooks," he said, looking in her direction, "I prefer to leave all my options open. One can never predict in advance exactly how matters will transpire and what will be most helpful in the end. If things go poorly for us, I will call as many witnesses to Mr. Tilney's character as possible, in an effort to sway the jury in our favor at last. Besides, holding a summons will ensure that you have seats in the courtroom. High profile cases often draw a crowd.

"Well, I suppose that covers the main points, unless you have questions or any new information for me." Mr. Cogsgrove glanced expectantly from face to face round the table.

Despite what Mrs. Brooks had said before – and despite her own promise – Catherine could not help looking intently at the woman across from her, hoping she would change her mind and speak up now. They would all, especially Henry, be spared further suspense, and Mr. Cogsgrove might be prevailed upon to transfer his efforts to defending her instead. Surely, that is what Henry would want.

Mrs. Brooks would not meet Catherine's eye, however, or Mr. Cogsgrove's either. She sat mutely, forcing Catherine to do the same. In the end, only Captain Tilney spoke.

"Mr. Cogsgrove, you are an experienced barrister…"

Mr. Cogsgrove nodded his assent.

"Well, then, not to put too fine a point on it, sir, but what do you think of my brother's chances tomorrow? And what happens if he is convicted?"

"Oh, Frederick!" wailed Eleanor in dismay.

"Must we discuss that dismal possibility now?" asked the viscount. "There are ladies present."

"I am quite aware of that fact, Jonathan," rejoined the captain. "But it does neither them nor my brother any good service to ignore the question. It only leaves us unprepared."

Here again, Catherine wished she could tell what she knew, especially for Eleanor's sake, tell them that Henry's danger was, for all intents and purposes, over.

"Please," said Cogsgrove calmly, "do compose yourselves.

For now, these weighty questions must be left to me. Speculation about what might or might not happen tomorrow is pointless, especially since juries are unpredictable entities. You may be sure that I will watch them sharply and respond as necessary, using my knowledge and experience to procure the best possible outcome for Mr. Tilney."

After Mr. Cogsgrove departed and Catherine said goodnight to her companions, she waited in her own room for half an hour before going to have a word with Mrs. Brooks. Their prior conversation had been abruptly interrupted at the sudden ending of their journey, leaving matters less than comfortably settled between them. That situation needed to be remedied before she would be calm enough to sleep.

Catherine knocked lightly and opened the door a few inches. "Mrs. Brooks?" she called softly. "May I come in?"

"As you please, Mrs. Tilney," came the reply.

"Oh Mrs. Brooks!" Catherine began, as she swept in and closed the door behind her. Facing the other woman, who stood in her nightdress a few feet away in the small, spartan room, Catherine continued. "How I wish you had spoken up when Mr. Cogsgrove asked! Things might have been settled already and poor Henry free. And surely, it will go better for you if you confess of your own accord, not waiting until the last minute. Still, I felt bound by my promise to you, though I was forced to make it in haste."

"I have made you a promise as well, Mrs. Tilney," Mrs. Brooks said evenly.

"So you have, and your pledge has given me great joy. It has indeed. Now, I will see Henry in the morning and tell him what I know. Then he will be able to advise us both."

Mrs. Brooks quailed at once. "Oh, Mrs. Tilney, you mustn't do that! Remember your promise."

Catherine looked askance. "I assure you, Mrs. Brooks, that I never should have given any promise if I had thought you meant me to keep what I know even from Henry! After all, he is my husband and the one most concerned in the business. And recall how confident you were that Henry would wish to protect you. I make no doubt it is true, too. That being the case, I should think you would be eager to place your fate in his hands."

"It ain't that, ma'am. It's the thought of the darling boy learning what I done. What will he say when he knows that somebody he trusted is responsible for his father's death? Not only that but the appearance that I have left him to take the blame." She began to cry.

"Take heart, Mrs. Brooks," said Catherine, patting her shoulder. "No doubt he will believe it was an accident, just as you say, and think none the worse of you. In any case, we are come too far to turn back now, and I simply cannot do without Henry's help. This thing is much too weighty for me to carry alone. Surely you can see that."

Mrs. Brooks reached behind herself for the chair and then sank into it. "Very well, Mrs. Tilney," she said wearily, offering no further resistance. "I suppose it must be, if you say so. I will endeavor to resign myself to it."

"Never fear, Mrs. Brooks. All will be well. Now get some sleep."

Thus, having relieved her feelings tolerably well, and with the sanguine expectation of seeing her husband presently set free, Catherine took to her bed, there passing a peaceful night. Downstairs the next morning, however, when Mrs. Brooks did not immediately appear with the others for breakfast, a portion of the old foreboding returned.

"Have you seen Mrs. Brooks?" she asked her sister-in-law.

"Not yet, no," replied Eleanor. "Why, Catherine, whatever is the matter? Do not distress yourself. No doubt Mrs. Brooks is still in her room and will be down shortly. There is plenty of time…"

Catherine did not stay to hear more. She left her friends

without a word of explanation and raced back upstairs. Not pausing to knock this time, since she was already convinced there would be no answer, Catherine threw open the door to Mrs. Brooks's room. It was empty.

THE MORNING OF

*I*t was with a slow step and a heavy heart that Catherine retraced her way down to the private dining parlor, where her friends continued to enjoy their breakfasts. When she came in, all eyes naturally turned to her. "She is gone," Catherine said dejectedly. "Mrs. Brooks's room is empty and she is gone."

The unexpected development left all those who heard it quite amazed and momentarily incapable of speech. Captain Tilney recovering first, he said, "What do you mean? How can Mrs. Brooks be gone? She knows she is wanted here to testify, and surely she can have nowhere else to go. This makes no sense at all."

"Nevertheless, it is true," said Catherine. She was still deciding how much of the rest she should divulge when Mr. Cogsgrove entered.

"Good day to you all," he said. "Mrs. Tilney, if you are ready, I will take you to your husband now."

Mr. Cogsgrove's timely appearance decided her. Catherine saw at once that it would be much better to explain matters to him rather than to her family. He could be trusted with sensitive information, and he would better know what to do.

"One moment, Mr. Cogsgrove," interposed Captain Tilney. "It seems we have a situation on our hands this morning. Mrs. Brooks has gone missing."

"Indeed?" Cogsgrove replied, with brows drawn together.

"Let us go, Mr. Cogsgrove," Catherine interrupted. "I will explain it all to you along our way." Reaching to take the arm that the attorney then belatedly offered, Catherine expertly steered him from the room in advance of any possible remonstrations from the others. Once safely away and in the gentleman's carriage, Catherine exhaled in relief.

"Now, Mrs. Tilney," said Cogsgrove. "Something tells me you know more about this business with Mrs. Brooks than I have heard so far."

"I do, sir, and yet before I speak, I must have certain assurances from you."

"What may I do for you, madam?"

"First, tell me again that, as a lawyer, you are constrained against speaking to others what is revealed to you in confidence."

"It is as you say, Mrs. Tilney."

"Very well. And are you also constrained to act according to your client's wishes? You see, I meant to tell Henry what I know first and allow him to direct you. But with Mrs. Brooks disappearing so unexpectedly... Well, there may not be any time to lose. I think I must tell you without delay and trust you to abide by Henry's requests later."

"By all means. Let us have no delay that might jeopardize your husband's situation. Speak freely, Mrs. Tilney. You have my word that I will keep your confidence and honor your husband's wishes."

And so Catherine told him nearly everything, only leaving out Mrs. Brooks's claim of being the general's sister, which was neither here nor there and, she judged, best left to Henry's discretion. So she gave Mr. Cogsgrove Mrs. Brooks's account of the night General Tilney lost his life, her fears of confinement, her solemn promise to confess if need be to save Henry, and her tenacious hopes that in the end it would not.

"...I think she became scared and ran off, Mr. Cogsgrove. She was terrified from the start at the idea of testifying in court, and now it would be ten times worse for her than I had imagined before. She is mortified that Henry must be told what happened – of losing his regard – for she thinks of him much like a son. And who could blame her for being frightened half out of her wits that the truth might come out and she be arrested?

"Oh, Mr. Cogsgrove, what are we to do? You said yourself that she is important as a witness to Henry's good character, but how much more than that now! It is all my fault, too, that she has gone missing, I mean. I mishandled the whole thing. I should not have oppressed her so last night... Or perhaps I should have done the opposite – shown no mercy. Now poor Henry may pay the price for my blunders!"

"On the contrary, Mrs. Tilney, without you, we still would be in the dark as to the true killer."

Catherine began to disclaim, but Cogsgrove held up his hand. "One moment, if you please. I thank you very kindly for relaying this vital information, but now I must think."

Catherine silenced herself at once, and in that silence she fervently prayed that Mr. Cogsgrove would be inspired with the necessary wisdom to rescue them from this latest crisis. To have had their salvation so close at hand, only to see it slip away again, was unbearable.

Sooner than Catherine had expected, Mr. Cogsgrove curtailed his ruminations and spoke.

"This is how I intend to proceed, Mrs. Tilney. First and foremost, I will send one of my men – a very capable fellow who is at my disposal – to search out Mrs. Brooks. He will start his inquiries at the inn, where he will also be in a position to reassure your friends. They need not know the details, only that the matter is well in hand. Meanwhile, you will speak to your husband of these things, so that we may both be informed by his wishes. Then we must hope that Mrs. Brooks returns in time to keep her promise."

"And what if she does not?" asked Catherine. "Cannot you explain to the court what really happened? Surely then…"

"Unfortunately, that will not do at all, Mrs. Tilney. I cannot go into court and tell the jury third hand what you have told me second hand, nor can *you* testify to it. That kind of information would not meet the standard of acceptable evidence. Still, knowing what I now do will help me in how to direct my questions. And I can always call you or one of the others as a character witness if necessary. I had preferred Mrs. Brooks, but we must play the hand we are dealt."

Even Mrs. Brooks and her whereabouts were temporarily consigned to the shelf – along with everything else – once Catherine was at the point of actually setting eyes (and lips and hands and other parts) on her husband again. Some faceless gaoler opened the door, and there was Henry – *her* Henry – in the flesh, his arms and smile spread wide to receive her. Then no force of nature or artifice could have held Catherine back; into his embrace she tumbled with tears of joy and murmurings of her steadfast love, of his many perfections, and of how fiercely she had missed him.

Henry responded in kind, clasping her tightly to himself and drinking her in by every means possible. Indeed, now more starved for his wife's presence and affection than at their last meeting in similar circumstances, fully five minutes elapsed before he could either countenance releasing her or tolerably contain his own emotions.

At last, Catherine's senses returned and she remembered the pressing business at hand. "Oh!" she cried of a sudden, "I have so much to tell you, Henry! Good news, I hope. You will be amazed, in any case."

"Then tell me while I hold you, for I will not give you up," he said into her ear, squeezing her more tightly than ever.

"But I must look you in the face. Do be reasonable and sit down, darling."

With a groan of protest, he finally loosened the embrace a bit, sitting down on the only chair and at the same time pulling his wife onto his lap. "There," he said. "This way, we both get what we want. You can look me in the face but I can still hold you near me. Now, my dearest, what is this news that has you so agitated? What can possibly be so very important?"

"The good news is this. I have discovered who the real murderer is... or at least who caused your father's death." Since Henry appeared too stunned to immediately respond, Catherine ran on, her words coming out in a rush. "I know it is hard to believe, and I daresay you have a right to doubt it, for I have had several theories before that turned out to be entirely mistaken. But this time, my darling, I know I am right for we have a confession... although Mr. Cogsgrove says that until the confession is made in court, which is a problem I will tell you about presently, no one may believe us. Still... Oh, Henry! This is the break we have been waiting for. Do not you see what this means? It means the nightmare may soon be over." She briefly threw her arms about Henry's neck before continuing. "Now prepare yourself, for some part of the story will not be pleasant for you to hear."

"Anything that releases me and restores my good name must be pleasant," said Henry. "Do go on and quickly, Catherine, for, as you might well imagine, I am rather impatient to hear this news you have to tell."

Catherine took a deep breath. "This is the unpleasant part, Henry, and we might as well get it over. It is your dear Mrs. Brooks who killed your father, you see, although she claims it was an accident. And the difficulty now is that she has run away."

Henry's smile faded as the weight of this pronouncement settled on his mind. Then Catherine proceeded, repeating to him the rest of the tale, answering his questions and hearing his various exclamations along the way. Catherine left nothing at all out this time. She only hesitated when it came to telling Henry that Mrs. Brooks might well be his aunt. Then she quickly decided he had the right to know this too and to know it now. For it would not do for the information to overtake him in a less private place, such as in court. Plus it was one piece of what he must consider before instructing Mr. Cogsgrove as to his wishes.

"…Did I do right in telling you, Henry? I hope this part of the news does not upset you overly."

"Certainly you were right to tell me," he said gravely. "We must have no secrets between us. As to my reaction, I am more distressed at the thought of Mrs. Brooks going to prison than at any other part of the news, for I must believe it was an accident, as she says. As for being a blood relation… Well, I suppose I have unconsciously considered her an honorary aunt, in any case. Now to learn that she may be indeed… That is one more reason I have a duty to protect her if I can. Still, she seems to have taken matters into her own hands by absconding, although I cannot believe she means to break her word to you, Catherine. There must be some other explanation."

Catherine frowned. "Darling, when you say you mean to protect Mrs. Brooks, please tell me you would not go so far as to willingly take the punishment in her place. I *know* she would not want that!"

"No, my dear; never fear. I am not looking for a chance to nobly sacrifice myself. I might be willing do so for *you*, but in this case, I flatter myself that you would prefer an ordinary man alive to a martyred saint for a husband." He laughed.

"Oh, Henry! How can you even joke about such a thing?"

"Sometimes that is the only way to get through life, my love. When the choice is to either laugh or to cry, I will choose laughter every time."

On the chance that Catherine was still put somewhat out of spirits by his macabre joke, Henry thought it best to say no more on that subject. Instead, he endeavored to distract his wife with something altogether different and more agreeable for her to think about – the kind of little husbandly attentions he enjoyed giving as much as she seemed to enjoy receiving. His pleasant ministrations, which began forthwith, met with admirable success despite the limits placed on them by their current situation.

-29-

THE PROSECUTION

There was no last minute reprieve – not in the form of Mrs. Brooks turning up to confess or otherwise. So the trial, assigned to the courtrooms of Booth Hall in Westgate Street, went forward as scheduled.

After being obliged to leave Henry, Catherine joined the rest of his family there. She found them in the chairs reserved for everyone holding a summons as a potential witness. This meant seeing some other familiar faces as well as a few Catherine did not know. General Courteney and the Marquis of Longtown each acknowledged her with a nod when she came in, as did General Tilney's lawyer, Mr. Wilcox. Sir Melvin Whitmore was present also, his grim face an unwelcome sight. When he did not meet her eye, Catherine was saved the trouble of pretending civility towards him. She recognized one of the other men as the doctor who had examined the body and testified at the coroner's inquest.

Catherine was glad the chair next to Eleanor was vacant so that she might sit there instead of beside Captain Tilney, or worse yet, Sir Melvin. The courtroom was filling rapidly, she noticed as she sat down, and the growing crowd hummed with expectant murmurings.

Eleanor took her arm, squeezed it, and said in a low voice, "No news of Mrs. Brooks yet. How odd of her to go off like that, although she did seem quite nervous about testifying. I suppose that must be the explanation. Now, how does Henry do? I trust he was very glad to see you."

Catherine's cheeks burned at the thought of what had so recently passed between her husband and herself – more than ample proof of Eleanor's statement. Fortunately, she seemed not to have noticed. "He is well," Catherine said. "Hopeful, I believe. Mr. Cogsgrove has a new line of defense that sounds promising."

Catherine could have said so much more – wanted to say much more – but she held her tongue. With Henry wishing to keep Mrs. Brooks's part in the crime quiet if possible, it would be for him to tell the family what he deemed best once his ordeal was finished, for him to recommend what should be done with the housekeeper short of turning her over to the law. That was, if the whole story did not come out during the trial, which seemed less and less likely with every minute that passed with no sign of Mrs. Brooks.

Henry, like Mrs. Brooks herself, hoped he would be exonerated without the need of directly incriminating her in the business. And Catherine, like Mr. Cogsgrove, was obliged to abide by his wishes.

If it had been left up to her, Catherine would have suffered few scruples at calling Mrs. Brooks to account as soon as she could be found. Indeed, she began to fervently wish she had done so the night before – told the others at once and made sure Mrs. Brooks was locked in her room for the night! With Mrs. Brooks's decision to run off, most of Catherine's past sympathy for her had expired. Many unexpected things could happen during a trial, she feared, and she would rather have left nothing to chance where so much was at stake. In the end, when the verdict came down...

At that precise point in her musings, Catherine actually heard the word "Guilty" clearly declared, followed by a noisy crowd response. She started violently and looked about herself, wondering if she had only imagined these things or had somehow conjured them by her fearful speculations.

"It is from next door," Eleanor explained soothingly. "The walls between the two courtrooms are notoriously thin. In fact, Frederick told us on our way here that the whole building is derelict and to be torn down as soon as a new and much better courthouse can be erected."

Catherine thanked her sister for enlightening her, but she had great difficulty settling her startled nerves afterward, especially when the proceedings got underway. When the judge entered, wearing scarlet robes and a wig, she thought to herself, "This is real, not a play or a story in a book." When the jury filed into the seats set aside for them, when they were sworn to do their duty, she acknowledged with some dread, "These are the men who will decide Henry's fate, and so my own." And when Henry himself was escorted to the dock and the charge against him read out by the clerk, it was all Catherine could do to keep from crying out, along with her husband's plea, "Not guilty!"

After that formality, Henry searched out his friends in the crowd, a task made easier by the fact they were all gathered together in nearby seats. His eyes came to rest on his wife, who returned his gaze steadfastly. For her part, Catherine wished she could join her husband in the dock. It was dreadful to see Henry standing there, alone and accused. And it was all wrong. Their marriage vows had made them one flesh, and her place was beside him, through thick and thin.

Then the prosecutor – a short, stout man by the name of Albany – began by laying out to the jury his theory of how the crime had occurred and why – much the same *motive and oppor-*

tunity rationale as Sir Melvin had effectively used against Henry before. And the line of witnesses called were a fair repeat of the inquest as well. Catherine heard nothing she had not heard before, at least at the outset.

General Courteney was called to establish what had occurred that fatal night at the ball, most specifically, what was intended to establish motive for murder: General Tilney's threat to revoke Henry's living. Then the Marquis of Longtown was called to corroborate all that General Courteney had said, as well as to witness to the fact that the dead man could not have committed suicide, since he had everything in the world to live for, including the prospect of a charming young wife – the Marquis's own daughter. These two revealed nothing new or surprising.

Unlike at the inquest, however, this time there was opportunity given for the defense attorney to cross examine the witnesses. Not that anything Courteney and Longtown had said was in dispute. Mr. Cogsgrove put only two questions to each. He asked "How long have you known the defendant?" to which both replied, "All his life." Secondly, "Do you believe Henry Tilney capable of murdering his father?" to which both men gave an unequivocal "no."

Although Catherine felt somewhat heartened by this herself, she failed to detect any positive signs among the jurors, all of whom remained determinedly straight faced and impassive.

Next, the prosecutor called Mr. Shepherd, the medical man who had examined the body. After Mr. Albany led him to testify that, in his professional opinion, the victim was murdered by means of being pushed from the rooftop, it was Mr. Cogsgrove's turn.

"Pushed, you say, Mr. Shepherd?"

"Yes, sir."

"That is very interesting. Would you be so good as to explain to the jury how you could be certain of that, doctor? Were there muddy handprints on the victim's back?"

Shepherd chuckled. "No sir, of course not. The evidence of murder is in the appearance and condition of the body."

"Aaah. Then, kindly tell us what difference in the body you would have expected to see if General Tilney, instead of being pushed, had fallen by accident or leaped to his death intentionally. Would the injuries from his impact with the ground have been any more or less damaging? I admit I am no expert, but I expect a thumb smashed by a hammer will look much the same regardless if the blow was accidental, intentionally self-inflicted, or struck by someone else."

Doctor Shepherd hesitated. "Well, there is some truth to that, I suppose. But there was certainly nothing in the condition of the body inconsistent with a push from the rooftop. So when I was told that's what had happened, I saw no reason to dispute it."

"*When you were told that's what had happened*... Yes, I think it is clear now how you came to the conclusion you did. Thank you, Mr. Shepherd."

This caused a mild stir amongst the crowd, and at least one of the jurors wagged his head in disapproval. Mr. Cogsgrove had hit his mark, it seemed. But the small victory did not last long.

The prosecution next called to the witness box a man by the name of Tommy O'Rourke. He was a pleasant enough looking fellow – young, fair, clean shaven – but Catherine had no idea who he was or what he could possibly have to do with the case. The prosecutor, however, wasted little time getting to the point.

"Now, Mr. O'Rourke, please tell the court how you come to have pertinent information about the crime in question."

"I were there that night, at Northanger, when the old gentleman – General Tilney, that is – met 'is end. I were one of the extra footmen hired to wait on tables and such."

"I see," said Mr. Albany, as if this were new information to him. "And did you observe anything that night that can shed light on the question of how General Tilney died?"

"I certainly did. I heard 'is son, Mr. Tilney there..."

"One moment, Mr. O'Rourke, but just to be clear, do you mean the defendant that you see here in the dock, Mr. Henry Tilney?"

"Yes, sir, that's 'im."

"Very good. Tell the court what you heard the defendant say, and what the circumstances were."

"Well, this is right after the body was found, you understand, and the general's family is all huddled up like, there in the front hall, frettin' and talkin' amongst themselves. I 'appened to be passing through, and as I were walkin' by, I hear Mr. Tilney say… He says, clear as anythin', 'He were a nasty piece of work from first to last, and I, for one, ain't sorry he's gone.'"

There was an audible gasp from the observers, including Catherine, and an almost imperceptible smile crossed Mr. Albany's lips. After a strategic pause for effect, he asked, "Were those Mr. Tilney's exact words, Mr. O'Rourke?"

"Yes, sir, or near enough."

"Very well. Did you draw any conclusion as to whom the defendant referred by this comment? Who was he not sorry to have gone?"

"Ain't it obvious? Had to be his ol' man, the general. That's the only person who had just departed this earth."

"Thank you, Mr. O'Rourke. You have been very helpful."

Catherine could hardly keep her seat through this testimony (and a look at Henry proved he did not bear it with complete composure either). Her not inconsiderable perturbation was a little relieved when she saw Captain Tilney rise. Perhaps he could do something to correct this travesty! He quickly but quietly made his way to Mr. Cogsgrove's side and whispered something into his ear.

When Mr. Albany was finished, Cogsgrove approached the witness, saying, "Now Mr. O'Rourke, you have testified that you are quite clear about what you heard."

"Yes, sir."

"I am wondering, however, if you can be just as certain about who it was that uttered those words. The reason I ask is that there were, in addition to two ladies, presumably *three* gentlemen in that family circle as you passed by: Mr. Henry Tilney, Captain Frederick Tilney, and the general's son-in-law, the Viscount Astley. Does that sound correct?"

Mr. O'Rourke squinted and lifted his gaze upward, as if looking for his answer there. "I reckon so."

"Very well, then. Since you do not normally work in the house, you cannot possibly be expected to recognize the different voices of those three men, can you?"

"No, sir. That's true enough."

"So unless you were looking directly at the man when he spoke, you could not say with any certainty which one of those three it was who said the words you heard. Could it not just as easily have been Captain Tilney or the viscount?"

O'Rourke crossed his arms over his chest. "I guess I must 'ave been lookin' at him, then, because I knows what I know, and it were Mr. Tilney there," he said, pointing to Henry in the dock, "who said how he's glad his father were gone." After fending off Mr. Cogsgrove's challenging glare a long moment more, Mr. O'Rourke was dismissed.

Catherine turned to Eleanor and whispered, "It is so unfair! Henry never said those things; it was Captain Tilney!"

"I know, I know. Bad luck that anybody overheard. That man is obviously mistaken, though."

"Or deliberately lying. I would wager that the prosecution has got him to say what he did to put Henry in a negative light."

"Mr. Cogsgrove was at least able to cast a little doubt on the witness's credibility. And remember, he will be able to call his own witnesses later."

But there was only one witness Catherine wished to see called in Henry's defense. She scanned the crowd again for the one face who could save her husband with a word... a sentence or two at the most. All Mrs. Brooks would have to say was, "I know for certain that Mr. Tilney is innocent. I know because *I* am the one who killed the general." But it had to be said in court, it had to be said by her, and it had to be said today. Catherine's searching eyes met with no success. *Oh, where was the woman?*

SIR MELVIN, WE MEET AGAIN

$\mathcal{M}$eanwhile, the prosecutor had called Sir Melvin Whitmore forward to testify. At least he must have, for Catherine came to herself in time to notice the hated magistrate rise from his seat a few feet to her right and begin making his way to the witness box. He held the Testament, pronounced the oath, and gave his name and address, just as the others had done. Then Mr. Albany began with his questions. What had he seen when he arrived at Northanger that night? What did the evidence on the roof reveal? Who had he talked to and what had they told him? As an experienced magistrate, what conclusions had he drawn from all this information?

"...It was clear from the start that General Tilney had been murdered, and we had a houseful of potential suspects. But, one by one, they were all eliminated until it came down to the defendant, Mr. Henry Tilney. He was the only one with clear motive, opportunity, and most importantly, no alibi," Sir Melvin confidently stated at the end of his several minutes of testimony.

Here again, the information was not new to Catherine; she had heard it all before, and in the same self-satisfied tone of voice that had irritated her from the start.

The prosecutor smiled. "Thank you, Sir Melvin, for your thoroughness and your service to this court. I have no more questions." Turning, Albany added, "Your witness, Mr. Cogsgrove."

Mr. Cogsgrove took his time approaching, as if carefully considering how to proceed. "Sir Melvin, we meet again," he began. "I, too, wish to thank you for your service. You had a Herculean task before you when you were called to Northanger that night. 'A houseful of potential suspects,' as you said. There must have been well over a hundred people you had to interview and eliminate."

"Well over that number, indeed," agreed Sir Melvin in a boastful tone. "There were precisely one hundred and seventy-two altogether: family, guests, and others."

"Quite a daunting task, Sir Melvin. One hundred and seventy-two persons with a connection of one kind or another to the victim. And yet, I understand that in little more than an hour, you had eliminated all but a handful of those from suspicion and released them. How was that possible?"

"I set the constables to the job at once, and it was easily done. The advantage of a crowded house is that nearly everybody has an alibi, because nearly everybody is in company with at least one other person all of the time, if you see what I mean."

"Yes, I do see, although the fact that it was a masked ball must have caused *some* difficulty. And then there were the legions of invisibles."

Sir Melvin looked confused. "The legions of invisibles? I do not take your meaning, sir."

"The servants, Sir Melvin. Those coming and going without anybody noticing them. It must have been more difficult to establish the whereabouts of each or alibis for every one of the score of servants in the house that night."

"Oh, well, nobody thought one of the servants had done it," the magistrate said dismissively. "The constables spoke to the housekeeper and the butler, and as many of the others as could be found. Nothing of interest turned up there."

"So then in actual fact, not every person in the house that night was completely examined and cleared. Some, particularly amongst the servants, might have been overlooked. Correct?"

"I must take exception to the term 'overlooked,' which implies some negligence. We were very thorough, I assure you, Mr. Cogsgrove, taking every prudent precaution. Anybody known to have a possible motive was verified completely. Time was not wasted inquiring after every disinterested housemaid and stable boy."

"*Anybody known to have a possible motive.* That was a very sensible approach, Sir Melvin, I am sure. And exactly how many of the servants did that include? How many did you consider suspect enough to investigate thoroughly?"

"Well... none of them. As I said before, nobody thought one of the servants might have done it."

"Do servants never hate their masters, then, or think of doing them harm? Never mind, Sir Melvin. I withdraw the question, for you cannot possibly be expected to know the answer. Allow me to put a more specific question to you, just so that I can appreciate the *thoroughness* of your investigation. What about... oh, let us pick a servant as a random example. What about Mrs. Brooks?"

"The housekeeper?"

"Yes, the housekeeper. You mentioned her a moment ago, so I know you are aware of her existence. And being so prominent a member of the household staff, I trust she would have been looked at as closely as any of the servants. So were you able to establish Mrs. Brooks's whereabouts for the entire hour in question? Did she provide you with the solid alibi you required?"

"I do not precisely recall... That is to say, I did not speak to her myself. But I believe she gave the constable some account of her activities during that time, an account he found quite satis-factory."

"So, if I understand you correctly, Sir Melvin, Mrs. Brooks provided no alibi to prove her whereabouts. You just accepted her word that she was where she said, doing what she said."

"That is essentially correct, I suppose."

"And yet you denied my client the same courtesy. When he provided you an account of his activities, you did not take him at his word. Can you explain this seeming contradiction, Sir Melvin?"

"There is no contradiction, Mr. Cogsgrove," the magistrate said slowly, with an air of infinite patience. "Your client had a clear motive to kill General Tilney; Mrs. Brooks had none."

"None that you *know* of," Cogsgrove corrected. "Thank you. I have no further questions."

Catherine rejoiced that the possibility of Mrs. Brooks had been suggested to the jury, and yet in such a way as to not accuse her of anything. She hoped Henry would not mind Mr. Cogs-grove having walked such a fine line concerning his wishes in the matter. Although her eyes rarely left her husband's face, she could judge very little of his thinking with any confidence. His command of countenance was so admirable as to give nothing away.

It had done her heart good, too, to see Sir Melvin brought down a peg, bested by a man of equal or better capacity. She was impressed with Mr. Cogsgrove's skill in maneuvering the pompous magistrate into admitting he did not know everything after all, and she began to think that they could not have done better for a competent barrister.

Periodically, another noisy eruption issued through the wall from the adjacent courtroom – not enough to determine what exactly went on, only enough to discern that the tide of judgment weighed heavily against the accused in a series of briefer trials. Time after time, Catherine distinctly heard a verdict of "guilty" pronounced and the crowd cheering their approval. On the other side of the Channel, she would have next expected them to cry out in unison for the guillotine.

Did those round about her feel the same, she wondered? Is that what they had come out to see – a prominent family beset by troubles of the worst kind and another man condemned? Did that make their own humdrum lives seem a little less dismal?

Catherine did not like to think so. Indeed, she preferred to think as she had before: that most people were basically kind at heart and that they wished nothing but good fortune for every stranger they met, just as they would for their neighbors and friends. Even aside from what this whole business had done to Henry and to herself, there was an additional weight upon her soul at having been forced into a better acquaintance with the ways of the world and the baser side of human nature. It was a loss of innocence, which could never be entirely recovered from. Even if this trial finished with Henry's full exoneration, she feared the shadow would always haunt them, hovering like a specter just out view.

She tried to catch Henry's eye, hoping to give him a reassuring smile – optimism she did not sincerely feel – to encourage him. He must be tired, she reasoned, standing so long there, alone in the dock. Why could he not have a chair like everybody else? The judge, the prosecutor, even the people in the gallery (at least those who had come early enough), they all had a place to sit. It was unconscionably cruel that the person under the most strain must continue to stand, perhaps hour after hour.

Catherine's musings had once again momentarily distracted her from what was going forward in the courtroom. Next thing she knew, the prosecutor had apparently finished, because it was Mr. Cogsgrove who was now clearly in control.

He called Mr. Wilcox, General Tilney's attorney, who testified that the general had never enquired of him about the possibility of revoking the Woodston living from his son, and that he had been summoned to Northanger on the first of November for an entirely different item of business. As expected, Mr. Albany, in his cross examination, took much of the air out of this news, pointing out that such information proved nothing. It only mattered what the defendant believed his father meant to do at the time.

"I call Captain Frederick Tilney," Mr. Cogsgrove said next. The captain stood at once and marched forward to the witness box. After the usual formalities, Mr. Cogsgrove posed his first question. "Captain, you are here because you specially requested to be given the opportunity to speak. What was your purpose in doing so?"

"My purpose is twofold," the captain asserted. "First, I wish to say that it is impossible that my brother killed my father. I know him better than anybody here, and I tell you that he simply is not capable of serious violence or the kind of mindset required to kill. Henry is a good man, but he would make a very bad soldier. He would sooner allow himself to be insulted than to fight. When faced with a threat, he would more likely make a joke of it than draw a sword. As a military man myself and a commander of other men, I have seen his type before, so I know what I say is true."

Mr. Cogsgrove allowed this to sink in a moment before then asking, "And what is the second thing you wished us to know, Captain?"

"Only to set the record straight about something that fellow said earlier – Mr. O'Rourke. It was not Henry he overheard; it was I who said those things. And what is more, I stand by my words. My father was a nasty piece of work, and I cannot honestly say I am sorry he is gone, except for the trouble it has caused. I had as much reason to kill him as anybody and more the temperament for doing the deed than my peaceable brother. I make no secret of that."

"That is quite a surprising admission, Captain Tilney. But

that being the case, I must ask the obvious question. Why is it, then, that your brother was the one taken into custody and not you?"

"It is simply that I had the great good fortune to have a sturdy alibi, and my brother did not. That is the only difference. Sir Melvin himself said as much at the time. He would have happily arrested me instead if the situation had been the reverse."

When the captain was dismissed, Catherine noticed a look and a nod pass between the Tilney brothers. She likewise would need to communicate her appreciation to her brother-in-law for doing what he could for Henry. That was at least one character witness in her husband's favor.

She wondered who Mr. Cogsgrove meant to call next. For a moment, he himself seemed undecided. Just then a man whom Catherine recognized – the one who had been dispatched to find Mrs. Brooks – approached close enough to catch Mr. Cogsgrove's eye.

THE CRISIS POINT

Cogsgrove asked for and was granted five minutes to confer before proceeding. He first listened without comment to what his colleague had to report. Then there were a few whispered words between the lawyer and his client. Lastly, Cogsgrove approached Catherine and the rest of the family, who leant in to hear what the barrister had to tell them.

"Unfortunately, my man has been unable to locate Mrs. Brooks," he said with a significant look at Catherine, the only one amongst them who knew the full import of this news. Catherine's heart sank, but Cogsgrove carried on. "Without her testimony, I must fall back on what the rest of you can contribute. I do not like the look of the jury, and I'm afraid the mood of the court – especially from next door – is not in our favor either. So we must do what we can."

With that, Mr. Cogsgrove went back to the business at hand. He called a friend from Henry's college, an esteemed professor, and then it was Eleanor's turn. These three made more sympathetic character witnesses than the captain, but their information was much the same: Henry was a good, kind, and principled man, who could never have committed the crime he stood accused of.

Had it been enough to sway the jury, though? Who could know for certain? Catherine studied the faces of the twelve men for clues. To her untrained eye, at least, there was nothing useful to see.

She tried to prepare herself, assuming she would be the next one called, for there was no one else left, as far as she knew. But then the judge, who had been fairly unobtrusive until this point, spoke up.

"Mr. Cogsgrove," he said wearily, "how many more witnesses to your client's good character do you intend to call? No doubt all Mr. Tilney's friends think he is a very fine fellow, but that is hardly evidence of anything except their own opinions. This court has indulged you just about as far as we intend to. Move along now. Let your client make his speech in his own defense, and have done. There are other cases waiting to be heard."

Mr. Cogsgrove hesitated. "Only one more witness first, your honor." He turned neither in Mrs. Tilney's direction, as she had expected, nor to anybody else in the designated witness seats. Instead, his eyes searched the gallery of spectators, traveling back and forth, then higher and into the balcony, until at last they came to rest. Then he nearly shouted, "I call Mrs. Brooks, housekeeper of Northanger Abbey."

Great was Catherine's surprise when Mr. Cogsgrove called out Mrs. Brooks's name. At the same time, hope flared within her breast. Her head quickly turned to follow the direction of Mr. Cogsgrove's gaze, to see if the missing woman would materialize before her eyes, as if by magic. Yet the face she sought failed to appear.

"Mrs. Brooks," Mr. Cogsgrove repeated sternly over the general hum of anticipation that filled the air. "You are wanted in the witness box."

Several more seconds passed with more anxiety and more excited murmurings. Was it nothing more than a brave bluff on Mr. Cogsgrove's part, Catherine wondered, or had he really seen her?

Then the judge asked, "Does this woman hold a summons, Mr. Cogsgrove?"

"Yes, sir! I placed it in her hand myself last night."

"Very well, then." The judge motioned for the agitated spectators to quieten down before he spoke again, more loudly this time. "Mrs. Brooks, if you are present, you are solemnly compelled by this court to step forward and testify, or you will be held in contempt."

A small movement near the back of the balcony caught Catherine's eye. "There she is!" she cried out, pointing.

Mrs. Brooks was indeed coming forward, slowly but surely, with every spectator straining to see this apparently important personage emerge from the anonymous crowd.

Relief flooded through Catherine at the sight, and she presently looked to Henry, wanting to confirm that he shared her feelings. Henry, however, looked uneasy instead, which in turn tempered Catherine's own inward celebration. Of course. He, who had hoped to spare the beloved maternal figure precisely this kind of pain and scrutiny, could not rejoice at the prospect of Mrs. Brooks being made to testify against her will, Catherine realized. Her charitable husband could not delight in another's danger and discomfiture, especially on his account.

Then there was still the mystery of what Mrs. Brooks would say. Would Cogsgrove simply ask her to endorse Henry's character, as originally planned? Or would he, against his client's wishes, press for more? It seemed the tension and suspense of the past days and weeks were not yet resolved;

they were in fact a palpable presence, now building to the crisis point.

The room had grown very warm, and when Mrs. Brooks took the witness box, Catherine found that she could barely breathe. She was not the only one in distress, however. Mrs. Brooks herself was noticeably trembling and began wringing her hands before Mr. Cogsgrove could even address her. Accordingly, his first words were more of a soothing apology than a reprimand.

"I can see that this is very difficult for you, Mrs. Brooks, so I thank you most sincerely for answering your summons today."

"I only done it for Master Henry – Mr. Tilney, I mean," she mumbled.

"A bit louder, if you please, Mrs. Brooks."

"I said, I done it for Mr. Tilney."

"Very good. Now, could you please tell the court how long you have known Mr. Tilney and in what capacity?"

"I known him since he were just a babe in arms. I were a nursery maid at Northanger Abbey back then, you see, before I worked my way up to being the housekeeper."

"So you have been with the family for over two decades. And I daresay you must have been held in some considerable regard to have risen so high from humble beginnings. Did you get on well with your former employer, General Tilney?"

Mrs. Brooks eyed Mr. Cogsgrove suspiciously, as if he had laid a trap for her. "He were a hard man, sir, so I did my job and tried to stay out of his way. That's all."

"Is Mr. Henry Tilney much like his father, would you say?"

Mrs. Brooks became animated at this. "Oh, no, sir; not one bit! He took after his sweet mother, may God rest her soul. She were as amiable a creature as you could ever hope to find, and Henry's just the same. I've never had a cross word from him in all my life."

"Really? Boys will be boys, after all. Do you mean to say he never gave you any trouble at all, even as a child?"

"Oh, well… he were a regular boy, right enough, and as good at gettin' into mischief as the next. But he never done nothin' really bad, nothin' mean spirited, only things in jest. He were always one for a laugh and a joke."

"I see. Knowing him as well as you do, then, Mrs Brooks, do you think it is likely that Mr. Tilney is guilty as charged in this case?"

"No, sir! Not likely; not even possible. As far as I know, Master Henry never hurt a single soul in his whole life, much less his father. He would have far too much respect for his father's authority…" Mrs. Brooks broke off with a choking sound. Finding her handkerchief, she brought it to her eyes. "I'm sorry," she added a minute later.

"That's quite all right, Mrs. Brooks. We are nearly finished," Cogsgrove paused to look inquiringly over at Henry, who shook his head ever so slightly. The barrister sighed and returned his attention to his witness. "Just one thing more, Mrs. Brooks. You heard the judge's remarks a little while ago, when he said that a witness to a person's character is merely giving evidence of his own opinion." Continuing very deliberately, Cogsgrove asked his final question. "Mrs. Brooks, is there any reason this court should give your testimony more weight than that? Think carefully before you speak. If there is anything more – anything at all – that you would like to say in Henry Tilney's defense, *now* is the time."

Waiting to hear what this last and most important witness would answer to the barrister's very pointed question, Catherine Tilney held her breath. Perhaps she was not the only one who did so in the considerable suspense of the moment, but Mrs. Tilney was most likely the only one in the courtroom that day who fainted at that precise instant. Although this would have been a dire distraction if indeed she had crashed to the floor as a result, instead she merely slumped quietly in her chair, and no one at all noticed except Eleanor beside her.

Consequently, Mrs. Tilney did not hear what Mrs. Brooks said then. To her everlasting shame and regret, she missed witnessing the housekeeper's full and free confession. She remained oblivious through all the tumult that broke out as a result, the judge's repeated calls for order, and that failing, the eventual ejection of a host of unruly spectators from his courtroom.

When Catherine at last came to herself several minutes later and her eyelids fluttered open, it was her dear Henry's face she beheld, wearing the guise of concern which then melted into a warm smile. It was his strong arms that cradled her so reassuringly. It was his familiar and perfectly formed lips that met her own once more.

"What happened?" she asked, without making any attempt to right herself.

"It is over," Henry said. "My darling, the nightmare is over at last!"

EPILOGUE

*W*ho can doubt what followed?

With Henry free, acquitted of all charges, the Tilney clan soon retreated from the harsh glare of Gloucester notoriety to the quiet retirement of the country, gathering together first at Northanger Abbey to reflect and console each other for all that had happened, and then on to their own respective establishments.

There was some melancholy, especially on Henry's side, for the one of their party they were obliged to leave behind. Mrs. Brooks was detained by the authorities until such time as the case against her should be decided and the appropriate penalty meted out. Although the Tilneys were leaving, Mrs. Brooks would not be abandoned by the family with whose fortunes her own had been bound together since before her birth.

"Never fear," Henry told her when he and his wife were allowed to visit the prisoner before their departure. "We will not desert you. I shall write and visit as often as I can. And Mr. Cogsgrove remains in our employ, only now transferring his good efforts towards defending you instead. He assures me that the consequences will not be too severe for what was, we all agree, essentially an accident. Any judge will take that into account, as well as the fact that the family is requesting leniency."

The charge would not be murder, but a substantially lesser offense such as involuntary manslaughter. That much was settled already. And it was Mr. Cogsgrove's opinion that it might mean as little as a year of confinement for Mrs. Brooks and a fine commensurate with her means.

In the same visit, Mrs. Brooks redeemed herself somewhat in Catherine's eyes by explaining her behavior on the day of Henry's trial.

"I never meant to break my promise to you, Mrs. Tilney," she said apologetically. "What happened was this. I lay awake all night, thinkin' and a'worrying about one thing and another. I thought how the next day everything might change, and perhaps I would never be free again, which made me remember how my mother's grave was not far away and that I should have liked to visit her once more. So I rose at first light, took myself off to the place where she rests, and had a good long talk with her. Then I plucked up my courage and went to the courtroom, thinking I'd keep an eye on things from the back and be prepared to sing out if I was needed. It was wrong of me to worry you, though, and I am sorry for it."

Henry, who had forgiven her at once, fully intended to shoulder the burden of Mr. Cogsgrove's fees himself, but his much wealthier brother would not hear of it.

"*I* will pay for Mrs. Brooks's defense," Captain Tilney declared during their family conference at Northanger. "Whatever that entails: Cogsgrove, fines, sureties, and the like."

"That is very generous of you, Frederick," said Eleanor in surprise. "I did not think you much cared for the woman."

"Indeed, I do not. Still, if she carries Tilney blood in her veins, as Henry tells us, we owe her something. And as the head of this family, it is my responsibility to do what I can for her – a cost I am willing and well able to bear," he finished magnanimously.

There now! At long last we glimpse a clear sign of hope for the improvement of Captain Tilney's character! Or perhaps it has occurred to some – some of a more skeptical nature – that his philanthropic gesture may at least in part stem from a different motivation. Would it be uncharitable to suggest that perhaps Captain Tilney considered he owed a debt of sorts to the one directly responsible for his dramatically improved circumstances? Accident or not, his main source of frustration had been permanently removed by the hand of Mrs. Brooks. With no effort and very little expense, he now found himself master of a prosperous estate far sooner than he had dared to hope only six months before. He was consequently free to judge for himself what was right to be done with it and what would make him happy.

What would make him happy, he soon concluded, was to give up his military life and make Miss Virginia Holt the next mistress of Northanger Abbey, which he did without delay. If society felt an inclination to complain about his wife's humble origins, then society and its antiquated expectations could "go to the devil."

In due time, the viscount and viscountess returned to the noble house and grounds of Astley Park, where they hoped to soon produce an heir and then a spare, in order to secure the line and title for another generation. Although no one could have shown herself, by unpretending merit and long-suffering, more deserving to receive and enjoy felicity, Eleanor could not have been happy whilst her favorite brother remained wrongfully accused. Henry's release thus freed Eleanor's own heart as well.

To the general satisfaction of all her acquaintances, her ladyship then resumed the life of her own choosing with the man who had long been the prime object of her affection. Even the distance from their dearest friends proved no material evil to the couple's joy. For when one has an exceedingly generous income, good roads, and the choice of several comfortable carriages, what are fifty miles?

With the formidable patriarch gone and the new master of Northanger considerably softened and settled by marriage, all impediments to cordial intercourse in the future were soon removed. Thereafter, a month rarely expired without one part of the family finding it convenient to visit another – first, for their own pleasure, and then later on, to ensure that their growing band of progeny should also be on the most intimate terms of friendship with one another.

It is well to know that Eleanor's future and felicity are secure, how Frederick is much improved, and even Mrs. Brooks left in good hands. However, as this tale comes rapidly to a close, you will be wondering about Henry and Catherine. You will wish to be assured that they are also safe and well, to witness for yourself their early perfect happiness at Woodston restored, and to catch at least a glimpse of the years ahead.

Far be it from me to deprive the reader this satisfaction, although we must agree to be discreet. We must grant them a degree of privacy. After all, they are still essentially newlyweds. And yet I owe you this much:

The young couple returned to Woodston, once again taking up the quiet life they had, against their wills, left behind some months earlier. They both did their best to carry on as if nothing unpleasant had ever intervened until the time came that it seemed so indeed.

Henry resumed his former good offices in the parish, becoming much beloved for his service to the needy and for his remarkably short sermons – short but to the point. He kept chickens, worked with his horses and dogs, and was always on the lookout for improvements he could make in their domestic arrangements – the house, the stables, the gardens, the grounds –

anything that could enhance his wife's happiness or keep them in good stead with their neighbors.

Catherine set about ordering their home and training herself up to be a proper lady, now with the added help of Patsy – the maid whom she spirited away from Northanger, as promised. Young Mrs. Tilney had been in training for a parson's wife all her life, of course, by observing her mother's excellent example. But to this she must now add the refinements expected within the elevated society she had acquired by marriage. And what better way to start than to install her own personal lady's maid within the home?

Not that the young couple needed wealth, position, and social trappings to be happy. After their recent ordeal, they only wanted to be together again and a return to their snug home at Woodston.

In truth, however, the newlyweds did not wait for Woodston to be happy, nor even for their two-night stop at Northanger along the way. They wasted no time at all in becoming fully reacquainted after their long, enforced separation. Why, only minutes into their carriage ride away from Gloucester... Well, as I say, we must allow Henry and Catherine *some* privacy.

Later, still reclined and entangled in a rather awkward embrace – the best that could be managed in their present surroundings – Henry commenced to praise his wife's perfections. "What a clever girl you are, Catherine. I have always admired your beauty and your spirit, of course, but I do not believe I have given your sharp mind enough credit until now."

Catherine raised her head from its comfortable place on Henry's shoulder, so that she might see his face and judge if he were teasing her or not. It seemed he was not. Blinking at him in some surprise, she said, "Thank you, my darling. Really, I am quite touched by what you say. I hardly know what makes you think of such a thing at this moment, but I suppose you must be referring to how I solved the mystery of your father's death at last."

Henry smiled and grunted, noncommittally.

Catherine rested her head in its former place again, saying presently, "I believe you give me too much credit, though. If I had been really astute, I should have got it right the first time instead of accusing your brother, then Mr. Oberton, and then your brother once more before at last discovering Mrs. Brooks was the one who did it. It was a very roundabout way to arrive at the truth, coming nearly too late, too. I shudder to think of it." She held her husband more tightly, burrowing as close to him as was humanly possible.

"Nevertheless," said Henry, smoothing her recently disheveled hair. "You discovered the answer when no one else could, and I will be eternally grateful to you for that. But in truth, I was thinking of something else entirely," he added archly.

"Is that so?" She asked, eyeing him again. "Whatever can you mean?"

"Indeed, I was thinking what a stroke of genius it was that you had the foresight to bring this carriage with you to Gloucester. If not for that great inspiration of mind, we would this minute be sharing the other one with my brother, my sister, and her husband. As much as I care for them all…"

Catherine laughed. "Yes, I see what you mean. There are certain… certain advantages to having one's privacy, especially on a long journey with little else to keep one occupied." She shifted position to kiss him again – slowly and comprehensively – in proof of what she had been saying.

"Exactly," said Henry, when they paused for breath. "Genius, pure genius."

The End

AUTHOR'S POSTSCRIPT

$\mathcal{T}$hank you for reading *Murder at Northanger Abbey*! I hope you enjoyed this continuation of Henry and Catherine's story as much as I thoroughly enjoyed writing it. Do take some time to savor their escape from jeopardy and their blissful ending!

Although I personally believe the young couple will be happiest where I left them – in their quiet, comfortable life at Woodston – I also know there are readers who might have been imagining a different outcome, who might possibly have even preferred to see them wind up living large, ensconced in the grandeur of Northanger Abbey itself. And I did consider that possibility.

Jane Austen must have faced a similar decision when writing *Mansfield Park*. With Tom Bertram, the irresponsible heir, teetering on the precipice between life and death late in the book, it must have occurred to her that with one small nudge she had the power to see that the great estate would fall into better hands: into Edmund's and Fanny's. But perhaps she didn't want her favorites saddled with so much responsibility and the corrupting power of wealth, so many worldly cares. As I have for Catherine and Henry, Austen chose a comfortable but simpler life for them. She did the same for Edward and Elinor in *Sense and Sensibility*.

Nevertheless, I thought it would be a fun challenge to write an alternative outcome as a bonus, allowing you to decide for yourselves which you prefer. And this variation may not be any more improbable than Jane Austen's own ending to the original novel, where she performed a little sleight-of-hand to achieve her happy ending:

The anxiety, which in this state of their attachment must be the portion of Henry and Catherine, and of all who loved either, as to its final event, can hardly extend, I fear, to the bosom of my readers, who will see in the tell-tale compression of the pages before them, that we are all hastening together to perfect felicity. The means by which their early marriage was effected can be the only doubt: what probable circumstance could work upon a temper like the General's? The circumstance which chiefly availed, was the marriage of his daughter with a man of fortune and consequence, which took place in the course of the summer – an accession of dignity that threw him into a fit of good-humour, from which he did not recover till after Eleanor had obtained his forgiveness of Henry, and his permission for him 'to be a fool if he liked it!' (Northanger Abbey, chapter 31)

You may choose, as I suggested earlier, to simply savor the original version, at least for a time. But what follows is an alternative ending for your consideration, if and when you decide to read on. It is perhaps less consistent with a typical Jane Austen story and more suggestive of the Gothic tales that inspired her to write *Northanger Abbey* in the first place. As with the rest of the book, this is played a little bit tongue-in-cheek.

The action picks up in a revised Chapter 23, where Catherine is traveling with Captain Tilney to confront Mr. Oberton. Her personal radar sounds a warning, as before, but this time it is no false alarm.

AN ALTERNATIVE ENDING

$\mathcal{C}$atherine's mind buzzed with equal parts fear and self-recrimination, leaping quickly from one thought to the next.

She wondered how it could possibly have happened again. How could she have allowed herself to be...? No, it was worse than that. She had done this to herself! She had once again blundered into trouble by depending on her own questionable powers of deductive reasoning, so sure of her mad theories and conclusions that she charged ahead without proper precaution. Since initially setting eyes on Northanger Abbey and letting her imagination run wild, it seemed she had learnt nothing at all.

First she had been absolutely convinced of Captain Tilney's guilt. Then, as of this morning, she had been equally convinced she was mistaken and that the villain was Mr. Oberton instead. But now that it was too late, she had to consider that she might have been mistaken about being mistaken! What if her first conclusion had been correct after all, in which case she had now placed herself in grave danger. She was alone with a murderer! She was under his power, and worse still, nobody knew it. She had told no one where she was going and with whom. As far as she was aware, nobody at Northanger had even seen her leave with Captain Tilney. So when she could not be found, it would be as if she had simply wandered off into the woods on her own and got lost.

Perhaps, if Captain Tilney knew about her accusations against him, which seemed all but certain now, he had only been held back from acting against her before by the chance of being discovered. Now she had played right into his hands. She might easily disappear forever into a gully choked with brambles – exactly like the one she remembered passing a few minutes before – and wild animals would disperse her bones far and wide. Now there ran a rushing river beside the road they traveled. What a convenience! With very little trouble, a man bent on murder might tip her in, allowing the turbulent waters to carry the evidence of his crime away to the sea. No one would be the wiser.

Captain Tilney was a highly capable man, as she had just been thinking only moments ago, and he was strong. It would be nothing at all for him to overpower a small woman and dispose of her body somewhere along this road. He probably would not even disturb his hair or soil his immaculate clothing in the process. She would stand no chance against him, of course, and if she should scream, who would hear her in this lonely place?

There would be some sort of search undertaken when she was missed. She believed Eleanor at least cared enough to insist on that. But they might have no idea where to start. In all likelihood, there had been no note dispatched to Mr. Cogsgrove about Mr. Oberton before they left, and for all she knew, this might not even be the road to Compton Court. Besides, Captain Tilney would have some clever story prepared so he could deny any knowledge of what had happened to his 'scatter-brained little sister-in-law.'

The greatest heartbreak was that poor Henry would never know what had become of her. Then, with no one to save him, he would go to the gallows in his brother's place. All was lost indeed. The only thing either of them could look forward to was being reunited on the other side of that great divide. Catherine choked back a sob. It was every bit as tragic as any novel she had ever read!

Captain Tilney slowed the gig to turn onto the bridge that had come up on the right. Catherine peered down at the dark, icy water below. She knew at once this was the moment, the ideal opportunity the captain had been waiting for. She only hoped he would be mercifully quick about it.

In the exact center of the bridge, Captain Tilney pulled the gig to a stop. Catherine immediately discarded the idea of leaping from the carriage to make a run for it. Where would she go? She had no idea in which direction the closest help might be found. Besides, she would probably not get ten feet before being overtaken by Captain Tilney. It would be better not to provoke him, at least while there was still a chance of things ending in less than total disaster.

"Why have we stopped," Catherine asked in a tone she hoped conveyed only natural curiosity.

"Oh, no reason in particular," said the captain, "except that I thought you might enjoy the view from here. The river rages so violently this time of year, especially after stormy weather. It is quite a sight, do not you agree?"

"Yes," she admitted, staring down at the roiling torrent fifteen feet below until it had almost hypnotized her. Coming alert again, she said hopefully, "But should we not continue on to Compton Court without delay? We both agreed it was a matter of urgency, and surely there will be time for views later."

"No indeed, Catherine!" he boasted confidently. "There is no hurry at all. We would not find our killer at Compton Court, even if we should go there." He shook his head and laughed loudly. "How surprised Mr. Oberton would be to know of your wild assertions about him! I daresay he would find the idea quite diverting. Perhaps I will tell him sometime or other. Not today, however."

"But you said you were as convinced as I that it was Mr. Oberton!"

"Does a gentleman never tell a lie to please a lady or to get his own way? My dear Catherine, you are so ignorant of the ways of the world. Allow me to explain. I knew the business with Mr. Oberton was nonsense, but I could hardly refuse the call to adventure, I could hardly refuse the chance for... the chance for this stimulating outing, just the two of us alone together. It was the perfect opportunity."

Catherine shuddered to think what he meant, but she asked anyway. "The perfect opportunity for what?"

"I wanted a private word with you."

"You did? I cannot image why."

"Can you not? I thought sure from your frightened countenance a moment ago that you had anticipated my topic of interest. Come now, Catherine. As you must know, I wish to speak to you about your *previous* theory for my father's death – your persistent favorite until this mad inspiration about Mr. Oberton struck and made you forget it. It would not last, however. When Oberton was cleared, as I happen to know he has been already, you would return to your favorite again, like an unrelenting dog to his bone. So to speak plainly, Catherine, I wish to settle this matter of your accusations against me, once and for all."

Catherine was too terrified to pretend incomprehension... or even surprise. Daring to look her tormenter in the eye at last, she saw there the confirmation of all her fears. If she had cherished any hope that she had misunderstood the situation yet again, she was that instant undeceived. Without a doubt, her brother-in-law meant to do her harm. "So you *did* read Mr. Cogsgrove's letter," she said fatalistically.

He shrugged. "The temptation was irresistible. And besides, I thought it my right to know what goes on under my own roof. Of course, what the letter revealed was nothing new to me. I had long understood that you favored me for the crime. And perhaps you will not think it unreasonable, then, that I have resented you for it. Still, I can hardly fault your instincts and your logic. You alone divined the truth. All I can say is 'God bless Miss Holt!' If not for her and her misplaced faith in me, you would not have been the only one. And who can say but what she may yet break down if you persist? Since I clearly cannot allow that, the question becomes, what am I to do with you? I am sure you can see my problem…"

As if he were giving a speech, the captain droned on with his self-serving justifications and round-about admissions to what he had done and meant to do. Catherine was only half listening, though, as the tension within her built higher and higher until she could bear the cruel cat-and-mouse game no longer. Did he really expect her to sit calmly by, waiting in suspense to be murdered, wondering when he would stop toying with her and pounce?

He had her boxed into a corner, and he knew it. The power was in his hands. All this was undeniable. The only choice left in Catherine's control was whether to offer her paltry resistance or go quietly.

Then she asked herself what a true heroine would do in her position. That must be her guiding principle. If she could not change the outcome, she must at least run the race bravely to the end, to finish with honor the course laid out for her, though no one would know it. The picture then became clear. No true heroine would be so obliging as to succumb to her enemy without a fight, and therefore, neither would she.

Although Catherine knew she could not succeed, she determined in her heart to try an escape. She steeled her nerves and watched for the precise best moment to make her attempt.

"…It seemed I had little choice but to put up with you a while longer," Tilney continued. "Now, however, you have not only forced my hand but given me this unexpected opportunity…"

All at once, Catherine pointed and shrieked, "What's that over there?"

It was the oldest trick in the book, but effective. When Captain Tilney turned to see, she leapt from the gig, running as fast as she could in the opposite direction.

Before she had covered more than forty feet, however, her adversary was upon her, grabbing her arms, pinning them behind her, and dragging her back to the bridge. Captain Tilney was saying something unpleasant to her, but Catherine could not hear. She screamed for all she was worth, and she kept right on screaming until his rough hand flew up to cover not only her mouth but her nose. Now she could no longer speak *or* breathe, and though she struggled against her attacker with all her might, she swiftly felt her strength ebbing away. As her vision grew dark and she slipped from consciousness, she seemed to feel herself falling, falling toward the cold water below. When she hit bottom, her last thought was of her darling Henry.

When Catherine finally awoke again, she was warm, dry, and in her bed at Northanger, making her wonder how much of what she remembered – or seemed to remember – had been a dream. Then she saw Eleanor.

"Catherine, oh, Catherine!" Eleanor cried with equal measures excitement and relief. "You are come back to us! Allow me to fetch the surgeon for you." She immediately fled towards the door, calling out, "Mr. Murphy, come at once. Mr. Murphy, she is awake!"

Less than a minute later, Eleanor was back with a stranger at her side. The bearded man said, "I am Mr. Murphy, Mrs. Tilney. How do you feel?"

As the medical man went about examining her, there were more questions. Was she cold? Did she have any pain? Did she know where she was, the month and the year on the calendar, what had happened to her? Catherine answered as well as she could in her confused and somewhat alarmed state of mind. Except for a distant but distinct throbbing in her head, she had very little discomfort of any kind, she reported. Although she did still feel rather muddled.

"Perfectly natural after what you have come through," the surgeon assured her.

Eleanor saw Mr. Murphy out once he was satisfied, and then returned to Catherine's side, proceeding to rearrange the patient's pillows and tidy the bed. "Oh, my dear Catherine," she said as she went about this business, "what a fright you have given us. However, now that the danger is passed, all will be well again."

"But what did Mr. Murphy mean?" Catherine asked. "What did he mean when he said 'after what you have come through'?"

"Do you remember nothing, then?"

"There are things in my head – images and words – and yet I cannot tell if I should trust them as real," said Catherine.

This much was true enough, and she dared not risk distressing Eleanor by saying anything against Captain Tilney, in case it should be completely a product of her imagination. Only a nightmare: that was what she would prefer. And yet, with a closer look at her sister-in-law, she could see that all was not well. "You have been crying, Eleanor. What is the matter? What has happened?"

Blotting her eyes with the back of her hand, Eleanor replied, "It is nothing, only that you have been so terribly ill. You must not worry about me or anything else. Sleep now. We will speak more about these things later."

Catherine meant to object. She meant to demand Eleanor's explanations at once. Instead, the mere suggestion of sleep proved enough to overcome her strongest intentions to do anything else. Catherine thus did as she was told. Only later were her questions asked again, and this time Eleanor reluctantly answered them as they sat together in Catherine's room.

"Jonathan and I were nearing Northanger, returning from the village, when we saw Frederick's gig heading off in the opposite direction," said Eleanor. "I thought nothing of it, but when the stable boy told us you had been with my brother, Jonathan became uneasy for your safety. It seems he has never trusted Frederick, especially since my father's death. So he took his horse and rode after you, staying out of sight but within reach. He was near enough to hear some of your conversation at the bridge, which was enough to convince him that Frederick was up to no good – that he had a hand in my father's death and that he meant you harm as well.

"Oh, Catherine!" she continued, nearly sobbing now. "What a disservice I did you when I told you Frederick could not be the villain you supposed. You had been right all along, only I could not see it!"

"There, there, Eleanor," said Catherine, taking her sister-in-law's hand. "You were not to know, especially since Miss Holt had provided your brother a false alibi. But what happened next? I believe I ran, but Captain Tilney caught and held me. Perhaps I fainted then. I do not know. I just remember the sensation of falling. Did I go into the river?"

"No," said Eleanor soberly. "No, thank God Jonathan was there to intervene or indeed that might have been your fate."

"Oh! Yes, thank God!" cried Catherine. "But Jonathan, too. I owe him my life. Where is he, Eleanor? I must see your husband at once, to tell him how grateful I am!"

Eleanor dropped her eyes, saying, "Not now, Catherine. You must allow me to tell you the rest, though it may be difficult to hear."

Catherine's imagination instantly called up every kind of horror and her mind, every distressing question. Was the viscount injured… or worse? What had become of Captain Tilney? And Henry? Had she been unconscious long enough that the trial had come and gone. Had Henry been convicted? Oh, God, had the sentence already been carried out?

These were thoughts and sensations most painful to Catherine. In her agitation, her voice was unsteady. "Then tell me quickly, Eleanor," she said, "for I am fearing the worst."

"Be at peace, my dear. Everybody is well… or will be soon enough. All except Frederick, that is."

Catherine gasped a little at this implication but could say nothing until she knew more. She remained silent while Eleanor went on.

"When Jonathan saw Frederick…" Eleanor paused to gather her courage. "When he saw Frederick attack you, Catherine, and carry you towards the river, he could stay hidden no longer. He drew his pistol, made his presence known, and ordered my brother to release you. According to Jonathan, Frederick then dropped you to the ground, drew his own pistol, and fired, all in one motion. Jonathan was hit in the shoulder, and before he could get off a shot of his own or otherwise stop him, Frederick dived into the river. I suppose he knew the whole truth must now surely come out, and his only chance was escape. A search turned up his body several miles downstream."

"Oh, Eleanor!"

"He deserved no better, I know, but still…"

"Still, he was your brother."

"Yes."

The two sat in respectful silence for a few minutes, each clinging to the other's hand. Finally, Catherine said, "And Jonathan? He will soon be well?"

"Yes. Mr. Murphy has been attending him as well as you, and he says Jonathan was very lucky. The ball went straight through the muscle and out again without striking bone or any other vital structures. There is no sign of infection, and the shoulder will eventually heal."

"And what of Henry and the trial?" Catherine asked, holding her breath until she should hear the answer.

"Sir Melvin has been here to listen to Jonathan's account of what he overheard Frederick admit. He has also got Miss Holt to confess that she lied. He will wish to hear what you know as well, of course, but he expects all charges against Henry will soon be dropped. The matter need never go to trial at all."

Catherine's jubilation at this most excellent news may well be imagined – imagined but not described, for she herself was incapable of putting her feelings on the subject into speech. Indeed, intelligible words of any sort were beyond her ability for many minutes. Her relief in knowing the long ordeal was finally over flooded forth in the form of tears instead. She sobbed and wailed, wailed and sobbed. Eleanor, being a kindred spirit, understood perfectly and joined her, though in a slightly more restrained style.

Who can doubt what followed?

Catherine soon received word that if she cared to go to Gloucester, she would in fact find her husband set free and able to return home with her. The viscount – who was recovering well and whom by this time Catherine had been allowed to see and thank over and over again to her heart's content – suggested she take her pick of Northanger Abbey's fleet of fine carriages for the journey.

"Oh, no, I could not possibly!" cried Catherine. "I will send to Woodston for my own carriage."

"My dear," said Jonathan, kindly, "has it not yet occurred to you that this house as well as all its carriages *are* now your own?"

No it had not. Until that moment, Catherine had been quite contentedly picturing in her mind Henry and herself returning to Woodston parsonage to resume their simple life there. It took some little time to adjust her thinking and become resigned to the idea that that part of her life was in the past. Northanger Abbey in its entirety belonged to Henry now, and she was the new mistress there. She had no doubt that Henry would nobly shoulder his new mantle of increased responsibly; she only hoped she could do as well.

Catherine would in fact miss her home in Woodston, where she and Henry had been so happy. But it comforted her to know that they could return to visit there anytime they wished – for a picnic or just to admire the view from the drawing room windows. Besides, there *were* many advantages to Northanger, she admitted upon reflection. Think of the hours she could spend exploring the ancient edifice and grounds, now with no fear of castigation. And perhaps in time she would become so accustomed to its luxuries as even to wonder how she had managed to be content with less. As her father-in-law had once observed, a tolerably large eating-room, such as Northanger's, was one of the necessaries of life.

The truth was, though, that whenever and wherever she and Henry could be together, they would make each other happy. And, once reunited, they wasted no time beginning. That is to say, they wasted no time becoming *fully* reacquainted after their long separation. Why, only minutes into their carriage ride away from Gloucester…

Well, we must allow the young couple *some* privacy.

Later, still reclined and entangled in a rather awkward embrace – the best that could be managed in their present surroundings – Henry smoothed his wife's recently disheveled hair and commenced praising her perfections. "What a clever girl you are, Catherine. I have always admired your beauty and your spirit, of course, but I do not believe I have given your sharp mind enough credit until now."

Catherine raised her head from its comfortable place on Henry's shoulder, so that she might see his face and judge if he were teasing her or not. It seemed he was not. Blinking at him in some surprise, she said, "Thank you, my darling. Really, I am quite touched, but I hardly know what makes you say such a thing at this moment. Whatever can you mean by it?"

"I was thinking what a stroke of genius it was that you had the foresight to insist on coming to Gloucester on your own, and in Northanger's best carriage too. If not for that great inspiration of mind, we would this minute be sharing this comfortable coach with Eleanor and Jonathan. As much as I care for them both..."

Catherine laughed. "Yes, I see what you mean. There are certain... certain advantages to having one's privacy, especially on a long journey with little else to keep one occupied." She shifted position to kiss him again – slowly and comprehensively – in proof of what she had been saying.

"Exactly," said Henry, when they paused for breath. "Genius, pure genius."

The End (Again)

ABOUT THE AUTHOR

Shannon Winslow specializes in writing for the fans of Jane Austen. Her best-selling debut novel, *The Darcys of Pemberley* (2011), immediately established her place in the genre, being particularly praised for the author's authentic Austenesque style and faithfulness to the original characters. Since that auspicious beginning, Winslow has steadily added to her body of work – several more novels and one non-fiction piece – to make a total of ten books published so far:

- *The Darcys of Pemberley*
- *Return to Longbourn*
- *Miss Georgiana Darcy of Pemberley*
- *The Ladies of Rosings Park*
- *For Myself Alone*
- *The Persuasion of Miss Jane Austen*
- *Murder at Northanger Abbey*
- *Leap of Faith: Second Chance at the Dream*
- *Leap of Hope: Chance at an Austen Kind of Life*
- *Prayer & Praise: a Jane Austen Devotional*

Her two sons now grown, Ms. Winslow lives with her husband in the log home they built in the countryside south of Seattle, where she writes and paints in her studio facing Mt. Rainier.

Learn more about the author and her work at her website/blog: www.shannonwinslow.com

Printed in Great Britain
by Amazon